Acclaim for John McManus's previous book,
Stop Breakin Down

"Here is rage on the page. . . . It's a whole environment, with a new food chain, and yes, I want to know about it."
—*Los Angeles Times*

"Would I be happy to have written these stories myself? I wish I could have written them."
—Madison Smartt Bell, author of *Master of the Crossroads*

"Fast and furious . . . [An] exhilarating read."   —*Atlanta Journal*

"John McManus's short stories are the literary equivalent of drive-by shootings. . . . McManus is either going to become the next Celine or self-destruct before he turns thirty . . . but what this young author knows is as impressive as how he writes."
—*The Richmond Times-Dispatch*

"These stories will have young adults nodding their heads and parents shuddering. . . . McManus weaves dark and light into images that beg for our empathy."   —*The Boston Phoenix*

"Precise, brilliant language that evokes without ever having to explain. . . . His transcendent vision gives us devastating glimpses."
—Joyce Johnson, *ELLE* magazine

"Promising . . . captures the inarticulate without resorting to it."
—*The Village Voice*

"McManus straps [his characters] into a screaming, circular drop toward nothingness in what seems like one long, breathless take."
—Ron Franscell, *The Denver Post*

Also by John McManus

Stop Breakin Down

BORN ON A TRAIN

JOHN McMANUS

PICADOR
NEW YORK

Picador® is a U.S. registered trademark and is used by St. Martin's Press under license from Pan Books Limited.

For information on Picador Reading Group Guides, as well as ordering, please contact the Trade Marketing department at St. Martin's Press.
Phone 1-800-221-7945 extension 763
Fax 212-677-7456
E-mail: trademarketing@stmartins.com

www.picadorusa.com

The following stories were previously published: "Natcher Mountain" in *The Columbia Review*; "Fetch" in *The Oxford American*; "The Face of the Moon" in *Night Train*; and "Cowrie," under the title "On The Coast Highway," in *Tin House*.

Library of Congress Cataloging-in-Publication Data

    McManus, John, 1977–
      Born on a train: stories / John McManus.— 1st ed.
      p. cm.
      ISBN 0-312-30185-5
      I. Title.

    PS3563.C3862 B6   2003
    813'.6—dc21

                              2002192687

First Edition: March 2003

10 9 8 7 6 5 4 3 2 1

FOR SARAH

CONTENTS

BROOD   1

MR. GAS   29

NATCHER MOUNTAIN   47

FETCH   55

EASTBOUND   73

THE EARL OF CREDITON   95

THE FACE OF THE MOON   123

OLD TIMERS' DAY   139

AURORA   143

A FLOCK OF BLUEBIRDS   163

COWRIE   195

CADES COVE   213

DOG'S EGG   215

Mom: You gonna go live with your father?
Austin: No. We're going to a different desert, Mom.
Mom: I see. Well, you'll probably end up on the
same desert sooner or later.

—Sam Shepard, *True West*

BORN ON A TRAIN

B R O O D

Libby is also the name of a Confederate prison, two hundred miles east of here. It is short for Elizabeth, my middle name. Conditions there were marginally improved, says the calendar in Hiram's bathroom, but overcrowding remained the norm. Hiram is an old man's name, but his name on-line was Wheatboy. I had a list of all their names until I left my journal in California where Richard may be reading it now, learning what I thought of him, which I don't anymore, because he's much too far away.

On our third night at Hiram's house, I stood by the kitchen window listening through the wall as Mother spoke into the cordless phone on the back porch with a tissue to her nose. Hiram and his sons were asleep and snoring. I'll be so embarrassed if I have to leave again so soon, said Mother. I knew I should have picked the one in Georgia.

Ten seconds of silence.

The other one, she said. The freelance writer. No, you don't know that.

Five seconds of silence.

She'll see that no one loves me, Mother said. It's already happening. I feel so ashamed when she looks at me.

Silence.

I'm just doing this so she'll be happy, Mother said.

The blaring from the earpiece was finally loud enough for me to hear, although it wasn't language, only sound.

Polly, Mother said, if you were here I'd slap your face. She switched ears and leaned her head against the phone. Aunt Polly works with the Peace Corps in Uganda, where it isn't even winter, where the sun was maybe rising as she spoke. Hiram's a good man, Mother told the phone, and I like him a lot. She knocked her head against the glass twice as Polly spoke, and when she hung up she turned around and saw me through the open window. It'll work out fine this time around, she said to me. Whatever I say.

He buys you things, I said.

She nodded. That's one of the reasons it'll work out. He'll buy you things, too.

Hiram hasn't worked for several years. He sued a boy over a fender-bender and won a hundred thousand dollars, and he sued a Mexican restaurant for habañero pepper salsa that burned his stomach up, he said, and all inside his throat. He's suing now to make the neighbors cut down four magnolia trees that block his mountain view, because the house was there before the trees were ever born.

His three sons all have bright red hair. Eammon is six months older than me, with a driver's license.

Just think if we'd known him when he was thirty, Mother said on the fifth day.

You would have been my age, I said.

I mean if we were the same age, she said.

He could be your father, I said.

No, she said, I was born in Walla Walla. Hiram's never been out west before. She peered through the blinds and sighed. The landscape looks so different here, she said. The little ways.

I shook my head and said, He's forty-seven.

And I'm thirty-two.

Plenty of fathers are fifteen years old.

Name one, she said. Name one father.

I don't know any, I said.

I'm glad you've still got your sense of humor.

It's amazing how it stays there all over the country, whatever boyfriend it is.

I never knew about any boyfriends, Mother said.

Yours, I said.

Don't yell at me, she said.

I never had time to find one.

It'll be easier once you start up school again.

I'll go to school the next place, or the place after.

You'll go to school here, she said.

We'll be gone in a week.

Oh honey.

You don't even know the name of the school here.

It's named after a war hero, or somebody, or a founding father.

You don't know the governor. You don't know the mayor or the sales tax or the zip code.

We'll learn all that together, she said, trying to smile. When she stroked my cheek, I backed away and left the room and went to read my book. On our way to Virginia, Mother had bought me a field guide to birds so I could educate myself. The birds inside are rusty, green, raw umber. Hiram doesn't know it's the rufous-sided towhee singing *drink-your-TEA* each morning in the trees. Few birds display such geographical variation in their voices. Birds squawk at Hiram's dog, which makes it very sad. The dog lay at my feet as Mother flipped through the book and laid it on her lap and squinted and asked me what raw umber means.

It's a crayon, I said.

No, it's a bird.

I shrugged.

They probably meant lumber, she said.

They meant umber, I said.

I suppose you know, she said.

You're the one who bought it.

We're not talking about the crayons, she said. We're talking about lumber.

Lumber can't be raw, I said.

Of course it can be raw, she said. Anything can be raw.

Like what?

Like a stupid old mutt, she said. It was silent when Mother kicked its belly, because it wasn't a fighting dog. I don't know why Hiram picked a dog that wasn't in the war. He doesn't take it to his reenactments. He doesn't act like real soldiers, who raped and pillaged like the cowbirds. No one knows why cowbirds became brood parasites, laying their eggs in the nests of other birds. Perhaps they followed bison herds for so many million years that they never had the time to build nests of their own.

Let's rearrange the furniture, Mother said.

Jackson and Leroy, the younger boys, came downstairs as Mother pushed the hassock to the wall. They stopped at the landing to watch her unplug the lamps. Jackson's lips and tongue were purple from a Dum-dum. I imagined cutting off his head and switching it with Leroy's, just like Mother was switching the two coffee tables with each other.

Aren't you going to help? she said to me.

I like the furniture the way it is, I told her, but I didn't like it at all, either way. Leroy whispered in Jackson's ear. They grinned at me together. Mother folded up the bearskin rug and carried it outside to shake it free of dust by its flat, clawless legs.

Eammon said, said Leroy.

Sshhh, said Jackson.

He said to ask her.

Only if we want to.

We're spose to.

Ask me what? I said.

What thirty-six twenty-four thirty-six is.

It's a song, said Leroy. Eammon said you'd know what it means.

Eammon wants to know? I said.

Leroy nodded as Jackson shook his head no.

It's a rock song, said Leroy.

Then you know what it is, I said.

What is it?

It's a song.

Horses galloped across the pastel prints on the living room wall. We had another sister once like you, said Leroy.

She had purple pants, said Jackson.

They were pink, said Leroy.

What happened to her? I asked.

It was her mama, Jackson said.

What was her mama?

It was her mama that it happened to, said Leroy.

The young cowbird grows quickly, at the expense of the host's young. It steals most of the food. Sometimes it even pushes the other babies out of the nest. Every third stair creaked beneath my feet as I took loud, intrepid steps to Eammon's room where he sat at his rolltop desk hitting his keyboard with his fist. That's smart, I said to him, and he swiveled around in his chair and grunted, looking startled.

I pointed to his books and said, You reading those?

He pointed to my eyes and said, You always wear that shit?

A cowlick rose up from his pixie cut like an arrow toward old webs that dangled from above. I felt my hair for fallen strands of them. Eammon saw what I was doing and said, Things was cleaner in Eureka, and I wasn't sure if it was a question. I didn't see why he ever would have been out there himself. Are you much like your mom? he asked, and when I didn't answer, he said, You find you a computer man here, too?

No, I said.

Huh, he said.

Huh, I said. He removed his hands from the pockets of his jeans to finger an encrusted silver cross on his necklace. On a shelf above his head was a row of bulging Trapper Keepers— back to the first grade, I guessed—and comic books, and *Dune,* and a jar of hemlock pinecones for a bookend. He opened and closed the drawer that held his pens and white-out. I've got a waterbed, he said, stretching his chin down to his sharp clavicle.

Yeah.

Real good on your backbones.

I looked at the bed and said, I've never liked them.

You had one before?

Here and there.

His teeth were the worst I'd ever seen, except on poor kids. Did your dad melt down your braces to make bullets, I wanted to ask, but he was already talking. His high school had the second-highest rate of anorexia in Virginia, he said. Three state representatives had graduated from it, and the fullback for Nebraska. Tomorrow was a field trip to Sharp Top.

It'll be your school, too, he said. We'll ride the bus together.

I don't know whether that's going to happen.

The bus is number ninety-nine, he said.

I don't ride school buses, I said.

Well, I guess it used to be thirty, but then they changed it.

Who are you talking to? I said when an instant message popped up on the screen of his computer.

He minimized the window and said, No one. Friends.

From here? I said.

He grinned with only half his mouth.

Are you retarded? I said.

From other places, he said.

Where's your dad's computer? I haven't seen it.

It's the same as this one, Eammon said.

He comes in here and uses it? I said.

What do you care?

It's wise to jot down a drawing of an unfamiliar bird after the viewing. It will train you to notice small but important details that are easily overlooked. Eammon placed two printed pages in a drawer and locked it shut and put the key on the shelf above himself and rubbed the zit below his ear. When another window opened on the screen, he flipped the surge protector switch so the computer powered down, and I went downstairs. Learn to move quietly and to avoid wearing brightly colored clothing. I stood examining the teapots in the china cabinet as Hiram answered Mother's questions in the kitchen. Where else have you lived? she asked, and he said, Nowhere.

That's stupid, Mother said. You don't live in one place.

Yes I do, he said.

Not *you*, she said. One does not.

I guess one does, he said, picking at his ears as Mother grilled green peppers in a skillet, pouring spices into the boiling oil. She cooked for over an hour, and then we all ate dinner together. Hiram passed the dishes to Mother on his left, then me, then Eammon, Jackson, Leroy. The beans had been fried in Wesson oil, and Hiram spooned himself out a heap of them and said, These is good.

Mother smiled and said thanks.

You didn't get you a pork chop, Hiram said to me.

I don't care for Mother's pork chops, I said.

Mother smiled at me.

You ain't had one yet, said Hiram.

I've actually had several dozen over the years, I said.

These are nice big ones, he said.

I nodded and said, That's been the trend. Hiram looked at Mother and shook his head and sliced his pork chop and ate a chunk of it. I knew it would take him a long time to chew the meat, but I hadn't thought I'd be able to count to eighty before he swallowed.

I guess I'm not as young as I used to be, he said.

How old were you in the picture? said Mother.

What picture? he said.

The one you sent me, Mother said.

Hiram looked at Eammon, who nodded back at him. What difference does it make? Hiram said, his mouth already full again with beans.

Was it an old picture?

What's old?

I don't know, said Mother. I just wondered.

Hiram shook his head and didn't answer. Mother regurgitated stories about Idaho and California to fill the silence. As she told about the crippled irrigation engineer's arrest for arson, Eammon poked my side and leaned to mumble in my ear. What he said was unintelligible. You look out for that one, Hiram said to me. Boy's a real lady-killer.

Mother laughed politely. He's a handsome little fellow, she said.

Not that the others ain't, said Hiram with a jowly grin, and he rubbed his fingers through Leroy's flattop.

He really knows how to fill out a pair of jeans, said Mother.

To what? said Hiram.

Mother smiled as if trying to lighten the mood. So anyway, she said, we had our pick of anything in his house. I mean, what was he gonna do about it?

Who? said Hiram.

Dowell was his name, said Mother. I met him in Parlor Games, like Richard.

I stirred my food together into a collage of many colors.

How is everything? Mother said to me.

Deplorable as usual, I said.

Yeah, it's pretty goddamn good, said Hiram, nodding.

Thank you, Mother said.

I like the spices.

It's probably just the allspice.

Allspice, Hiram said.

Uh-huh, Mother said.

Allspice is Mother's favorite spice, I said.

Is that so, Hiram said.

Uh-huh, I said.

I don't reckon I've got a favorite spice, he said.

Libby's just teasing me, Mother said to him.

Maybe allspice is your favorite spice, too, I said. Maybe allspice is what brought the two of you together.

He didn't answer me because he was busy thinking about it.

Afterwards he moved onto the porch to smoke his pipe. When Mother sent me out to fetch his glass, the dog was draped across his lap like a sunning seal. Hiram patted it and turned to look at me and said, Tell me what your mama likes.

Okay, I said, but I'm going to lie to you.

Does she like cats? he said, his breath displacing cherry-flavored smoke.

She loves cats, I said.

We use to have cats, he said.

That's interesting.

When Eammon killed the kittens off, he said, the mama cat skedaddled to who knows where. Boy came and asked me, can I kill those kittens, and I said no, you can't kill those kittens. Ain't yours to kill. Went and done it anyway.

In the house the telephone was answered after half a ring.

You see that gunnysack over there? said Hiram, and I nodded my head but didn't turn to see. It's all bloodied up inside of it. Go look.

Maybe when I'm bored sometime, I said.

It was rocks, he said and hung his mouth open like he wanted me to answer. I took his empty pint glass from the rail and poured its dregs onto the wood between my feet. Spit stalactites joined his lips together like a cage that split apart when he said, I wasn't finished with that Bass.

It was empty, I said.

But don't worry, though. He don't treat people like that, like he does cats.

He kicked his tennis shoes into the yard. When I turned to go inside the house, the dog stood up and walked around in a circle and lay back down in Hiram's lap. They called it *she*, although it seemed to have a penis. In many species the male is bright and colorful. Sometimes the female can be identified only when one knows the male. They've all been dumb, I said to Mother when we were alone, but this one's stupid.

Her voice sounded like a stranger's when she said, Don't call people stupid.

I only call them stupid when they are.

But look at what he wrote me.

She gave me a piece of folded paper from the journal, and I turned it to the light to read its printout, starting somewhere in the middle. *You awaken a reservoir of zeal and emotion in me that overwhelms my mind. I see the same resplendence in your eyes that I had once.* I skipped a line. *Colorful and bright, like a color TV.*

It's so poetic, Mother said.

Like I am born upon the wind, the letter said.

I don't understand it, Mother said. It's so confusing.

Maybe you went to the wrong house, I said.

But he's good, though, she said, laughing emptily. When she left the room to smoke a cigarette I watched her through the window. She moved into the yard and dumped the birdbath's stale water onto the grass, and I turned the paper over and saw a list in Mother's cursive script, written in silver ink.

1. *Pack warm things. More than you think you'll need.*
2. *Little More Hesitant*
3. *Age*
4. *growth (benign?)* 5. *maps*
6. *glass candy from an Island*

Mother's script is thin with jagged edges. Penmanship should be genetic, like blood, but mine is round and careful like it came from somewhere else entirely. Upstairs Eammon cursed and stomped his feet on the floor. Leroy chased Jackson down the stairs and through the living room, their plastic firemen's caps ablaze and wailing as I folded the letter along its former creases. Mother held the hose up to the concrete birdbath bowl. She waved at the window, but I didn't bother waving back.

That night, like every night, I lay awake. The walls distorted Hiram's and Mother's whispers into whistles, hisses interspersed with strikes like he was whipping her with a belt, like she was pressed against the blue wall shared by our two rooms. On their side it was white. I couldn't identify all their noises. Hiram coughed from deep within his lungs and grunted like a hungry boar and snorted when he laughed, and then I was listening to their snoring. When Eammon's alarm went off at seven, my heart was racing from my fatigue. I went to school with him after all. It's good to meet the boys I'll never know. The girls were the same as at the last school. Everyone was lined up for the field trip. In the headcount I filled in for a cheerleader who was puking in the bathroom, so the teachers didn't notice me. The bus was loud and boring as it bounced along the mountain ridge, an hour to the trail, where we headed uphill through the mud that soaked my socks and feet through gouges in my sneaker soles. I walked on fallen leaves beside the drop-off.

You'll fall, said Eammon.

I'll be okay, I said.

He pushed me toward the inside of the trail. You're not as smart as your mom, he said.

You don't know my mom, I said. You've never talked to her.

She said a lot about you. She sent a picture.

I shook my head, and he nodded his. There aren't any pictures of me, I said, there's not even a camera, and Eammon pulled his wallet out and opened it to a year-old photograph of me with short, wet hair and Mother's hand on my shoulder, the rest of her body cropped off by the photo booth, and a ring on her hand despite the printed date that showed she was married then to Peter, six whole months before we left him for Eureka.

I'm the smartest one in my class, he said. My granny says I'll be valedictorian.

How would she know?

She's the guidance secretary, Eammon said. Plus she just knows.

Good for you, I said.

Plus who else would it be?

The rest of the class was ahead of us on the trail. Eammon said his shortness of breath and his red cheeks came from high blood pressure. The trail was too narrow for him to hold my hand, and he probably felt awkward when I jerked mine away from his. When we rounded a curve between high boulders, we came upon three boys sharing a cigarette atop the largest rock. Well, said the one in cargo pants, if it ain't Fifty Teeth Comin Outta One Place.

Eammon bit his lip and said, Hey, Frank.

How's it hangin, Fifty Teeth Comin Outta One Place?

You embarrassed him, said the middle one, who swung his jacket out and bounced its sleeve off Eammon's face. He's gonna pretend like that ain't his name.

You missed his teeth, said the third one, watching me.

I might of got one or two.

Forty-eight teeth comin outta one place, said Frank.

They laughed. In another half an hour we reached the mountaintop, where kids were scattered across the summit's tiers, four thousand feet high, better-looking than Eammon, learning how the rocks were formed and how Confederates had used the summit in the war. I matched them with the corresponding faces at the last school. Everyone was there. I counted the silos down below us, white-capped soldiers smaller than my fingernail. A sparrow flew into a wind that pushed it back toward pine green pimples rising from the piedmont, and I squeezed them.

Eammon really did have a lot of teeth coming out of one place. The sparrow gave up and landed to face the catcalls of the other birds. My ears were burning from the air, and Eammon's hands were so cold that I wished I could fall backwards off the bald rocks.

I didn't really do anything to those kittens, he said.

What happened to them, then?

They died, I guess.

How did they die?

Clouds cast shadows north to south along the jagged cliffs, but really it was just one cliff. Cars, said Eammon, shrugging with his cross between his thumb and middle finger. There's a lot of cars in town.

My eyes were watering from the breeze. I noticed hair like cat fur growing from his wrists and knew he'd killed them. Look at your hair, I said and ran my hand across its grease. You'll be bald by the time you're twenty-one.

The hell I will, he said.

I knew a guy in Utah who looked just like you. His fell out before his eighteenth birthday.

Eammon scrunched his chin up.

It's not what you look like, though. It's the consistency.

Do you like me? he said.

For the first time all day there were more things to say than just one thing. I only shrugged and didn't speak. What kind of answer is that? said Eammon. Fences in the fields below were drawn by pines and cedars. Five minutes, a teacher yelled from lower boulders, and I leaned into a ledge to jump down to the path between high rock walls, over boulders, waiting for black-berry thorns to prick my skin, but the boy in the cargo pants had trampled them so their stalks weren't twining anymore. Eammon pulled me into an alcove in the rocks, so my leg pressed up against his cold canteen, and he moved it along his belt so it faced the path. My dad was the one that killed them, he said into my ear. He got some barbecue meatballs from a can and soaked them up with antifreeze, and then he called the kittens over there, all five, and then they ate it.

Eammon stopped talking and snorted his nose a few times and took a drink of water. Four girls from the class walked by us on the path and didn't notice we were there. Three died right off, said Eammon. Dad told me the neighbors done it. An hour later the two black ones were still moving and crying. I stuck them in the freezer so it would quit. Took half the night to freeze.

Eammon nodded his head at my eyes, like he was proud of everything.

Why would Hiram do that? I asked.

Because that's what General Forrest did to Sherman's cats.

The whippoorwill says wurt-wull, wurt-wull. The loon says ree ree ree. I don't know how the wind could make those calls or why it happened only when I stood by Eammon, who was taller than our cavity in the rock. He crouched there like a half-wit. The trail wasn't as slippery anymore. I wanted to say, Shut up, Fifty Teeth Comin Outta One Place, but whenever I opened my mouth nothing came out.

The teachers led us to a graveyard at the bottom of the mountain, where I leaned against a sarvisberry tree and watched the corpses shine beneath the ground. They were older than the dead in California. Their surnames sounded like the hills. Look, I said to Eammon, Maybe that's your grandma.

My grandma's alive, he said.

Your other one, then.

You're fucked up.

At first I didn't push him away when he tried to kiss me. He tasted like the peanut butter crackers he'd just eaten. In the tree we heard a penetrating *preet*. The black shirts finally noticed me, demanded that I tell them who I was, and I said, I don't know, ask Eammon. When they did, he acted proud to be in trouble. On the bus I had to sit apart from him, and I ended up beside the dark-haired boy who'd trampled thorns, who said to me, You oughta stay away from Fifty Teeth, or yours could get like his. Which is the last thing you need. He hit a passing station wagon's hood with his used-up bubble gum. He drew an oval on my gums to check for foreign fangs that might have sprouted up like corn when Eammon had touched my mouth with his contagions in the graveyard, and I couldn't even move.

On that bus the thing was to wear as many bracelets as you could. Eammon gave me one that night at the house, a painted chain, and we stared at each other. It takes so long to think of how to say a sentence. By the end it's hard to locate the beginning. When he shut his mouth, he looked like certain prisoners, the good ones who can't help it. Lots of people look like that.

Don't you get lonely living everywhere? said Eammon.

Only when I'm around people.

That doesn't make any sense, he said.

Look it up in the dictionary.

Sense?

Lonely.

All we've got is the *Farmer's Almanac*, he said.

There's one on-line, I said.

Did you get on my computer without asking?

His chain was too big, and it fell off my wrist.

How do you know what's on there and what isn't?

Shut up, Fifty Teeth Comin Outta One Place.

There's a password.

I bet I could figure it out.

You couldn't.

There's only two or three things it could be, I said. Suddenly we heard Hiram moaning, the thumping of feet across the hall, and Eammon closed his bedroom door, embarrassed. The moans inside the wall were as constant as a radiator's hum, and I forgot them until they stopped when footsteps clomped along the hall, a door closed, a toilet flushed as Mother laughed and Hiram said, I can remember when you could walk out of this house and it would be 1975 outside.

The silence was Mother nodding, looking interested, Eammon pressing me into the waterbed to make waves. We rose upon the crests and sank into the troughs.

It wasn't carpet up here back then, said Hiram, his words distorted like he was saying them all twice. It was hardwood, just like the downstairs is.

When Mother giggled, I realized we might stay forever. I wanted to leave the house. Eammon had the keys to Hiram's car. He drove us up the mountain to the largest star on earth, an hour past dusk. Most naturally occurring stars are much larger. We walked to the wooden deck beneath the neon. I tried to force each tooth into its right place with my tongue. He smelled like a boy in a motel pool in Oregon whose name was Korin, whose voice was like he'd known me since our childhoods. I want to place my naked body on your naked body, he had said, and so I'd laughed at him until no one would ever talk that way again and here was Eammon forging grunts as thunder crackled, and he said, What would you do if I asked you to stand over me and piss on me? The clouds were ready to erupt on yet another mountain. The next time a boy speaks to me in Oregon, I won't laugh or be afraid. Eammon's head kept shaking as he said, You know I was just kidding. He must have had strong gums to hold those teeth together, one on top of the other.

I'll be gone soon, I said.

You're not going anywhere, he said.

Mother has been talking about the south.

Tower lights were red like a midnight highway into the west. Lightning didn't hit them, because they weren't any higher than we were.

This is the south, said Eammon.

Florida, I said. An island.

But she's in love with my dad, he said, sliding his arm around me like it was something we should share. Maybe Hiram was asking Mother to piss on him, too, and it was hereditary, and their ancestors had done it in the Civil War.

He's got a huge cock, said Eammon, is why they all like him so much.

We need to leave, I said, and pointed at the star.

We need to stay.

This is where the lightning's gonna hit.

Lightning isn't gonna hit the star.

If I were lightning, I would hit the star.

I took a shower with him when I was a little kid, is how I know, said Eammon.

I want to leave.

It was three times as big as mine was.

Of course it was, if you were a little kid.

I mean now, he said, annoyed that I had questioned him. I remember what it was.

I tried to laugh hard so he'd think he was ridiculous, but I stopped when it sounded fake.

You must of took a shower with your mom when you were little, he said. Did all that shit look huge just cause you were little?

I don't remember, I said.

You must remember something, he said.

All I remember is hair.

When we got to the car, he opened my door for me, and I slammed it shut and opened it again. He rubbed his hands together in front of the air vent and backed up.

Maybe they died while we were up here, I said.

Who? he said.

Your father, and my mother.

He narrowed his eyes and said, Why?

Ebola, I said.

You're weird, he said.

It would be even weirder if they were dead.

That's not weird, it's sick.

But if I predicted it just now, and I was right, it would be weird.

Eammon hit his knuckles on the Kenwood. My dad says to always keep some wood to knock on in your car, said Eammon, for when you think of something bad, cause cars aren't made with wood no more.

I don't see any wood, I said.

I don't have any, he said, like he was sad over it. I felt so tired my blood was only floating through my arms. An Oldsmobile circled up the mountain, and Eammon and the woman switched to their low beams at the same time. She was probably more connected to him then than I was, and he drove around a cardboard box at least a meter high and burst out laughing.

Just think if there was a baby in that box, he said.

What about it, if there was?

That fuckin baby would be fucked.

His laughter didn't stop until the radio played Bon Jovi. He sang along and nudged my upper arm and blew his horn. There was plenty of wood around, although it wasn't in the car. His voice erupted into a falsetto, and he shut up like he was ready to be ridiculed, but I didn't say a thing to him. The houses were all the same house painted other colors, rearranged so all the roads had different names. I faded into the turns. Each time I fell asleep I opened my eyes again until they were closed for good, and then I woke up in the middle of the night in all my clothes, my entire arm lodged in the crack of Eammon's waterbed. I used my other arm to lift it out. It felt like the appendage of a corpse as I rubbed it back to life. Moonlit clouds in the window fell apart. The squarest cloud was really the computer screen. Hiram sat at Eammon's side and whispered, No.

But I like her, Eammon said.

But she don't like me.

Not her, said Eammon. Libby.

She don't like me either, Hiram said.

Goddamn it, Eammon said. Don't screw this up.

You've got to find me another one.

Be quiet. She'll hear.

Get on there and do like you did last time. You got those letters saved.

You haven't even tried to make her like you.

You shut up, said Hiram. You don't know.

Buy her something expensive, like a stereo.

Get onto that computer now and make it hook up to the other computers.

Eammon folded his arms and shook his head. Tears were in his eyes.

Then show me how, said Hiram. I'll do it myself.

I won't show you.

I paid for this fucking thing myself.

I'll break it.

I'll beat your ass.

I'll run away, said Eammon. They'll take me with them.

I doubt they'd want you, Hiram said.

I can tell it in her eyes.

You can't tell shit in her eyes.

She loves me.

Her eyes love you about like her mama's do me.

I'll go to Florida with her.

Hell, said Hiram. They'll probly just stay here in town some-where.

She'll want to be as far from you as she can get, said Eammon. So do I.

Told me she might just settle down, said Hiram. Tired of traveling.

You don't know.

There's houses all over the place these days.

Get out of my room, said Eammon. I don't want you here.

I own this room, said Hiram.

Fuck you and your room. He turned the computer off and stomped out.

Hiram felt behind the monitor for a switch but didn't find it. When he turned to look at me I closed my eyes and listened as he quietly left the room. By that time my arm felt the same as the rest of my body, and it wasn't long until the sun began to rise. The cries of birds made complicated flowers with their calls. When I fell asleep again, they were having a war. Many of the species had developed explosives. The brown birds were neutral—finches, waxwings, owls—and therefore silent like the bombs that woke me up, killing everything, even the terrain, so there was nothing left to dream.

Libby, Mother yelled, the bacon's ready.

I timed the food from bed as it got cold. When my legs had tired of the mattress's relentless waves they stiffened up. Chirps and bleats crept upstairs from the Saturday morning cartoons. I still could smell leftover breakfast fumes when Mother began to cook lunch. I could tell her then or wait until we ate. I wondered if she'd get so embarrassed she'd run away on foot, leave the car behind so I could drive it to my own towns, find the shittiest city in America and get that one over with right now. She cooked for an hour and a half, using every stove eye and the broiler and the Cuisinart, then turned them off and frowned at each dish one by one with a curled, unhappy nose and twisted shoulders and carried them to where we'd be together, set them down. The duck stared up at us as we converged.

You must be hungry, Mother said to me. You haven't eaten since yesterday.

Is that a question? I said.

Mother smiled at me. Who wants to say grace? she said, but no one answered, and she looked around. Hiram? Don't you folks usually say grace?

Hiram shrugged.

Well, it's not like I'm one to say it, Mother said.

Eammon sat down, and then Jackson and Leroy did, too.

I guess we won't say it then.

However you want to do it, Hiram said.

Mother poured tea for everyone. We piled our plates high with hot, steaming lumps of food until the serving bowls were empty. I wished there were a way never to need to eat, never to sit in a wooden chair in a room of wooden chairs with ugly people trapped like wingless birds who try to eat and breathe and chew their food and talk to one another, all at the same time.

How's the duck? Hiram said to me.

It's better than the pork chops.

Of course it is, he said. It's a duck.

I see the same resplendence in its eyes that I once had.

Hiram kept on looking at his plate as Eammon set down his fork and stared across the table at me. Mother got up to fetch the pepper shaker from the kitchen. Eammon fingered the cross on his necklace and frowned and pulled it up so he could see its crusty coat of dried-up grunge. The silver band was tight against his neck. What's all this shit on my cross? he said, glaring at me again.

It's been there all along, I said.

This is gross, he said.

That's from when Jesus was on it, I said.

What?

It's from His smegma.

Mother's cheeks got bright. She slapped my cheekbone instead of my cheek, so it didn't make the sound she wanted, and she didn't seem to understand why she'd done it. Hiram stared at her with his fingers curled around his bugle.

Our Lord was circumcised, she said. He didn't have any smegma.

Maybe it came from somebody else's smegma, I said.

Like yours, she said.

I reached as if to slap her back, the right way, but I didn't.

You're the smackinest damn family I ever saw, said Hiram, and he licked a greasy film of mashed potatoes from his teeth. They weren't as crooked as Eammon's, although he'd never had braces either, it appeared. Mother sniffled as her nose swelled up like mine does when I cry, reddening long before the tears appear. Hiram put his bugle to his lips and played reveille right there at the table. He wasn't good enough to play upbeat. That's the kind of man who likes Mother. He didn't seem to care much about her anymore though.

For future reference, he said, don't mash the potatoes up like this, till they're goddamn diarrhea.

He sputtered a low note like a fart on his bugle, and Eammon giggled.

You went and beat the hell out of em, Hiram said. I take it with some lumps.

Mother nodded like she was almost smiling. Hiram adjusted his hearing aid, smearing gravy on his earlobe.

Just for future, though, he added. I reckon it's all right for just this once. Two brown cardinals landed on the kitchen windowsill, and Hiram blew the bugle until they flew away to other people's houses. Note the bird's behavior: is it alone or in a flock? What's the nature of its call? The loggerhead shrike has no talons, so it impales its mice and rodents on a thorn or barbed-wire fence, hence its nickname, butcher bird. It waits to tear the prey apart until a later time. Don't read at the table, Hiram told me, and I laid the book facedown upon the tablecloth.

Daddy? said Jackson.

What.

Do deaf people know it when they fart?

I'm sure they do, he said.

How do they tell the loud ones from the ones you can't hear?

Hiram shook his head. Mother tried to hook her eyes to mine, but I looked down, refusing to acknowledge her silent cries. Some species can be lured into view by an imitation of the sound of a bird in distress. Hiram drank his coffee from a tin cup with a pinch of salt and blew his bugle once again and laid his fork down suddenly and closed his eyes to say grace after all. He cleared his throat and thanked his mother, Jesus, God, the duck, the mother of his children, solemn-spoken names I didn't recognize, all the people who had died to make our lives so beautiful.

You know, I can do it too, I said to Mother.

Libby, sweetie, I don't know what you mean.

It doesn't take much. Say what state and give me three days' notice. I can keep up with you.

Hiram said, You better watch your mouth, little honey.

Why don't you let Big Honey be the one to tell me that, I said.

He shrugged and said to Eammon, Hurry up. I want to get an early start.

Where are you going? I said.

Why don't you ask Big Honey, Hiram said.

They're driving down to Bristol for the NASCAR race, said Mother.

That sounds like fun, I said. Eammon ate eagerly and quickly and didn't look at me anymore, only at Mother. He and Hiram left their dishes at the table and disappeared upstairs to change their clothes and then came back down and shouted bye and let the screen door slam, and then we were alone with only Hiram's dog and all the dirty plates. Leroy and Jackson played Nintendo in the living room. Mother dragged her chair to the wall and stood upon its seat and stretched to reach the pink wallpaper border. A house is a home where love dwells. She found a crack in it and tried to pull the banner off the wall, but just two feet came loose, and she crumpled up the strip and growled and laughed and cried and coughed. The *o* in *love* was a bubbly heart.

Libby?

What.

You could—

She stopped talking. I waited for her to finish.

You could do like Eammon did, she said.

Like he did when?

You could get on there and find me somebody.

Mother—

Because it's your age, not mine.

Then you know it was him.

It's your generation that knows all that talk. All those acronyms and symbols.

I don't know any acronyms.

The whole language of it all. I can't really even type.

I started to shake, although I didn't want to.

That's why I could never be a secretary, she said. The typing.

One two three four five six seven eight nine ten one two—

All those rooms of people typing, and it's so fast, it just goes right down the screen. Forty in a room at once now. The limit used to be twenty-three.

I don't know what you're telling me.

The ones who type fast look smarter than the ones that don't. It's not how you spell things.

Please be normal.

But in spite of it all they like me, over and over, they like me.

I just want you to be normal.

Honey, she said.

I want to sit here and listen to you be normal.

Say you'll do it. You could choose the place that way. The area.

I choked on what I tried to say, which wasn't anything.

Just once, she said. Like Eammon.

I'll never do anything like Eammon.

You don't care about me like he cares about Hiram.

He doesn't care about Hiram any more than I care about you.

Mother stared at me.

Stop staring, I said. Why are you staring?

Because it sounded funny, she said, about caring, the way you said it.

I didn't make the words, I said.

Of course you didn't. I was saying them before you were even born.

We piled all the dishes in the sink. Mother squirted streaks of Joy across the pots and plates until she'd used it all up, and she placed the empty bottle in the cabinet. I could tell from how she nodded her head like a dove that we'd be leaving soon. Mother followed me into the living room and said, Look up what kinds of birds they have in Georgia.

You don't look up Georgia. You look up a specific bird, like robins.

Look it up then.

She opened the closet door and got her iron and wrapped its cord around the handle and poured the water into a potted corn plant.

I'm sure there are robins in Georgia, I said.

Mother was crying, of course, and I felt guilty. I wanted to pat her shoulders, but it seemed awkward. We're so mean to each other, she said.

Her warble was less musical than the chirps of finches on the porch, and weaker, with tinkling trills like weeping.

What day is it? she asked.

Today.

It could be my birthday, and you wouldn't even know.

This isn't spring, I said.

You wouldn't even know it if it was.

Robins are considered a harbinger of spring, although in winter they frequent mostly cedar bogs and swamps. As with many birds, their mortality rate is about eighty percent a year. Their song is a series of rich caroling notes: cheer-up, cheerily, cheer-up.

Jackson and Leroy played video games as Mother packed her things. They shared a glass of milk, because it was the last of the gallon, and the house was empty of food except for spices. Hiram wasn't coming home until tomorrow. I hoped the boys would have enough sense to walk down to the Mick-or-Mack and buy some dinner, although we didn't leave them any money when we left.

M R . G A S

Mama said the way to keep a diary was to write down the opposite of everything that happened, so she gave Jason a blank book so each night he could tell how all the boys played kick the cans until the bogeyman came. How the plumbing still worked in their old bungalow, how Mama could still walk, and how her black hair fell onto his face when she tucked him in with his dolls and stuffed animals lined up to save him from dying inside the crack between the wall and his twin bed.

Won't I remember it the other way? said Jason.

You'll read it this way, she said.

Then I'll remember both ways, he said.

That's your kid memory. When you're grown you just remember a year.

You remember the wreck, said Jason.

That's just cause you remember too, said Mama, her rainy

voice pointed at the gray sky, which the bedroom window chopped into eight rectangles joined by crows that flew across them all and suddenly were dead, because Jason was fifteen now, reading of how he'd crossed the creaky woods at night and mooned trucks on the highway with his friends, but he couldn't remember their names or what they were the opposite of. He'd written nothing of their faces, only Mama's. Once a month a truck delivered groceries from town twelve miles away, but Mama needed milk each day so her bones could grow back. Jason would walk through the woods to the minimart to buy it. He could buy nineteen months of milk with all the coins they'd rolled, and that wasn't the opposite of anything; it was just true.

Get two today. The white kind.

It's all white, Jason said.

The bottle cap, said Mama, and Jason nodded. He walked the trail to Mister Gas where the sun scorched junebugs on the highway beneath a row of jack pines. Shawn was a hawk-faced boy who looked up at the pines while he pumped gas. His blue-white eyes cast a radiant shield over the whole service station. He talked like his mouth was scraping underground on broken bricks: Where is it you walked from.

It was a mile and a quarter through the woods to Mama's house, and it was another mile to the abandoned limestone quarry where fallen cranes sank their rusted fangs into two pits of murk.

Up yunder? said Shawn, pointing at the hillside.

About a mile, said Jason. They'd never spoken to each other before. A flatbed truck hid Shawn in a cloud of dust that rose up as tall as the treetops. Coke lasted me fifty miles, said a leathery face when the dust settled. When the bottle hit Jason's shoulder instead of the trash bin, Jason hoped Shawn had seen it; he thought of the scent of Shawn's sweat, how it had smelled in his dream about the cowhide lash. He'd thrown his underwear away so Mama wouldn't see; he'd left the trash bag in the woods on the way down to Mister Gas. He bought two jugs of milk and stood on the concrete island as Shawn filled the tank of a red Tundra. He didn't want to walk back home. He'd heard about faraway places where you slept outside at night, where adults were only fourteen, deserts or something, but the milk was getting warm, so he started back up the hill and thought about tomorrow, which was only June first even though the junebugs had already died.

What were you thinking about while you walked? said Mama back home.

Jason paused. The trees, I guess.

I felt it, she said. Both my legs twitched.

I forgot my watch, said Jason.

Think about eleven minutes ago, she said.

Jason remembered thinking of Shawn pressing him into loblolly pine bark, naked in mud as the rough ridges of bark mashed into his chest. The opposite of eleven was negative eleven. Twelve minutes now, she said. I felt it working.

I don't think it was, said Jason, but he didn't want her legs to be his fault.

Think how you did it, she said. I felt your steps.

I can't remember.

Was it my face? My voice?

When Jason met her eyes, she nodded.

The voice, she repeated.

Jason tried to nod his head, but it was a lie; there hadn't been any minutes.

We'll order a tape recorder from the Penney's catalog, she said.

I stepped on all the roots like you told me to.

Good, she said, nodding so hard that the mole on her neck shook. Jason wished he were excited too. They hadn't shared a moment in a long time.

Check and see if the minimart sells them, Mama said.

Right now?

Tomorrow.

Yes, ma'am.

Ma'am, she said. I never taught you that. It's not even a word.

It comes from school, said Jason.

Like lice, said Mama. Her smile was gone now. Did you even think of me at all?

Jason nodded. I thought about the milk.

I'm not the milk, said Mama. I'm a completely different thing.

You were the reason I went there.

No, she said and shook her head, you'd get it anyways. Just to get out of this house. She talked like she was pressing the words out of her intestine. Jason remembered Shawn's arms lifting crates of milk, and he turned away so Mama wouldn't know how he wished those arms would squeeze him, but it was too late; she rubbed the birthmark bird that watched him from the back of her neck, its marbly eyes the ones that saw into his head where bodies writhed beneath the setting sun. The only man who'll ever touch you again is the coroner, she said, but Jason was too far away to answer. He wondered if he had a birthmark too. At the bathroom sink he cut his hair so short he looked like a boy again, but there was nothing on his scalp. No one even saw it but the glass. He didn't know if a mirror's opposite was cold or warm, so he imagined the frigid metal crane touching his one side while Shawn's flesh warmed his other, whipping him with a black belt that fueled the breeze above the quarry, while at the house Mama danced so cheerfully as the night kept dying until the moon was down so no light showed what he'd created.

I don't want you to go back to school, she said.

It's still three months away.

I get so lonely.

There's the TV, said Jason, but then Mama busted it with a pretend kick of her leg. Jason tried to think of something good to say, but she made it hard to stay for long inside the world. He poured her another glass of milk. Come here and put my legs up for me, she said. He wanted to shave them for her again, but she was too stubborn to let him. Jason didn't understand why. He tried to remember the last time he'd said no to anything. Whatever Jason wanted, Shawn wanted the same thing backwards. It was incredible, but he watched the sky for helicopters, wheeled machines, because he knew there were people who didn't understand.

Stop that, said Mama. It's like you're not even in the house.

You're the one that gave it to me, Jason said. He saw in every impatient sip of milk how Mama wanted the sip to be finished, how liquid and glass and the air made her so mad she could almost move her toes again.

I mean thinking in general.

I'm thinking about getting a job down at the station.

I don't want you working, she said immediately.

For money to fix the car.

Money won't fix that car.

We could go places again when I'm sixteen.

Gas fumes give you cancer.

I'd be inside the store, he said.

Cancer goes through walls.

I wouldn't get it till I'm old.

You'd never be here, she said. You wouldn't work the puzzles anymore.

That's not true, said Jason. He found a thousand-piece puzzle in the closet and dumped its pieces out and brushed the jigsaw dust onto the floor. There, he said, and he pushed edge pieces toward Mama, who wheeled herself up to the table and reached for piles Jason made of clouds, of purple lupines on a lakeshore. He worked on a steeple to divide the hole in the sky into two parts. At every piece he fit he tapped his finger twice, and Mama fell asleep. Her head leaned limply forward like a jack-in-the-box. The time was nine and ten and nearly midnight. Jason went outside and tried to break a bourbon bottle's neck against the woodpile, but it just bounced off the wood. He smashed it on the concrete gutter drain. He cut the stalks of eight white irises blooming in a bed of weeds beneath the hickory. With his shirt off he wet his hands in the birdbath and rubbed his chest so that the cool teeth of June night air scraped water off his flesh, the back door open to the breeze, and Mama woke up at twelve-nineteen, like always; she was thirty. She rubbed sleep from her eyes and said, What's this.

They're for your birthday, Jason said.

Those were the only flowers in the yard.

They're still in the yard. They're just inside instead.

Mama began to wheel herself back and forth. Dead, too.

Not yet, he said. There's water.

Why do you treat me so nice? she said.

It's not nice, he said; it's just normal.

I haven't done anything nice for you.

What's the word for just normal? Jason started to ask, but he stepped backwards when she trembled. He wanted to cover his face and run. She spoke so slowly.

I was having the most terrible dream.

Why was it terrible? said Jason.

The flowers. The white things. Sweat was on her face. Mucus moved audibly in her throat. Why are you here? she said and spun the vase. It didn't fall. Flowers weren't what people liked.

Just say I'm just an old bitch like in the dream.

Jason shook his head. It helped his heart slow down to close his eyes.

Don't you forget that word, said Mama, wheeling into the bedroom. You'll need it if you ever wanna be a man in this town.

Jason wondered what town she meant. He hadn't seen one all summer. He wished Mama didn't even like him, and he'd keep walking one direction away from home. If he felt like crying, he'd just cry. He hadn't in three years, not since the green diary, the one he'd burned with the leaves last fall.

That night at the quarry Shawn tied a hangman's noose to the oak and placed a cinder block upright. Jason's stomach rose and fell at the touch of strange hands, the smell of motor oil. I'm sorry I ran away, he said softly, and he put his head in the loop. It calmed him to wait for Shawn to kick the block away, because they'd never have to grow old together. They'd never see the ugliness in each other.

But what if that's all you remember about me?

Jason shook off motion sickness when he looked at Mama's voice.

That I hate flowers. And I don't even hate flowers.

Jason saw nightbirds flying too slowly to form jet trails.

I don't even know what I hate, said Mama. It's all out in the world. She wheeled herself to the kitchen again and labored at the puzzle until the Church of the Good Shepherd was complete except for one missing piece. I feel wrong, she said. You're old enough. You know that.

Jason removed edge pieces from the puzzle and reattached them.

Don't you start to feel wrong too.

I feel okay, said Jason.

I never should have tried to hook our minds up.

That's just a game, said Jason.

The walking times. The roots. It was so selfish.

But nothing happened.

I felt a twitch.

I wasn't even thinking about you.

You got infected, she said. It's like cancer, but in your mind.

I don't have any cancer in my mind.

I know how you look at that grocery boy.

How do—

Ronnie.

Ronnie? said Jason. But he's ugly.

Mama stared at him like an ulcer was eating her stomach, and he knew he'd said the wrong thing. An ulcer was someone's fault. He wasn't ashamed of what he and Shawn had done together, but he understood the need to hide their actions. It had been shortsighted to let Shawn brand him with his black initials like a dog tag. He wanted to get scared and make everything burn, but it wasn't a year yet, so he lay awake and counted stars and shaped them into profane spires, distant furculae of the night. At the quarry Shawn swung from vines whose handles grew like human toes, but cold, and the animals and squirrels were his friends; when he quacked they said quack quack. When he hooed they hoo-hooed too. Mama snored just once every thirty seconds, but the noises pierced the night like foghorns. Jason tried to think what dream could be catching fire like that. What if she choked on the snores? He entered her room and unfolded her wheelchair and sat down to guard her; he wasn't tired. The crescent moon was rising. Fireflies that lit the field outside her window were the only darknesses in a ruthless swell of light that closed in on him and Mama together like a choke collar.

Melissa, she said in her sleep.

Jason closed his book in a hurry. He didn't know a Melissa. His eyes burned as he watched for signs of consciousness. Maybe it would have been his name if he'd been born a girl, or maybe she was real. Mama had smiled when she spoke the name. Jason looked around for her diary, but his hands were tied to metal fists that rose like inverted trivets from the crane. Shawn's face twisted up with every breath, stretching all its shadows into pieces. There, Mama repeated like the words were snores, her scratchy voice masculine and deep. Her face was a hybrid of many faces; somewhere in the world was a boy with her real eyes, and she had his, and someone's nose and Adam's apple. Jason wondered how his own face had turned out the way it did when Mama's was so harsh and sharp, and he felt evil for having wished she'd die, even though it was for her happiness; she always wanted to.

He pinched his nipple tight until his face clenched up and she wasn't in his head. Harder, he whispered. It excited him to know he'd feel ashamed when it was over. Shawn's skin was twitching everywhere like stinging wasps. They breathed together like two chimneys of the same burnt-down house exhaling their last smoke into the frozen night.

Two suns rose into the sky that morning. He didn't even know how to explain it. They hovered in the vacant space above the quarry: not a sick moon or some exploded star, but two distinct and shining balls of fire.

Mama was still snoring at eleven. She hated watching the soaps by herself, but this way they'd have something to say to each other, because she could tell Jason what had happened.

He tied his tennis shoes in double knots. His bones shrank when he stayed awake so long. He turned on the humidifier and closed the blinds and locked the door and in the yard a white splat fell from a tree and barely missed him. He wished he could shit straight back up at the bird for revenge, but it was already gone. Everything became a dream as long as he was alone. Shadows were falling opposite their usual paths. In twenty minutes

he was at the service station. Shawn cast a narrow shadow from
a ladder against the marquee. A plastic number nine lay on gravel
below him. The sun bathed his hair and skin in a coppery glow
like burnt celluloid. He dropped a two. He dropped a one. Jason
gathered the numbers.

There's bird shit on your head, said Shawn above him.

Jason rubbed his hair quickly with both hands.

Psych, said Shawn.

What's psych?

It's a lie.

Jason looked at his hands. He squinted up at Shawn, who
was descending the ladder now. Did the price go up? he asked.

We ran out of that kind of gas.

Don't you get more?

It sank down into the ground, Shawn said.

He stepped off the ladder and took the numbers from Jason
and tossed them onto a trash pile of planks and oil cans. So you
better watch out, he added, or you'll blow up. He took a lighter
from his pocket and held it up to Jason's face and flicked it.

Boom, he said. He laughed when Jason flinched.

I was thinking of applying for a job, said Jason.

He turned red when his words came out in a quick mumble,
but Shawn understood him anyway. You ain't afraid of gas inside
the ground?

Should I be? said Jason.

Boom, Shawn said, louder than before, and Jason flinched
again. He waited for Shawn to hit him; flinching was two fists
on the arm. His voice sounded high, transparent next to Shawn's,
and he wanted not to be embarrassed anymore. He wanted to
be eighty years old, so everyone who'd ever heard his voice would
be too old to remember. He followed Shawn into the minimart,
where four men were playing poker on a three-legged table. Did
I stutter? said a bald man sipping Coke that dripped onto his

beard and glistened there. Saw two, up three. The sloe-eyed man laid down his cards and glanced across at Shawn and up at Jason, who stood now in the doorframe blocking sunlight. The man tugged his overalls, and he was tall above the others; tobacco bulged in his jaw.

Are you still hiring? said Jason, and the men laughed at the lurch in his voice.

How old are you? said the tall one.

Sixteen, said Jason.

My boy wudden shit for it till seventeen.

For what? said the bald man.

For gas, he answered.

All the men at the table laughed, and the bald man nodded his head at Shawn. Eighteen Sairday week ain't you.

Pumps good gas now.

They all chuckled. Jason chuckled too, but he didn't want there to be a father. He watched them watching his reflection on the freezer window. The tall man told him what kind of job it was, how he'd mop the floor and scrub the bathrooms down. Jason nodded, but the man coughed and said, I'm the one that does the okay.

A woman in bleached overalls called out, Mosby, are you runnin a store?

The man who did the okay went to the counter and bagged her beer. When she was gone he sent Jason out to sweep the lot with a broom as wide as Mama's wheelchair. We'll see how you do with that. Jason took it out into the heat and stood there looking across the mashed bottle caps and dried-up gum. He was proud to be holding the broom when a truck passed by on the highway. Tomorrow he'd wear a white V-neck shirt like Shawn, who was pumping a GMC Savana full of mid-grade. He pumped five dollars' worth into an old Impala. He pumped pressure into

the hissing tires of a Talon. The air was sticky; everyone was
sweating. Men in their cars were sweating. When Shawn spat a
loogy across cracked concrete he looked satisfied to have reached
the grass.

You see the sundog?

Where? said Jason.

In the sky.

Jason looked at the sky.

Not now, dumbass.

When? said Jason.

When it was there.

When was it there?

You could just say no.

No for what? said Jason.

No you didn't see it.

A moving van pulled up to the diesel pump. Sundog. Sundog.
Jason wanted to dribble the word onto the asphalt with gasoline
so he'd remember it until he could write it down. The diary was
on the floor. He pictured it there. He realized it was on the floor
by Mama's bed. The rope was wet and fragrant from the dew.
Shawn wasn't pumping gas; he was watching Jason's face go
white. Life at the quarry was simple. You're the only one, he
would repeat to Shawn. Sometimes he felt an empty sadness
where Mama had been. The rope was creaking in the wind so
loud, shut up, shut up. It made him want to stab himself.

You froze? said Shawn, who looked so calm he didn't seem
real anymore. Jason felt his cheeks go red from heat and now
this voice that pointed to his turquoise ring and said, You got a
girl up at that mile and a quarter house?

Just Mama, he said.

He imagined her eating his stomach lining with her antacid
pills. He continued sweeping so that he could look away, so
Shawn wouldn't see inside his head.

Shawn shrugged and said, I let my mama wear her own ring.

Jason nodded with his back turned to Shawn.

She the one that drinks up all that milk?

Most of it, said Jason.

She a cow or somethin?

No, said Jason softly.

A cow don't even drink milk.

So why'd you ask?

You know who drinks a lot of milk?

Jason shook his head.

Loretta Lynn, said Shawn.

I thought she's dead.

Then watch out for your mama then.

She's all right, said Jason.

She sick? said Shawn.

Mostly she just coughs.

It helps her throat.

To cough? said Jason.

Naw, Loretta Lynn's throat.

Do you listen to that? said Jason.

All I listen to is metal.

Like who? said Jason.

It don't matter, said Shawn. Long as it's loud.

Jason tried to keep talking in spite of all the teeth embedded in his heart. He shut his eyes and told himself his words were coming out clear, clear, clear.

You know what time it is? said Shawn.

You're the one with a watch.

It was time for a cigarette break. Shawn fetched two orange drinks from inside and handed one to Jason, and they sat down on the oily concrete. Shawn's head blocked the sun. He lit a Marlboro but didn't offer one to Jason, who felt sick to his stomach. He didn't care about opposites anymore. Eighty years wasn't enough; he wished it were a hundred, and anyone who'd ever seen his face would be dead.

It scared him to sit so close to Shawn. It was worse to be nervous than to be alone. The drink's orange dye fed the twinges in his bowels as he tried to think of how to leave. He couldn't run away forever; it was the only place to buy milk.

When he sliced his middle finger open with his pocketknife blade his eyes stayed as still and furtive as a prowling cat's.

Ow, Shawn said when he saw the blood.

It doesn't hurt, said Jason.

It's a knife.

Once I did it to all ten.

What for? said Shawn.

It changes your fingerprints.

There ain't nothing wrong with my fingerprints.

So they can't ever catch you, said Jason.

I ain't done nothin to be caught.

Jason flinched at the word. He was dangling by the quarry in the breeze; there'd be a breeze when Mama found them. Shawn would remove his belt and hoist himself onto Jason like a deadweight pendulum, gripping his shoulders so they could swing together, two acrobats sharing a trapeze. Mama never read until her soaps were over, because of her eyes. He'd never heard her say some of the words he'd used; he wondered if she knew them.

Come back here with me for a second.

Jason was sweating so heavily his shirt was plastered to his skin. He laid the broom down on the concrete and said, I need to run home for a minute.

When Shawn laughed at him he turned red.

I forgot to put the fire out.

A fire in June? said Shawn.

Jason shook his head. The oven.

Shawn laughed again. Call your mama.

There's no phone.

Shawn pointed to a pay phone by the road.

I mean at the house, said Jason.

What happened to it?

We can't afford one.

You don't afford a phone, said Shawn, you just get one, and Jason's shoulders burned when he tried to move them for a response. He wondered if he should walk to the left or the right on the road to hitchhike to another state. He knew every direction had a state in it.

Pa ain't gonna let you go.

It would just take half an hour, said Jason, but he didn't even want to go anymore. He might as well work the whole day if he was going to run away afterwards.

Come back here with me for a second.

Back where?

Shawn pointed to the trees.

Jason wanted to be alone, so he could feel nervous on his own. It made it worse to have to talk at the same time. He didn't understand what Shawn could want with him. He followed Shawn into the thick woods where birds had defleshed the skeletons of rats. The air smelled like bourbon as they passed beneath an upside-down hammock of dead vines, and Shawn stretched his arms into the heat. You talk the same way I talk, he said.

Jason froze. What kind of way?

The way you say words.

Jason put his hands in his pocket to stop their shaking.

I learned it up in Knoxville, how you tell.

You're from Knoxville? said Jason, looking away.

Shawn shook his head. It's not just the words.

You said your pa didn't want us to leave the station.

He don't really give a shit, said Shawn.

Then I should run to the house.

Shawn put a hand on Jason's shoulder.

What are you doing? said Jason.

There's this place where they learned me how to tell.

What kind of place?

This bar, said Shawn.

Jason nodded.

It has to do with your fingers.

Jason looked down at his fingers and Shawn's fingers.

How long they are, said Shawn. He held his hand up to Jason's, which was bigger, and pulled it back and said, Just against theirselves, not the whole thing.

The sun was beginning to sink. Jason looked at the sky and saw fire.

Don't get nervous.

I'm not, said Jason.

I could tell it from your fingers.

Shawn moved up against Jason's body until his face was blurry. It hurt Jason's eyes. He hoped he'd know how to move his mouth right. Shawn had a chipped incisor. His lips slithered like two wounded animals, pressing Jason's whole body into the soft pine needles, and Jason shut his eyes. He hated that Shawn was being so gentle. He didn't even look the same as he had at the quarry; his eyes were smaller, rodentlike. He smelled like cologne. His hair didn't look like straw anymore. Jason had taken the wrong hill from his house down to the wrong highway, to a station that was separate from his mind. This wasn't Shawn. The sun was setting over the wrong woods in the wrong west, and Jason struggled to breathe. His throat retreated down into his guts like a withering root.

You're not paying attention, said Shawn.

Jason's windpipe closed up. He thought about his bedside table at the house, where he should have hidden the diary, where his yellow asthma inhaler lay in a drawer. He hadn't used it in nearly two years.

Can I pull a hair out of the back of your neck? said Shawn.

Jason felt like bladders were filling up within his shut eyes.

You won't feel it.

Yes I will, said Jason.

No you won't.

Why do you want it?

Why don't you want me to have it?

Get away from me. Don't touch me.

Shawn grinned. But I've already done it, you big baby.

Jason put his hand to the back of his neck to search for where the missing hair had been. When Shawn held it up to the dying orange light Jason's skin began to itch all over his body. He scratched himself. He wanted water.

Now I can clone you, said Shawn. I have your DNA.

Shawn wasn't supposed show affection. It oozed from his fingertips like tobacco spit. Jason picked up a fallen tree branch, because Shawn was worthless to him. Shawn watched him lift the knobby staff and grinned as if he wanted to be lashed, but the stick fell into three pieces. Jason hadn't seen its rottenness in the dark. He understood now why Mama had always hated sunlight. The sun dripped glue into his eyes, all day long, and it made no logical sense. What was the point of a molten ball that caused him only pain? He picked up a rock, because he wanted the rock to be a part of their world. It made a thud. Jason felt tranquil as he waited for Shawn to tackle him. It was taking a long time, but he had a lot to think about. You little son of a bitch, said Shawn, rubbing his leg like he was the opposite of everything, and Jason relaxed, because Shawn was talking the right way now.

NATCHER MOUNTAIN

It was two things Lonzoe done, it was the tree farm and the gas stations. It was Annie who he done it for, that night was quite a night, the wind chimes in the wind. It rained and rained. Clyde come in at Billiards slams his money on the table, drinks the honey wheat. Was they out of High Life. Clyde said no Lonzoe I just took a likin to the taste. Lonzoe says you think I give a lumpy shit. Don't take no fence. Don't tell me what to do. Clyde starts shootin eightball, Lonzoe lines up lucky number 7. Hey Lonzoe I guess you and Annie have one of them open relationships. Drug it out like real slow words. What ye mean. Seen her with the Breeden boy at Hatcher's Store for beer they's headed for the lake. How the hell would you know. Why else would they go that way.

Usual Lonzoe was real practical. When he heard the song about the cowgirl on the ceiling he said that don't make no sense. The one about the lost highway, he said that's Highway 72 how it got swallered when they put up Tellico Lake. He whups Clyde three straight games and Clyde he blabbered this and that and if he'd had his glasses on and Lonzoe said eat shit and wandered off. Where's Lonzoe. There he was against a table like to crush it. I'm gonna kill him Jasper he tells me. Who. That Breeden boy, I'll slash his throat. That's what all folks says. I ain't different from all folks. Went to the pay phone come inside said what's the number. Call Annie first. I did and she ain't home. They run that Christmas farm, go look up Smoky Mountain Trees. As if they run the whole damn Smoky Mountain. I don't know why I said it though I should of known to shut my mouth when his eyes was slants like that. Went out again come in again. You with me fellers. The football game ain't over, Clyde says. Vandy ain't even gonna score. I still wanna see it. You big faggot. You cuckold. What the hell's that mean. It's what you are Lonzoe if it's like I seen.

I don't know where he gets those words, it's like it's a big box full.

Lonzoe lunged for Clyde but Clyde moved forward, Lonzoe's on the floor, why don't you save it for Johnny Breeden.

Lonzoe drove.

Lonzoe smokes. He takes us down the 411, flicks his cigarette. Maybe you should of took the Mint Road. Maybe you could hush so I can think. It was some big rain comin. I wondered if we'd kill Johnny Breeden. I hoped it would be Annie in his stead that died, I never got to drink with Lonzoe anymore, that's why I come. Clouds like big black nightmares right there in November, they was dogs, they was the trees. It looked like they was little bits of shot. Lonzoe cussed on Sixmile Road to make the truck go. What are we gonna do. Quiet, I'm still workin it in my brain. I don't get quiet for no one else but Lonzoe. He was real mad. I'd never put no stock in Annie. Her skin's all green like it's the bottom of a lake. In the trees they was no leaves. Lonzoe pulls in Breeden's driveway, no lights on and rocks is in the air. Fists against the door, they weren't no answer. Johnny's at the lake, them fenced-up dogs all karf karf karf, they weren't no other sound. Lonzoe got hisself so mad he took their big ceramic nigger eatin fruit, he smashed it on the porch. I love to watch him smash it. Run down to the shed. Come out had a chain saw.

Jasper I'm gonna cut every tree on this farm.

He looked into my eyes seen I was scared.

No you ain't. You watch me. Chain saw's loud. They ain't nobody home nor in this valley. Mick Jenkins up the road. He'll be stone drunk. Don't do it. If you get the other saw it's twiced as fast, the rain is comin hard. Growl just falls down timber, timber, water felt so good. Trees would fall whichever way you pushed. Halfway up the trunk it wasn't only sell em anyway. I don't know what kind of trees it was. I wished them trees was all the men at Billiards, Lonzoe'd saw them till they died except for me we'd click our chain saws then we'd drink a beer. Everybody in the world was split in two, I'd be the only one, he'd talk out loud about the things inside his head. Now all he said was Annie Annie Annie. The clouds they had the moon in them, the rain. Look what just two drunks has done tonight. The stumps was warm, I said you never have such fun with Annie, fuck her, move back up at Natcher Mountain. My fingers still was shakin from the saw. I went to piss I didn't see him get the rifle out. They was four slow spaced-out shots and then no barks. Why'd you go and do that for. Cause Annie's mine and I'll make sure that everybody learns it.

Two of the dogs was dead the other two just crawled. Ain't you gonna shoot again. He shook his head. What had come over Lonzoe. He come from purebred mountain stock, it clogged him full of meanness. Pit bull crawled behind the truck before it died and Lonzoe backed right up and all this blood and Lonzoe said,

I'm right pissed off, it made me glad. I said how Annie was no good. I was the only one he'd tolerate to say it, he'd of clobbered any other man, I would of watched it. He drove me home he come in for a beer. Jasper, he says, real serious, and then I thought he would of said a serious thing.

You think we'll get in trouble.

I don't know.

I don't either.

The mountains back behind us, was that all, we thought two different things about each other, it was tangled. Clyde calls up and Breeden's down at Myrtle Beach, three weeks, my heart beats fast. How the hell do you know. He works with me at Denso. Who was that with Annie. Who knows cause every day she's on a different guy. Oh well it's done now. What is. Things. What things. Hung up cause that's what Lonzoe would of done he hated Clyde, Clyde was ugly. Lonzoe's passed out snorin on the floor, the bottle's empty. What was it but go to sleep, the sky was black as black. The trees would turn to brown next day I thought but it was green for way past Christmas. When they jailed his ass I wanted in there too but Lonzoe didn't rat me out, I didn't visit, he had other friends inside that jail. I didn't want to see. He got hisself probation and the grocery went and fired him. Annie left for Rufus Reaper, fuck you then, he said, I won't even beat him up, that's how much I give a shit. He had to pay the court, he had to make the payments on his truck. He opens up the *Daily Times* about how terrible he is, they wasn't on his side. Jasper, you got to help me get some money.

I said alright.

You ever robbed a man before. No one I ain't related to. Who would you steal from. Rich folks. Who's rich. Lamar Alexander. He don't live here no more. Reggie White. He runs a church you shit for brains, that made me mad, I told him figure out your money for yourself. I went home and they was snow up top the mountain. I wanted to drive and see the snow but fuck it, I could see the snow from my porch. How come you hear about a avalanche in other places, never here. I thought how Lonzoe wished he drove a truck but now he can't because of jail. We use to drive the mountains just to drive. What if it snowed till everyone was dead. I got so piss ass drunk and meantime Lonzoe robbed the Amoco, he robbed the Mister Gas, he robbed the Walland Highway Citgo. He stole a car which I don't know why he did that, he wasn't never scared. I don't know how to tell him things. He saw the coppers in his driveway so he drove out here to my place.

Guess what. What. I'm fucked.

We pitched horseshoes. He got to thinkin loud how Annie'd spent up all his money on her perfume and her clothes. She never bought a thing for me, he says, she threw my tape of Slayer out the window, called me stupid. I never cost you a penny I said. She smacked me on the head most every day he says. He got to thinkin all the miserable things she done. Can you drink a beer in prison. Don't talk like that, you're my buddy don't go get yourself in jail no more, I told you all along what Annie was, she even got the cross eyes.

Lonzoe just laughed.

Don't you care if you get locked up. You know I don't think he did give a fuck.

How old did we start drinkin he said. I said fourteen or so. It's been a long time since it felt like then he says and now the only fun is to fuck shit up, the trees was fun, the Amoco, the tires I slashed at Billiards they was fun.

I didn't know you done that.

Clyde's, and just the one.

We stared into the dark.

You know what.

What.

I never give a shit about that bitch Annie.

Bull shit I said.

I never even liked her.

Well I'll be.

Does that mean you don't like me cause I lied.

I like you.

Good cause I was scared he said.

You was? I said.

I ain't no good.

Bullshit I said but as for Annie she can rot.

I always liked you better, Lonzoe said. The stars jabbed down like helicopter search lights, we watched it gobble up the black. It felt like we was kids deep in the woods again beneath the insulation house and twigs blew off the trees they must of been as many stars, they twinkled where the hemlocks was, the cops won't never find us, we were shadows.

Anyways.

Clyde comes over Lonzoe picks a fight. You want a good kick in the balls. That's what he got, he's moanin like the devil girl that died. You alright there Clyde. Stay out of this, said Lonzoe, just you lay there and be drunk.

That's exactly what I did.

You was happy Annie left me. You had your scummy little eye on her and Clyde moans no no no. Lonzoe kicks his legs like he was doin it for me. It made me proud how fast he kicked his legs. There was Clyde all tied up in a chair. The towrope from my truck. You know the things on oaks the strings of fuzz well Lonzoe scoops a handful up and shoves it in Clyde's mouth and spit hung down all right you little prick, we'll try it thisaway. He picked up more and shoved it up Clyde's nostrils with his finger. The sky was upside down just like a cowpond and the moon trapped up inside of it, I felt like I was with someone. I thought of Annie gettin it from Rufus, I wished Clyde didn't have no eyes to see the 2 of us together in the yard, me layin down and Lonzoe over Clyde hey Clyde your nose is all stopped up. Ow ow it hurts. Shut up you baby. Lonzoe took some rope and wrapped it round.

Say sorry or I strangle ye.

Lonzoe starts a laughin, wouldn't stop. I don't think he meant old Clyde no harm. I knew I'd fall to sleep account of everybody's half alive and doin things they never would of done inside my head. Woke up in a foot of snow the coldness burned my blood no one's around. Every morning after black outs when I wake I think of what I can't remember. It could of been a hundred thousand acts. He could of thought that I was Annie. Scrap of paper in my jeans said Jasper, gone to hide myself at ma's house well his fingers put it there, it wasn't mine, it wasn't Clyde's.

Every time he gone he come back different. I know how it is down there in Georgia.

Drank some Busch, I drank some Wild Turkey. Where's the cops, maybe I'll go down to Georgia too so I can change like Lonzoe is and then we'll stay the same. The air so cold my sweater mashed that sweater fuzz inside my belly button. Get out. Get out. Poked my Buck knife up there like it's a cave. I was drunk or else it would of hurt me somethin fierce. The twists and turns inside of it. They wasn't nothin in that hole, but it must of bled for upwards of an hour.

FETCH

What a pretty bird, said Leila—the gray and yellow one. Patrick stomped on it, along with all the other babies in the nest. He cleared his throat. The tiger moths all got away, but it was fall, and they probably died later in the month. I don't know how the birds had stayed frozen all summer like that. I guess they weren't frozen anymore, really, but thawed and baked and rotted.

Which one?

The one that hopped up like that, she said. Like a pogo stick.

It didn't hop, he said. That was me.

Leila loved him because of his curls, his locked silver necklace, but mostly his face. It was smooth like an eighteen-year-old boy's. He would sit in the graveyard sewing chains of Queen Anne's lace, and he wore them until the sap drained. Make your own, he said to Leila; she liked that too. Once he made one for me, and it lasted eight days.

Leila and I lay below him in a field of grass as he straddled a crooked fencepost and thought of what to say to us. When he held the flask of vodka to his lips, his fingers made a brine-smoothed whelk. Power lines rose like lasers from a distant valley. Take it all in, he said, and I tried so hard my temples ached.

Then Leila had to go out to Tacoma for a few months; her sister had been in an accident with glass. Leila couldn't afford the phone rates, so she wrote Patrick a letter nearly every day. I sat on crisp leaves on the porch of our old house and read them slowly, and then I took them inside to Patrick and said *Read aloud* and sank into his voice.

I shot up today. Forgot how it bursts my mind apart, bends the notes of songs. I wonder do you remember either. You have this thing you call your only heart but its twin somewhere wants you to score a gram on Friday night, share it across the continent with me.

Around then was when he first got a job with Manpower, worked all day, built some muscle. Would you leave her if I were a girl? I asked. He had lips like silent eyeballs. You wouldn't have thought he had muscles; he stood there like a flower petal, smiling. You know the horses drawn on walls of European caves, ten thousand years ago? That was him.

I'd had never entertained the thought until Leila had come along, because he was my friend. We were standing on the back deck of our run-down house where wind stole all the yellow leaves away. The walnut tree bore thousands of brown asteroids, and when Patrick didn't answer, I was happy: he had deemed my question difficult. We lived up in the gables by the thunderstorms. It was the kind of place where if Leila broke a jar of olives across the floor, they worked their way into deep cracks in the hardwood. The rooms were bright and airy with secret passageways. Stop this, I screamed, holding Leila away from him. You love each other. You looked at her, Leila shouted, and the glasses rattled. Well, this is what happens. Patrick clenched his fist. You wuss, Leila taunted, you wouldn't know how. It was just some Longbranch bartender she was mad about, but I wished it had been me. When I let her go, she dropped his weed into a bottle of glass cleanser. They screamed in foreign scales I'd never heard before, words I couldn't understand.

What a hot day for September. I opened all the windows for a breeze. The wind felt best in the living room. When Leila turned over a chair, I saw an electrical outlet we'd never used before, hidden for an entire year. It made me sad—four lonely slits and two round holes, such a noise. They really did love each other, though; you could tell by how they cleaned the glass up together. I had a few drinks in my room. Later, when I came home from buying hydrogen peroxide at the drugstore, I sat on the front porch and saw a green olive that had made its way down through the house, its pimiento forced halfway out. I wanted to eat it, but it was covered in soot.

Leila ran off to go shopping somewhere the rest of the day, so I got to hang out with Patrick. I don't remember what he said, but I remember the dimple in his cheek twitching when he said it. I knew his face from sixty different angles. Everyone in the past had his voice now.

So he read the letter and the new ones that came on Tuesday, Wednesday, Thursday, and I went with him to visit his father, who was a diabetic. I promise we won't stay long, said Patrick in the car outside the peeling duplex. We didn't knock. Plastic covered all the furniture, like always. You been doin anything bad with that little girl of yours? Patrick's father called as Patrick rummaged in the kitchen for the cardboard box of orange-capped syringes. Come in here let me smell your hands.

When he laughed, he boomed like a tuba. I heard the crackle of aluminum foil. There isn't shit to eat in this house, said Patrick, reentering the living room, and already it was time to go. The car ride home was silent. What if I just don't have anything to say, I thought, ever. What if that's just not what I'm meant for. The roads were crowded. If everybody drove a car, no one would have a shadow anymore. Back home Patrick held a pregnant needle up. I wanna take this into N.A., he said, do it in front of everybody. I really, really want to. Like a chain.

He smiled at me. I watched his eyes and watched him breathing; he did it even better than in the dream, when his hair was one inch longer, just enough to blow the wind across his eyes and I said fall was my favorite season and we shaved our one-day beards together in the bathroom mirror with the window open to yellow maple leaves that spun and floated like they had so many ways down.

Can you hear me through the wall when I have sex? said Patrick.

Leila's gone, I said. You don't have sex.

I mean did you used to, Patrick said. She's coming back. She's not gone.

No, I said, only when you jerk off.

He carved his name in our old kitchen table, and Leila's name, and half of my name, as much as he could write before the needle was fully blunted.

The letters were piling up. He didn't pay attention to anything. I could have asked him if leaves were still on the trees and he could have said *yes* or *no*. But he was looking out the window when I stole a two-day stack of papers and put them in my drawer. He must not have wanted them. Maybe he wanted me instead. I made sure to look well-groomed and wore cologne each day, black shoes instead of sneakers. I stopped showing him the mail at all; he was always at work when it came, anyway.

The job wasn't going well for him anymore. He dropped a stack of bricks on someone's foot; he spilled a bucket of mortar. He picked the wrong guys to try to borrow money from. They asked him why he never ate his lunch. He came home in a sour mood and smoked weed on the roof. Then he got fired and came home at two, just after the mailman. Still no letter? he asked me. I wanted to give him that day's, that whole week's, but I was embarrassed to explain why I'd withheld them in the first place.

> I saw the Pacific Ocean today. I don't know what you were thinking while my eyes reeled in the waves but you weren't thinking about me; I didn't feel it. I hope you know the smack idea was a joke. We're done with that, you know.

I hated her for being able to write to him, for him to listen. She really was pretty, I suppose. I liked going to the mall with her so all the straight boys would envy me; I liked it when she whispered, in the middle of the night, on the roof with me, when she couldn't sleep.

I just want to pretend we're sixteen again, said Patrick. Take any day from that year. I want to make this that day.

So we had cheeseburgers and fries at Wendy's. We went to West Town Mall and bought some nitrous whippets and got high down by the river ten times each. We rolled a joint beneath the railroad trestle and said we wished our older brothers were home from college to buy us beer. We drove up and down the strip and looked at U.T. girls. Patrick shouted *penis!* at one with a green backpack. His eyes met mine. I almost took his hand.

We don't have any money, he said. If we were sixteen, we'd have money.

I parked right in front of the bar.

I don't want to be sixteen anymore, he said in the booth at Hanna's; we had a Turbodog apiece. I asked how old he wanted to be now. Each time he said *I don't know*, it was the saddest thing I'd ever heard.

We could be twelve and run away to Chattanooga, I said.

I think I want to be ninety, he said. Then I can just sit there. I won't have to do anything at all.

I had sat down opposite him instead of beside; he had chosen first, so it was my decision. I don't know why I didn't tell him how I felt. I wouldn't even have needed to think of the words myself; I had a dozen love letters to choose from. We couldn't afford another beer. We couldn't afford a tip.

I've got nineteen cents, said Patrick.

Why didn't you ask your dad for cash?

He's only got enough money to last him till he's sixty-six. He figured it out on paper.

I shrugged; I was broke too, on unemployment at the time, which wasn't much but it bought me a beer now and then.

Please tell me there's Steel Reserve at the house, said Patrick.

I think there's some.

We can use your card at the package store.

It's maxed out.

Please Jesus is there still a Steel Reserve. We walked up the hill to the house, and there were four. We drank them on the roof till they were gone. Patrick said he had a plan, and I followed him downstairs and back outside. As we walked down Clinch across the viaduct, the mountains were as hazy as my vision. We walked forever. We must have walked two miles. The pawn shop man with two bronze eyes and a steel-capped finger

held Patrick's engagement ring up to a slit of light and frowned.
He offered forty dollars. I was tired by then.

Forty-five, Patrick said in the dark room.

Forty, the man said.

Forty-two.

Forty.

Forty plus three quarters so I can buy a Coke. For the love
of God.

I felt all sorts of years breathing in that space. Did the pawn
man know he could have opened his blinds to see a bare mul-
berry tree, squirrelly power lines, the raised interstate? I didn't
say a word as Patrick's fortieth dollar came to him in silver
change. We were rich; we brown-bagged liquor down Broadway
beneath the freeway. Horns were blowing everywhere like
chopped-up trains. Outside the Salvation Army a couple
screamed at each other. I wonder what that felt like. Under the
bridge the road turned upside down.

I wish I still had my skateboard, Patrick said.

Looping like a wheat sheaf, his straw hairs and his shirt
pulled toward the earth—I wished so too.

If we keep walking this way for six hundred miles, he said,
we'll be in New Orleans.

But first we'd have to cross the river.

He nodded and said, I want to cross it on a railroad bridge.

If we really did it, we'd cross on a real bridge.

What's not real about a railroad?

Nobody goes on it, I said, just coal.

Leila took the railroad out to Washington.

No she didn't. She rode the bus. The railroad's like two hundred bucks.

Not this time, he said. A long time ago.

We were halfway home. I wondered if there was a new letter
yet. By now I felt bad about the entire situation, but Patrick was

looking at me more, and I had a chance with him, I thought. I knew I needed him more than Leila did, and anyway her letters were getting weird. She wrote about auras and said hers was a deep, dark red. Patrick didn't need to be worrying about that.

She called while Patrick was gone buying gin. It was dark outside. Rory, she said to me, I'm so glad to hear you.

Glad to hear me what?

Just to hear you, she said, but I didn't trust her.

Where are you?

In my bedroom.

She said Patrick had sent her three letters. Acts like he hasn't seen mine.

He saw them, I said.

Did he like them?

He's not much of a reader.

Where is he?

Longbranch, I said. Went to meet a friend of his.

Who?

I don't know.

You know all his friends, she said. You both have the same friends.

I can't remember her name.

For a moment Leila's aura changed from red to cold, fiery blue. We recalled the broken olive jar together. It conjured the taste of soot only for me; Leila remembered the glass. The Northwest was rainy and cold that time of year.

Do you want to leave your number?

I'll try back later, she said.

She left me with nothing to do but hang the phone up and walk outside. My stomach hurt; I really was uncomfortable. Patrick brought back whiskey in place of gin. It fits my mood, he said. The bottle had come with a free pack of cards, and we played some rounds of poker. I thought of unplugging the phone, but I didn't even need to do it; she never called again.

The last day before Leila had departed, we drove to Pigeon Forge to race go-carts, just the three of us. We could still afford things then. We went to the track by the waterfall. Mothers watched us speed around their children. I was so high I forgot I had a brake pedal. A man was bungee-jumping at the tower next door; he screamed past my helmet's glass and Patrick won the race. Afterwards we ate funnel cake with strawberries, and Leila said, Forty-eight hours, because that was how long her trip would take.

You can write me a letter the whole time, said Patrick. We were walking on the sidewalk past hotels.

What a selfish idea, she said and jumped up to ride his back. She pointed at me and said, I'll write to him instead. Every day. She beat on Patrick's shoulders. He spun around five times until she giggled and fell off. You can't have fun like this while I'm gone, she said. Promise you'll save it all for when I'm back.

I promise, he said.

Promise you'll feel just wretched the whole time till I return.

We'll be completely miserable, I said, and Patrick just smiled. He was sucking on a Dolly-pop. By then we were driving. Patrick had his finger on the wheel's pulse, and through him I felt every sports car that passed us on the parkway. I'm glad I'm leaving him with you, Leila said to me. Patrick touched his fingerprint to her labret. We drove up the mountain on a back road; soon it turned to gravel. Patrick pulled us off in the woods by a creek overgrown with mountain laurel. We had forty-ouncers in the trunk.

I want to build a dam, Leila announced.

I took my shoes and socks off and waded with her into the cold water. The rocks were slippery with algae. We filled gaps between large stones with sand and gravel. Patrick sat on a root and watched us quarry rocks from beneath the water. It was frigid; we were standing near its source. I chose bigger, stronger stones than Leila did, and they blocked more water, bridged the streambed faster. They were cold and calcified, and Patrick could see the flexing of my frame. I hurried with the gravel. I was winning. Mountains had risen so I could build that dam.

You'd better have a job by the time I get back, Leila told me. I'll be the housewife.

Won't pay much.

I didn't care. I had the money for six weeks' rent, food, beer, I figured, and she was leaving me alone with Patrick's chest, his shoulder blades, and there we stood on the ankles of Gunnel Mountain. I loved the air. Motes of dust rose from the water. I stood so cold but bathed in yellow sunlight. Skunk cabbage was dead and underground, existing only as roots and dried leaves. Blocked water splashed above the rock row. I built it up with stones like stillborn children, gray and heavy and folded in upon themselves. I stirred up silt as I widened the base; it sank in fingery spirals into mortar.

The best part was the cemetery beneath the sunset. A yellow-jacket chased me around the grave of Carson Crawford. Red umbrellas hung by threads from treetops. Leila showed us where we'd sit amongst the stones if we were feng shui artists' chairs. Patrick was east, I was west. Leila had a bed of acorns gathered in a hole beside her leg and bats flew well past dusk above our picnic.

You look perfect against that stone, Leila said to Patrick. Don't you think? she asked me.

I shook my head. It's a conjurer's trick, I said. He's kind of ugly when you think about it. Patrick swatted my leg. He'll have every Knoxville girl on him when I'm gone, said Leila.

That sounds good, he said.

If they do, they'll end up like the one in the song, she said.

I don't remember the song.

Both of them died, I said. They floated down the river out of town.

But there's a dam there, Patrick said.

It was a long time ago, I said. It was before the dam.

Leila told us all to stand up. Look for a grave that died the day you were born. I walked down a mossy row of lumps and clover and read dates that were abbreviated, fading. More children had died in winter than in summer. The trees were mainly cedars, their sap ripe in my nose, and I forgot what year we were in, with all those numbers.

Here's my birthday, Patrick said, but it's 1930.

I wondered if the bones survived as lodes of powder in the soil.

Keep looking, Leila said.

People weren't buried here that late, we're too young.

But Leila found it: it was mine. Her name was Jannie Carpenter, and she'd died at ninety-one and had a husband dead beside her. They had mothered and fathered three dead baby boys.

It's so quiet here, said Patrick.

Imagine if we all just started screaming, Leila said. As loud as we can go, until our throats burn.

Or digging, Patrick said.

What would we scream? I asked.

The dead babies, Leila said. And the spiders. They were all over her shirt. Below her nose a shadow swung darkly back and forth. It got black at night there like it didn't get black anywhere on earth. The graveyard had made us into corpses. I saw the first star in the sky in Patrick's eye, reflected. The stump he sat on had no stone to mark its death.

Who drives back? said Leila.

They hit their own palms twice with fists, and then Leila made a kite's shape with her thumbs and index fingers. Patrick waved his hands like rain, then tossed the keys, and Leila caught them. You always do diamond, he said.

Diamond cuts glass, glass draws blood, blood stains diamond. I sat in the back again and stretched across the imitation leather. Leila dragged her gold ring's plain surface across the window of her door. She'd never owned a diamond, never carved her words indelibly into glasspanes.

So we sat now at the kitchen table drinking whiskey, playing poker, betting pennies; one-eyed jacks were wild, and Patrick couldn't bluff to save his life. A cold breeze filtered through our bleak apartment; I was winning all the pennies, which I planned to use to buy a fifth of gin, which was what I'd wanted in the first place. I've always hated whiskey.

I don't even know her number, Patrick said. The rooms had secret shafts of moonlight, blue flames in the stove's eyes.

You could find out, I said, knowing he thought it too complicated, too arduous somehow to call long-distance information; after all, it was three thousand miles away.

Raise three.

See it and two.

Call.

It was so stupid to play poker with just two people; we might as well have played war, or built castles out of cards.

I think I've fucked my stomach up, he said. I feel full after I eat three bites, like I'm gonna burst. He was skinny; it was a perfect ratio of emptiness to flesh. This was his seventh day off heroin, and his face had begun to glow again, which isn't to say I'd stopped wanting him while he was paler, or ceased ripping his letters into small, uneven pieces.

Maybe it's the drinking.

He shook his head. That's the one thing tried-and-true, he said, is drinking.

There was a cold, blue light between us; there were chipmunks in the walls that scurried down the slopes of tunnels shapeless to my eyes. Oak leaves brown and rigor mortis-stricken fell into the shelter of our room through the deck door, the dusty oven window. I was wrong about the stove; it didn't bloom that night; it had withered in the afternoon and died, when a handsome man from United Cities Gas turned off our pilot light. He had bent so that his torn ear like a tomcat's watched me—two flowers dead: our stove had but the two eyes.

Patrick was sitting up tensely on his elbows. He closed his mouth and opened it and closed it. He wanted me to help him speak, I knew; he had his leather coat on. For fourteen months I'd processed Leila's moans at night through a crooked wall and willed myself into her skin to hold a hundred eighty pounds up by my haunches: he was shivering, he was six-foot-four, and if I die before I wake I prayed that I'd be resurrected in her mold.

Once I'd walked in on them, on purpose, just to see him. They moved like cellophane. Probably they won't again. I've never dismantled anything so intricate. Leila was a pretty girl who played the clarinet, spoke with a soft, kind voice, made necklaces for friends of friends she barely knew. Her letters bore a script like boys' eyebrows. I thought of that after I'd torn them all apart. Once when I was seven years old I rode down Johnny Boone's yard on a Big Wheel with his silver hamster in my hand and my dog ate it. Johnny cried. My stomach had felt the same as with the letters: all the dead men in heaven were looking down at me, watching for reasons not to be my friend.

We should just go somewhere, said Patrick; it's no good being here. Looking into my eyes he said, I'm drunk enough to do anything.

Out to see Leila? I asked.

Have you— he began and stopped. To leave it unsaid he poured himself a drink but the bottle held none, or else a few last drips, and he took his jacket off. His skinight rayon shirt was ribbed and black, like something I would wear to go dancing, to be cruised. We drank the vinegary dregs of week-old wine that glistened in its bottle on the counter. Patrick said things like, I'm too old to meet anybody new; things like, I'd guess they've got phones out there in Washington.

They have area codes and stuff, I said.

We could see the whole city from that window, thunderclouds that bore so many lights and blood-red brakings down on Western Avenue reflected off the Sunsphere's ball of glass and mirrors sixteen stories high. I saw Patrick working up to something: he'd curled up his eyebrows, his face like a helium balloon. All the water in my body parted with the music, and Patrick sang along and swayed to the rhythm. *I just want to dance in your tangles, to give me some reason to move.* When he said, Have you ever been attracted to me? he pushed it out of his mouth in one breath, his eyes aglow but moving nervously across my face.

Brennan's golden retreiver has a litter of puppies. As I was stroking their supple coats of fuzz I began to think of your beautiful head. Brennan went into his toolshed and emerged with a mallard corpse, its broken neck as flaccid as a tail. He was training the puppies to fetch. They ran to the duck. They disemboweled it and it died another death and catalyzed my thoughts of you.

I had tried to slice the skin of my palm with that letter, but Leila's stationery was too thick. I ripped it into halves until I held a

stack too big to tear and walked it to the Dumpster like all the
rest. It's hard to blame me; I was young, just a boy, really, and
I was drinking a lot even then, didn't see the big deal in right
from wrong. I liked to say things like, You can't fight fate, but I
didn't mean it; it was just an interjection.

Every minute of every day, I said.

You're the only two people I'll ever care about.

You're only twenty-four, I said.

I'm too old to bother with new people. It makes me tired.

It made me tired too.

I don't think she's coming back, he said, and I nodded. It
was the conclusion I probably would have drawn as well. I
thought you were cute, he said. It was why I sat down to have
lunch with you that first time, back in seventh grade.

That was thirteen years ago, that day in school. Suddenly my
legs were heavy, mortarlike. I remembered the time I'd cut a wire
in my mother's red sedan so she wouldn't go to work, so she'd
stay home with me, but then I learned she'd been laid off the day
before anyway and it was a very expensive wire. Everyone was
sorry.

Patrick scooted himself around the table. He wasn't perfect
either. Take those baby birds, the dead ones that he'd stomped
on—he wished they were alive. He wanted to have killed them.
They didn't bleed the way that houses did when they decayed. I
held on to my chair because I'd dreamed of this for so long. My
heart beat wildly. He smelled like musk. I imagined that I had
sliced him full of scars with our biggest carving knife, that the
gashes on his chest formed words in Leila's penmanship. It was
dark outside, but on the west coast the sun was only red and
setting. He deserves it anyhow, I'd said about the letters, if he
won't hook up with me. He sat around high or in a k-hole all
the time. You can mold unhappy people how you choose. You
can't recall what happened to the summer. Boys on the rainy

street still look the same, but they're shut down for the season, like waterslides. Patrick was waiting for me to lead, like we were equal; he smelled like I did. Whiskey, dirty fabric. When I pushed him away, he whispered he was sorry. I shook my head and pulled him to the couch and held him tight and horizontal. I cried so that he couldn't see it, couldn't hear me, so that any touch of tears was just my tongue's tip on the zenith of his cheekbone.

The alcohol made us brave that night. We walked right into the downstairs apartment and stole a case of beer from the re-frigerator, and we drank for two more hours, just staring at each other. The next day at noon Patrick sipped a steaming cup of JFG and glanced around uneasily, like rats might munch on his toes, like he was cold not from the outdoor frost but from me. I don't want leaves to fall from the trees yet, he said.

Of course you do, I told him.

It's just October seventh. It's so early.

This was the day it happened. The trees were bushy, and then the trees were bare; their waste made falling whirlwinds every-where, up and down the street. Cars had to turn their windshield wipers on to see past all the fallen leaves. We would go back to the pawn shop to sell my bike, his fishing rods, his drum set. We'd drive this time.

But that's what October *is*, I said. I was jealous of him. Those were the kinds of thoughts I wanted for myself.

I was about to tell him about the letters when he looked into my eyes and stopped me. I don't think I can ever be with you, he said. It seemed to make him sad. I asked why not, although I knew each answer possible—not pretty enough, not a good kisser, not a girl.

My life isn't going anywhere, he said. I'm not good for you.

I shook my head.

I smell like you this morning, he said, his voice hoarse, and he changed into a T-shirt that was draped across the space heater.

We had some beers left over from the case we'd stolen, and I opened one for each of us. I wanted to speak, but my throat decided not to.

I could never scream at you the way I scream at Leila, Patrick said. And the way she screams at me, the way we scream at each other. I like you too much.

We ate beef jerky at the table, leaving only beer and rotten mushrooms in the refrigerator. I spun the glass ewer, whose Queen Anne's lace had now been dead for quite a while. They were hardly flowers anymore, except for the stalks that looked the same as always, diffracted halfway down the vase by old water. I shivered, because the house was cold without our gas turned on. We sat in silence for about half a minute, until Patrick corrected himself and said, Screamed.

EASTBOUND

Letitia was brushing her long white hair when her sister's Chevrolet sedan broke down on east I-40. She usually wore it in a bun. She'd just taken her insulin, because they were on their way to Shoney's a mile ahead, but then Wendy gripped the wheel and screamed across the lanes, the middle one of four to the right-hand shoulder, which was only five feet wide because of road construction. It happened on a bridge across another highway. The car scraped a concrete wall and stopped as traffic blared by. Letitia's brush was tangled in her hair; she forgot it was there. Wendy took a heart pill from the glove box. She was sixty-eight years old.

The cars are so close, Letitia said.

They're not going to hit us.

The car was one inch narrower than the shoulder. They're—

Not. They're not they're not oh Lord don't hit us. She shut her eyes. Earthquake, she said, earthquake, oh my God.

But it wasn't an earthquake at all; it was a car carrier. Seven shiny Toyota Tundras thundered past and shook Letitia's body in the little Cavalier that shuddered like it might explode. Everything inside the car made loud vibrations, all of Letitia's bones, her rib cage and the brittle cuboids in her feet. They were one year healthier than Wendy's bones, a year and two months softer; they were shaking with the passage of every car and truck three feet from Wendy's door. They were hovering above a busy exit where Letitia saw the neon flags of fast-food restaurants, motels, department stores, a multiplex, an office building made of native stone. She didn't see a single blade of grass. She shook so many times she couldn't count them.

What did you do? she said.

It just stopped, Wendy yelled. It just cut off. She snapped her fingers. Just like that.

Turn the key.

I did, said Wendy. She turned the key again and nothing happened. Four Rodeways in a line rocked Letitia back and forth until her neck hurt. She choked on spit and coughed it up in a panic, and Wendy hit the steering wheel hard and hurt her fist. She rubbed it. I hate this car, she said.

It might not even be the car, Letitia said.

Wendy looked annoyed. What else would it be? she said, if it's not the car? Is it someone else's car? Is that the problem?

The traffic will all stop, Letitia said. It's rush hour.

Rush hour means you speed up. It's over anyway.

It's not an hour, it's two hours. It's been that way since the eighties.

Get on the radio, Letitia said, and we'll call for help.

What radio, Letitia? This radio?

I don't—

Which band do you call for help on? AM or FM?

No, I—

Should we try a rock station or a country station?

Letitia shook her head. She didn't understand the stereos anymore, with all their symbols. She was embarrassed for having made a bad suggestion, so she sat in silence. She didn't usually talk to Wendy much, because they already knew what the other would say. Letitia had been aware of all of Wendy's thoughts for a long time. She didn't speak for fifteen minutes, and the traffic sped faster and faster, seventy-five miles an hour now, she guessed. She couldn't remember the last time she'd touched tree bark. She was handicapped and didn't often go outside, except on drives with Wendy. Her children lived in Florida and Arizona, which were long drives. The cars were tailgating each other, weaving in and out of one another's spaces like a flock of starlings. Letitia guessed it was only a matter of time until a high-speed collision pushed them through the concrete and off the bridge to their deaths.

I told you not to take the interstate, said Wendy.

But you're driving. You're the one that took the interstate.

It was your idea. You said it would be faster.

Wendy, you make your own decisions. You always have.

If I took Kingston Pike, you would have sat at every red light thinking how we should have taken the interstate.

I don't even *like* the interstate, Letitia said. It just happens to be faster. She was shaking from the cars and from her nerves. She had taken insulin just a while ago. She was glad she'd finished the injection before the breakdown, or the lurch might have driven her needle right through her stomach.

It's not so fast now, is it? said Wendy.

Letitia pointed at the trucks that rocked her body steadily, and Wendy's body and the car, and said, It's fast for all those people.

Crippled old ladies shouldn't take the interstate.

Letitia tried to nod her head, but it was hard while traffic trembled in her like a live wire; she had to pause to figure out a way to move her body in two directions at once.

We shouldn't even leave the house, said Wendy.

Of course we should leave the house.

I can't even open my car door.

Wendy sounded hysterical; Letitia wished she would just calm down. She gauged the space between the left side of the car and the trims of passing vehicles; they ran as close to Wendy as she sat. She counted blurry faces. Wendy's car had tinted windows so no one could see in; Letitia shifted in her seat, invisible to everyone but Wendy, who didn't look but only frowned at the buggy windshield.

It's fast, said Wendy. What a perfect reason.

I didn't say it.

It's so fast, we'll die here, she said, that's how fast it is, and Letitia, who wasn't hypoglycemic quite yet, shook her head. She hated it when Wendy jumped to all her miserable conclusions. Wendy got scared of things, and so she didn't like them. That was probably why the car had broken down at all; Wendy was just scared of traveling fast, so she willed it dead.

Things were fast now. The interstate was fast. That was why the government had built it. Men had arrived to buy Letitia's childhood home and all its land, the fields around it, the four-square Dixon farmhouse, which was slow; it never even moved. Sometimes it creaked at night like wildwood owls but it wasn't ever fast till November 1959, when it was dynamited, dirt shoveled high atop its stone foundation. In its place the interstate shone. The lanes were drawn with bright, reflective paint. It reached the heights where only birds had flown before; it was a miraculous piece of road. It took some time to build up psychic resonance, because it was a new place, disconnected from the ground. It was like Letitia's condominium, just across the freeway from Suburban Center—it didn't have a soul yet. Developers had built the condo several years ago, in the nineties, but they ran out of souls in 1983, and houses had to grow them on their own now.

Wasn't our farm near here? Letitia asked.

Wendy shook her head. It was farther west, by Lovell Road.

I think it was here.

You can think it was here, said Wendy, but it wasn't.

Letitia was getting light-headed, so she looked out at the scenery. She didn't see the parking lots and restaurants she'd seen before; instead she saw a field. The light was falling differently; thick white clouds were shadowing the land. A child in a bonnet raked up yellow hickory leaves. She stood beside a cantilever barn, and she was crying. She covered the dead cat with leaves like golden arrows; she basked in the warmth of it, rubbing soreness from the rake off her palms. She didn't seem to hear the rumblings of the interstate above her. The highway was built on bridges, mounds of dirt, on pylons, and it reached the height of geese migrating north. It was almost primed.

See there, Letitia said, I feel it. It was here.

I don't care if it was here, said Wendy, or if it never was anywhere at all.

Letitia squirmed in her seat. I need to pee, she said.

That's just because of your blood sugar, Wendy said.

I know that, said Letitia. You don't have to be so logical.

Wendy's tears were making saltstains on the steering wheel. I'm not being logical, she said. You can't help me.

Letitia patted her on the shoulder.

We're helpless, useless women, Wendy said. She waved inside her window at the trucks that couldn't see her, couldn't stop. They went so fast she barely saw the bodies operating them, the faces. Her vision was bad. Poor Susie-cat, she said. She needs her Tender Vittles.

Letitia nodded. Mmm.

She'll claw the carpet at the door, said Wendy. We'll have to use the butter knife again to open it.

It's only been a day that we've been gone.

Cats don't know the days from weeks, said Wendy.

Susie knows.

I don't know.

She knows the sun.

Wendy shook her head uncertainly. Letitia watched the child move across the field below the highway. She was a pretty girl, eight or nine years old; she looked familiar. She hid the cat below so many leaves no light would ever find the way down to its dead and open eyelids. Letitia frowned; she'd done that to a cat once, buried it too shallow. The dog pack came and scavenged it to shreds and made her cry. She found the kitten's eyeball in the cow pasture. What if it woke up and it weren't a cat, but just an eyeball? She buried it below three feet of rocks, checked it every day so it never could awaken with the sunrise, but she never found the other eye, the left one, except in nightmares.

Land flows the same here, Letitia said.

The same as what?

As Daddy's land.

There's not a creek.

They buried it.

There never was a creek here, Wendy said.

How do you know? Letitia said.

It doesn't feel like water.

But Wendy hadn't lived in the farmhouse very long. She'd gone away to boarding school in Alabama when she was ten years old. It was a school for dance; Wendy was going to be a ballerina. She had a tutu Mommy made; she wore pink tights from Sears and Roebuck's catalog. She didn't pay attention to the animals, didn't know which cats were living, which had died. Letitia wrote her sister letters listing names of newborn kittens and their colors, whether they were nice or had sharp claws already. She missed Wendy; she wondered why her sister never wrote her back. She figured she had the wrong address; maybe she was spelling Tuscaloosa wrong. It was a long word, and hard to write; she didn't see why Wendy would go to such a place. Dance was boring. Letitia tried performing a ballet inside the barn with all her cats, or she made what moves she thought might compose it, but really she'd never seen a ballerina. It hurt to balance on her toes, to bend her knees. Even at the age of nine she had the symptoms of arthritis.

Do you remember Snarly? Letitia said to Wendy, who was holding her lower lip to stop its quivering.

Wendy shook her head. Was that a boy you took to the school dance?

Snarly was my calico.

A calico can't be a boy, said Wendy.

Snarly was a girl, Letitia said. She had that bony litter Carrot drowned. Carrot was their younger brother, the only one of four who still was living. He was too young to have been Letitia's friend; he grew up in the fifties, when things were more fun, when girls got to wear pants, when Carrot and the other boys played cowboys and Indians in the field and hollered names of horses, names of guns, but Letitia was a mother by then, and working, and she didn't care anymore what clothes she wore.

Carrot did no such thing, said Wendy.

Black ones. He tied them in a burlap sack and drowned them.

Wendy shook her head. The Probe that nearly scraped against her door was black, with neon plates.

You don't believe me, said Letitia.

It's not a very nice thing to remember.

I can't help what I remember.

I don't see why not, said Wendy. I'd forgotten those cats were even there.

But every barn's got cats, Letitia said. You know the barn, don't you?

I suppose so, Wendy said. What did it look like?

Big, and new.

What color was it?

Red, but then it faded, said Letitia.

What did we look like?

Like that, Letitia said. She pointed at the girl who lay in clovers now with a kitten on her chest, cradled like a nursing baby. It was a Siamese mix but gray from tabby blood; it swatted at the girl's ears and touched its nose to hers and clawed her chin, and Wendy, her brown eyes squinting south to where her sister's finger gestured, said, It's just a parking lot.

But the girl on the grass.

I don't know how you see that far, said Wendy. I don't see a girl. I don't even see grass.

It's there.

I didn't say it's not there, Wendy said. I said I didn't see it.

The girl was picking clovers now, looking for one with four leaves. Letitia blinked her eyes, because her vision wasn't any better than her sister's. She was starting to feel uneasy; she was perspiring. She didn't understand why Wendy saw a different picture of the land beside the highway. The field was blurry at the edges of Letitia's thick trifocals but the girl's face was sharp and clear; she stood and took her shirt off, unaware of any interstate above her. She swayed and moved her body like a wand. Letitia tried to remember how it had felt to move like that. She touched her arm and smiled.

We'll die here, Wendy said.

We were born here, said Letitia.

I'm sure it was at least a mile west.

But I can see the watermelon patch, Letitia said. Where the girl was walking now, kicking at rindy galls amidst the brambles, where she traveled from the barn across a wispy-flowered slope to reach the tanbark trail where she rose up closer to the road, where she ran her gentle fingers through her hair and walked up trickly dogwood roots and when she came up to their vehicle Letitia was transfixed; Letitia touched her sister's hip and said, We looked like that. That was us.

Wendy looked right through the girl's head and said, We looked like Best Buy?

Letitia was sweating. She didn't know what to say.

The girl's legs were bonded with the guardrail now. It was a solid metal rail. It grew right through her ankles.

Letitia blinked her eyes. She wiped her glasses on her blouse.

I can barely see cars in the parking lot, said Wendy. It's all a blur.

When Letitia donned her glasses again, the grass she saw was green and gray at once. It had a coat of many colors, made of metal.

The girl shifted in and out of focus. Kids these days all look the same, said Wendy. Letitia shifted in her seat uncomfortably and touched her three chins all at once and didn't know which one was real, which ones were only fat deposits, until the girl touched her own chin with an aster so that Letitia's top one itched and tickled. She sneezed as the girl sneezed. The girl walked into their car and through their bodies and stopped inside Letitia, where she bent to pluck a four-leaf clover from the earth.

From this valley they say you are going, she sang. *We will miss your bright eyes and sweet smile.*

The rush of cars on the interstate was quieting. Letitia heard no sound except her body's learning how it had felt once, how it used to move, the fraction of herself she used to occupy. When the girl rose and took another step, Letitia's newfound knowledge vanished; it sounded like a balloon deflated just too far to pop. Tractor-trailers ground their gears inside her ear canals. She saw no grass. The girl skipped away and galloped toward the barn, and fast-food logos rose into the dusk like pony sticks.

It was a five-leaf clover, said Letitia, but she wondered for a moment where she was. I remember now, she said. It was like the blades of a star.

There's no such thing as a five-leaf clover, Wendy said.

But I found one, said Letitia.

Then it was a completely different kind of weed.

The ground was thick with clover, said Letitia. It was nothing else.

Anyway, a five-leaf clover would be unlucky, Wendy said, if such a thing existed.

It's double the luck, Letitia said.

No, it's like a double negative, Wendy said. It's bad.

But it's not negative to begin with. It's positive.

Wendy sighed and coughed and tried to stretch the cramps out of her legs. I never saw what the hell was lucky about four-leaf clovers, she said. They're mutants. They're deformed. They're like babies born retarded.

They're pretty, said Letitia.

That's the real reason people pick them, Wendy said. To kill them. To put them out of their misery.

Wendy, a clover doesn't have any misery.

Wendy shook her head. You're right, she said. Not when it's dead. The neon signs of restaurants and hotels went dark. Their extinguishing caught Letitia's eye, and grass grew once again and this was no bridge; it was the top of a gentle slope beside a copse of trees, and Wendy frowned and didn't see the girl tear a leaf from her clover to make its number four.

No, she said.

Yes, said Wendy, her voice soft like it was far away.

Sixty years and Letitia still remembered how she'd robbed the clover of its symmetries. She'd thought the four leaves might spread out to fill the fifth's space, but they didn't move at all; she'd killed them, marred their form with a cavity. She pocketed the broken leaf inside her dress and looked for where she'd picked it from the ground. When she found a thumbnail patch of dirt between two buttonflowers, Letitia tensed her jaw and yelled, In me. You picked it here, in me, but she couldn't bridge their senses; the girl heard nothing, only placed the stem upright in dirt and stood and faced the west and never felt two lanes of eastbound traffic enter her and leave again so quickly, their engines hot, their pistons firm. She walked away. She felt sad about the clover, but she wasn't going to cry, not about plants, nor leaves; not anything. Wendy was the only one who ever cried, even though she said emotions were stupid, only told the body when to eat, when to use the bathroom.

Letitia had lain down on the grass and watched the clouds go by. She'd leaned her head far back to see how round the earth was, perfect like a clock face, and she hadn't known what lanes she lay across, or why the ground had always rumbled since she'd first gone out to wander through her father's fields. Why amidst the pasture's eerie silence she was touched by angry energies, minds jacked up by coffee, drivers who hated one another. She felt uneasy when she dug a hole for her uprooted clover, but she never learned until the ninth of September, 1999, what irate brutes were struggling through her body to be born.

When you're a skeleton, said Wendy, you'll be skinny enough to fit through that door.

I still won't be able to stand up, Letitia said. My joints.

You won't have joints. Just bones.

Letitia lifted the handle of her door. She opened it six inches until it hit the bridge's concrete wall. Even if it could have opened farther, she knew her knees were far too weak to stand up unassisted from such a low position. Her cane was in the hatchback. She looked back toward the only door that offered them an exit, and she knew ten years had passed since she could have maneuvered through the car to reach it. Eleven years since Wendy could have done the same. She had followed her sister to stomach trouble, crippling arthritis, a cane. Wendy had pulled her down that path, she'd led the way. It was her fault. She had always been the one to end things. One day horses weren't exciting anymore.

Last night I dreamed about you, Letitia said. I dreamed about your horse.

Which one?

The gelding. How they'd ridden him together, late at night across the dried-blood hay bales, how her only clothes were dresses, so she rode him in her underwear and how the horse bucked, and Letitia cried Stop, make him Wendy tell him to whoa. But Wendy stared and steered them forward in a loop around the muggy property to the barn where they corralled Spyglass for the night, and in the dream forever, because the barn had burned him and Katy Cruel and Falconer and Gideon to the ground and never made a sound, and in her dream Letitia couldn't even find their bones among the ashes, but in life, on that hot October evening back in 1942, she sat with Wendy on the porch beneath a brand-new oscillating fan that Daddy'd nigger-rigged, he called it, with a hemp rope, and they played canasta, laughing. The air was wet and eerie like an endless, dismal swamp and she laughed but Daddy wasn't laughing. Shuffle, said Letitia.

You.

You.

Letitia held the deck to her yellow dress. The paper angels didn't bend like usual; she knew by their rigid gloss not to deal another hand. She felt the urge to pee but knew she couldn't go inside; she felt like foreigners were racing back and forth above her head, balanced on a fleet-foot snake and Mommy came to her, not to Wendy but Letitia, chalked by all the reddle in the world and said, Which one of us? You pick which one's to leave.

Leave where?

Here, screamed Mommy.

Are we going to the store? Letitia whispered.

A spider clambered up the railing of the porch as Daddy made his presence known by saying calmly, Keep it in the house.

This is the house.

This is the porch.

Letitia didn't notice she was shuffling cards. Mommy wasn't going to the store. Letitia tensed her toes as Mommy crushed the spider, as Mommy pocketed her dainty hands, and yelled, Money's not any shorter than you are, and picked up steam each time she said, Which one, which one, which one of us, loud so Letitia never forgot again what color Mommy's eyes were; they were green. They were from Bean Station. Daddy came from Georgia; his eyes were blue. You, Letitia whispered; her eyes were by the spider. She saw its death up close. It was a porch spider, it was as black as Daddy's patent leather boots and if Letitia had a needle, she could spin its pool of viscous fluid into webs whose words spelled you you you, the words she spoke out loud when she imagined all the webs unspun forever by the spider.

Which you?

The you I'm looking at.

Mommy looked like she was dreaming.

You you you you you, Letitia said, because she didn't like it when people screamed. It made her eyes go blurry. She didn't know why they did.

Wendy never said a word till they were gone. Daddy in the house again, Mommy in the Ford, chauffered to the L&N by a lanky sharecropper named Drake. Guess what card I'm holding, Wendy said.

The four of clubs, said Letitia.

I'm not holding the cards, silly. You are.

Letitia separated suits on cedar planks. It was evil to play cards. She shuffled them till midnight when the horses slept and Wendy too and a bright pink sky hid the stars. She didn't understand why it was pink, why it glowed like industries that wouldn't rise for years of time to come. Daddy had said, Night; Wendy had said nothing, had slept for one last night in the bedroom Letitia shared with her. It was time to go learn ballet, tap dance, choreography, though not really. She got in trouble with a boy from town when she was thirteen, and she had to come back home. Spyglass came to be Letitia's; he died in the barn, of stomachache. Drake and Daddy dragged him out with ropes and burned him by the creek; he smelled like engines made of worms.

In tears Letitia said, You're supposed to bury him.

You wanna be the one to dig the hole? said Daddy.

Letitia shook her head and cried. They burned the barn at nightfall, like the dream. The cattle died of rinderpest, the chickens all were slaughtered, twenty-four of them, their necks like drinking straws. The sun was setting. The farm began to fade into the future where the world was made of steamrollers, backhoes born in factories.

It was stupid to take your insulin before we got to the restaurant, said Wendy.

We were almost there.

It was just really so stupid.

Someone will stop.

Who? said Wendy. Who can even see us? We're invisible.

Really? said Letitia. Her head felt funny.

Wendy rolled her eyes and mocked her: Really?

The highway men will stop.

The highwaymen? What are they gonna do, steal our purses?

Not that kind of highwaymen, Letitia said. The kind that works on highways.

This is nineteen ninety-nine, Letitia. There aren't any high-waymen.

Letitia didn't answer; she was sweating. She pushed her shirt inside her folds of fat to soak up the liquid. She wished the little girl would come back; she tried to map the child's journey with her thought. Beyond the clover's planting was the creek. She'd knelt to soak her silk bandanna in the water, she'd wrapped it round her mess of auburn hair. Water had dripped down her neck and back, under her dress. She hated dresses; she hated shoes. She was walking barefoot along the creek on red-dirt ground, burrowing her toes into the malleable clay like acorns, and she took her dress off. She rolled in mud and stood and let it cake in the breeze upon her skin and stomped on the dress like grapes fermenting in a vat and soiled it till she saw no yellow anymore. Yellow was what Nana had worn; it was a dead color, Nana was dead. The dress was a birthday present, only weeks before her death. Strokes ran in the family, just like diabetes, arthritis, diverticulosis, high blood pressure, obesity. Letitia didn't have her stroke until the age of fifty-nine. She couldn't talk right anymore. She walked with a duck-head cane. Wendy's came at fifty, but it didn't cause much damage; it only made her tired. She looked older afterwards, and her mouth hung slack. Only the women in their family had these problems. The men were tall and strong and healthy.

Carrot comes home from work this way, Letitia said.

He's retired, Wendy said. Four years now.

Four years?

It wouldn't matter. He worked the night shift.

Maybe he'll drive by anyway.

We don't know what kind of car he drives. He doesn't know this car.

Maybe he's out shopping.

Maybe.

Letitia strained her neck to look for the girl. Their custard-colored Cavalier was so much lower than the rigs and SUVs that shook their car and nearly sideswiped Wendy's door they came so close, thrice per second in this heavy traffic.

You have to try again to squeeze out, Wendy said.

I can't.

Try.

She pushed her door six inches open and slammed it shut again, then repeated these motions. She was thirsty. She weighed two hundred and fifty pounds, and her throat was closing up. She didn't want to talk anymore. You're fading, Wendy said, but what was really fading was the freeway; lanes and traffic patterns shifted. Translucent tractor-trailers displaced air opaque with the fog and sleet and smoke of sixty years, and then it cleared. She saw green grass and trees. The air tasted fresh upon her tongue. Her mud-daubed counterpart was on a grassy knoll and climbing to the chicken wire; she crossed it, she wore her dirty dress around her head wrapped like the turban of a sheik, and a cut was bleeding on her arm. She had a drink in hand, and when she sipped its sugary fluid Letitia gasped; her throat was tightening. She couldn't breathe right. It was Nehi orange. The ghosts of Fords and Buicks angled through her field of vision; she couldn't breathe, she couldn't talk but she could move again, she could float up to a sweeping panorama where the child held corncob dolls and sat upon a stump atop a hill. Letitia remembered everything about that stump; it was an elm struck down by lightning in a summer storm. Its trunk had formed a bridge across a murky stream to another hillside. She didn't see it now. The child made the voices of her toys.

You, said the little doll that was Letitia.

I brought you into this world, said Mommy, who was larger.

You keep having babies. Go have your babies somewhere else.

They're your brothers.

I don't want brothers, said Letitia's doll. Just cats.

Wendy tried to dance a fox-trot, but her corncob wouldn't bend that way; it cracked.

You can talk to us now, said Letitia's doll to Daddy, whose body looked exactly like Letitia's, only bigger. Tell me about when you were a boy. Why do ghosts fly through our house, why do comets streak each night ten feet above my bedroom, but the doll refused to say a word; it lay in silence on the stump. It had a glint in its eyes like woodfire.

Why do the signs glow? What do the spaceships want? She saw them every night above her ceiling. She didn't like her house. Daddy said it someday could be hers, but she didn't believe him. It wasn't long for the world. Yellow war machines would come, exhume the dirt, the buried skeletons of kittens. Chariots would crash into each other in the sky and lie as bait for wailing sirens, ambulances, trucks with shiny ladders mounted on the sides.

I love you, said Letitia's doll to Mommy.

It's too late, was the reply.

I didn't really choose. I flipped a coin.

You flipped wrong.

Letitia shuddered. Her mind split wide like separating highways: she was floating there above the farm, she was in the Cavalier with Wendy, she was dizzy from her body's need for sugar. Her eyes were closed, unconscious; she was the girl. She knew where all those corncobs ended up: in the graves of animals, in ashes like the horse, in Mommy's grave. Mommy had died young, of blood clots. They tore up her grave when they built the interstate. Letitia was a wife by then, a mother, overworked; she didn't pay attention. Graves were only sentimental things. She never said good-bye to her cemetery of dead brown cats, years and years of them, each with its own rock headstone etched

by gravel. None had ever died upon the road, but now ten thousand cars a day ran over them.

There was the rabid Burmese tom, there was Flavia whose
tail had two kinks. There was lynx-point Louis, killed by
Wendy's boyfriend Truss, the dreamy blond-haired boy with pale
blue eyes, a serpent's nose, a lisp. He pushed it down the chimney. It was August so the hearth bore neither fire nor starter log
when Louis shattered like a brick. Ashes dusted his ruffled fur
and stained the lacy frills of Letitia's dress. She carried him to
the creek bank, where a weeping willow's branches hid the joined
forms of Truss and Wendy, and she sneezed when the willow's
branches touched her nose. The cat had died with all its claws
on point, and she threw it forward. Truss screamed. His supple
body bled from four matched sets of holes, and Wendy held him
back. He screamed words Letitia had never heard out aloud—
they were words the spaceships' pilots used to curse each other,
morning noon and night. She listened more closely after that;
she'd never known they might be speaking straight to her. She
was older by then—fifteen or thereabouts. She grew her hair
long.

Wendy wept that night for hours. All I told him was piss into
the chimney, she told Letitia.

Well, that's not what he did.

No, Wendy cried, it's not.

I don't think I like you anymore.

Please don't tell Daddy.

Why would I tell Daddy? said Letitia. He wouldn't care.

He'd kill me.

Letitia wanted to cry too; she had desecrated Louis's corpse
by throwing him on Truss, whom she liked too, whom she could
never like again. Does it make you feel better to pretend that?
she asked Wendy.

Stop it, Wendy said. Don't be mean to me. Shut up.

I like to pretend things too, Letitia said.

Like what?

Letitia shook her head.

What? said Wendy. What?

I'll never tell you what they are.

Don't be mean to me, said Wendy. Now of all times.

When then? said Letitia. Tomorrow? Fifty years from now?

Wendy shook her head and cried herself to sleep. Letitia rocked in a hammock on the porch. Don't ask me questions anymore, she told her sleeping sister. She wished everyone would go away, but Truss returned next morning and flipped her hammock over so she woke up crashing on the porch's planks of wood. He climbed the stairs to Wendy's room and married her and named a son in six months' time, and five more by the age of twenty-seven. He left to be a trucker. Every few weekends he would come home, and once he even brought a cat himself, a rip-eared sablecoat. He died in a car crash when Wendy was still half-pretty, and the cat lived on. Wendy moved to Myrtle Beach to be a waitress and when she came home twelve years later the chimney was gone, as well as the house, as well as the barn. The hills were flat; the creek was underground. Wendy said she didn't care that the house had been destroyed; she was a pragmatist like Mommy. It was ugly anyway, she said. It was too square.

Already Mommy's face was gone. It was a white plate, smooth, not shattered, featureless. She had been rich and fat. She was You, because that was Letitia's only memory of her mother's nose and eyes and how the varicose veins were highway clover-leafs upon her legs from where Letitia always sat and wished she had some other girl to play with, but it was the countryside. She tried to remember why she'd even said it, but she had trouble remembering how old she was, or whether she was allergic to certain flowers.

If you can see the future, why can't I?

Because you're too old.

Letitia looked at herself and saw that it was true. Her wrinkles ran deep, and she quivered. She touched the girl, even though her memory held no record of a crippled ghost who stroked her hair, caressed her cheek. The meeting of their skins was like a sonic boom. You, she said, and brought their worlds together. The road buckled like continental plates colliding when her family's farmhouse materialized a thousand feet behind her car. Only the roof and gables rose above the surface of the pavement, only the brick chimney, the old black oak. Speeding cars were trapped inside the attic. A Toyota Previa was sliced in two by the eastside wall; its front half crashed into a red Eclipse that slammed against a Ram. The girl blinked her eyes. In an instant trees grew centuries tall and felt the head-on impact of a fleet of Schneider trucks that mashed their bark to powder, dust. Letitia flinched and cried out, Wendy, who was crushed by an Eagle Vision, and she passed away too soon to see the cats' graves rise from beneath the roadbed, all together. How they danced. The cars didn't even crush them; all the cars had crashed, and the road was free of traffic. Now Wendy could open her door safely.

I'm glad we broke down, Letitia said. I never would have seen these things again. The cats, the silk bandanna Mommy gave her, the trees she'd climbed: they rose. Mommy gave her many things—diseases, kittens, fears inherited, the swath of ruby silk that rose up through the ground along with all the things she'd ever lost, like poltergeists aglide as timelines merged so Wendy lived again, so she was in Alabama, dancing. The girl led Letitia through the catacombs of all her old belongings, through the house where cars had fallen through the floor into the kitchen, to the cellar shelf where Daddy kept his wine that turned to vinegar. It made her mad to feel what it was like to float, to know what had been stolen to have lived inside her body. She hadn't moved like that for thirty years. She was jealous of the girl, wanted to make her cry, so she opened her mouth wide. This is what you're going to look like, Letitia said. For many, many years.

But the girl wasn't listening. She cradled corncob Wendy in her arms. We've got the okra planted, she was saying. Me and Daddy did it on our own.

The crop will fail, Letitia said. There will be a drought.

Things are starting to come together, the girl said.

They can't come together, Letitia said. You're dead.

I'm glad you don't hate me anymore for what I said to Mommy.

She'll always hate you. She'll never, ever change.

But even as she spoke Letitia knew she lied. Wendy was changing—she was stiffening, her blood was giving up to gravity. Her lips were curling inward to greet her dentures. The men and women in the wrecks had died. Their bodies looked like husks in which no blood had ever flowed. They weren't solid; their air was spread across the decades. They bled no blood and sank into the earth and then an interstate was built, and when they died again in forty years they fell down where they'd died before and lived again forever. No one stopped the second time to give a lift to Wendy and Letitia, nor the sixth or the one-hundredth, nor did dust clouds ever cease to billow when the house fell.

Cats kept dying, every cycle. Letitia's knees grew weak and fat; it never failed to happen. Her cells developed insulin resistance; her pancreas broke down. She bought the same cane, every June in 1984, unto infinity, at Sears, and it always cost nineteen ninety-five. She got wider with the interstate, which grew and grew until it was reborn and Letitia grew; she saw bulldozers adding new lanes to her life. She watched the smoggy sunsets from her condo as they smoldered in the sky above the interstate.

THE EARL OF CREDITON

Barbara was lonely. Her parents and sisters and brothers and Granny were always around, but they didn't play soccer; they were too selfish. She was lonely and hot—the sun sat in her lap, slid down her throat in the back of the pickup, a hundred degrees, two in the afternoon. The heat was intoxicating as she leaned against a ridge of Duraliner plastic. Her sister Sheila's head hid houses one by one as they rode north.

Garrett stuck his middle finger up and pressed it to the window. He was Barbara's cousin, the only child of her dead uncle, and he was a hateful snitch. He sat inside the cab flipping Barbara off whenever he remembered to. When Barbara scowled and knocked against the window, her father reached back with a fist and hit the glass twice as hard. Barbara flinched. The truck swerved, as did the car behind them, and she laughed at that car, whose color was a dull gray; it had a dent in its bumper. She wished everybody in the world had a dented bumper, even her father. She kicked Sheila's leg and said, You know what Mama's gonna buy you at Kmart?

Sheila took her thumb out of her mouth and said, No, what?

Absolutely nothing.

Sheila kicked Barbara back.

Barbara liked the sound of *absolutely*. Again and again she said it: absolutely nothing, absolutely nothing. Floyd, her older brother, told her to shut up. He held Rhonda, four years old, in his lap; she was crying. He didn't tell her to shut up like he told Barbara, but he stroked her sand-blond hair. Barbara took a ragged pair of jeans from the truck bed and held them over the side, where swiftly moving air inflated them so that the legs crackled like whips. She had to hold them tightly. When Floyd saw what she was doing, he grabbed the jeans and swatted her in the head with the stiff denim waist. A belt loop hit her in the eye as Floyd said, If Pa sees you doin that shit, he'll pull over and whup you good.

Floyd tossed the jeans through the open window into the cab, where they landed behind Granny's head. After a while she shifted her body so that they fell behind her, but Barbara couldn't tell that she'd noticed the new cushion at all.

Pa had said he'd buy Barbara a new soccer ball. It was the end of the month, and he'd finally been paid. Barbara had been waiting for weeks. I'm only gettin you the cheapest one, Pa said, so I don't want no whining. Garrett was going to buy a rifle so he could shoot squirrels. His father had just died so he had a hundred dollars. He wanted a .22, he said, just like his father, who'd shot squirrels with his eyes closed. The more Barbara told him not to shoot squirrels, the more squirrels he killed. Soon they'd all be dead. Barbara stared at Garett's neck hard enough to burn flesh, but Garrett never moved, not even to breathe.

Crap, Rhonda yelled, her *r* unformed, and Floyd slapped her.

It was the hottest day of the summer, and the sun was almost too much to bear. Barbara used the stomach of her shirt to wipe sweat from her cheeks and forehead. Her father drove them into town past kudzu-covered trailers long uprooted from their foundations, past new and high-priced ranchers and split foyers. The truck sputtered like it spat out metal shards onto the road with each full revolution of the wheels.

Crap crap crap, said Rhonda.

Sheila looked uncomfortable in the heat. It was hard to tell, because she always looked unhappy; that was just how her face was shaped. Barbara felt bad for what she'd said. What if Pa really didn't buy Sheila anything at the store, she thought. Hey, she said to Sheila, I'm sure they'll buy you something, but maybe there wasn't enough money. They pulled off the highway by the children's home on the hill and coasted into Kmart's parking lot and stopped. Barbara climbed out of the truck. Her throat was parched; she felt like she'd sweated all the water out of her body. Rhonda and Sheila smelled like little-girl sweat, and she moved away from them. Mama got out of the cab with the baby in her left arm and fanned herself with a torn cloth diaper, and Garrett hopped down behind her. Granny didn't move. Get out, old woman, Pa yelled at her, or we'll lock you up in here.

You hush up, Mama said, and Granny blinked her eyes. Mama leaned into the truck and yelled in Granny's ear, Granny, we're here.

Granny looked at Mama blankly.

Who's got the pants? asked Pa.

Barbara had em, said Garrett.

Barbara didn't know how to hold em right, said Floyd. I threw em up front.

They looked inside the truck and saw the jeans behind Granny's neck as a pillow againt the glass. Good Lord, woman, said Pa. He reached inside and grabbed them from behind her. Her head hit the glass and bounced, but she didn't seem to notice.

You be careful, Mama said wearily.

She don't need a pillow.

Help her down.

Will you quit tellin me what to do? Shit. Floyd, help her down.

Floyd carried her out of the truck as the rest of them walked inside. He kicked the door shut behind him and set her feet down on the pavement, holding her hand to help her balance. God helps those that helps themselves, Pa said, turning his head to look.

You should have left her home then, Mama said.

No I shouldn't have. This is family business. It affects all of us. Inside the store the air-conditioning hit Barbara like an ocean wave. She closed her eyes and basked in it, and Garrett pushed her from behind. Get out of my way. Barbara stumbled and moved to the side and followed her family past the cash registers and swallowed spit to ease her thirst. Sweat tingled icily on her cheeks in the cool air.

Now don't yuns be runnin all over the dang store, Pa said. We got some business first. Yuns are gonna stay right here.

Can't I just go look at the sports aisle? Barbara asked.

What did I just say?

He led them to the returns counter, where he leaned forward toward the young clerk who adjusted the cash drawer and reached below the counter for a paper. Hey, Pa barked at him.

Just a second, sir, said the clerk without looking up.

Pa laid the jeans flat on the counter. These is my boy Floyd's, he said loudly, and then, Hey. Look. He spread the jeans out so the clerk would see the dirt stains all across the ripped and shredded fabric, a two-inch hole in each knee, the ragged cuffs, thick grass stains, a broken zipper. The seat was streaked with axle grease that zagged down to the hips in three black lines. These is my eldest boy Floyd's, Pa said again. They didn't work out too good.

Now then, sir, may I help you?

These is my boy Floyd's, Pa said again. He picked them up by a narrow belt loop and dropped them.

The clerk carefully touched the hem of the left ankle and raised his eyebrows. These pants? he said.

You see some others?

You're bringing these back?

Pa nodded his head. They didn't last too good.

What is it you want?

I want a new pair, is what I want. Pa crossed his arms and stepped forward so his legs pressed against the hard plastic counter. He looked around.

You can't exchange these.

Sure I can. Look at the durn things.

The clerk looked blankly out at the store. Floyd came forward to the counter, holding his mouth open, and said, They're all screwed up, nodding his head at the clerk. Pa scrunched up his nose.

You can only exchange unused clothes, the clerk said.

That's a lie, said Pa.

It's our policy.

It's a goddamn lie.

I beg your pardon, sir, the clerk said.

As he picked up the phone to call the manager, his face looked funny, like he was trying not to giggle or choke. Barbara stood behind Pa and Floyd, a foot shorter than either of them, and counted her breaths. She twirled Sheila's hair with a finger, and Sheila slapped her hand away. She watched Mama nurse the baby and remembered how thirsty she was. Can I go buy a Coke? she asked. As she spoke, Granny whispered that she needed to sit down.

Crap, Rhonda said.

My girl's thirsty, Pa told the clerk. Why don't you give me some new pants so I can get her a Coke?

The manager's on his way, sir.

And my granny needs to sit down.

Ain't you got a chair or something? asked Floyd.

Chairs are back in lawn and garden, said the clerk, back by tires. He pointed behind himself and to the left. As he did, the manager appeared from behind a tall shelf and came to the counter, and Pa showed him the jeans and explained his guarantee. He got irritated and began to raise his voice. No, for the last time I ain't got a receipt.

Do you remember when you bought them?

It was summertime. It was for the tomaters.

This summer?

Pa shook his head.

Last summer?

I don't recollect what summer it was.

Sir, if you'll just look at these jeans for yourself—

You think I ain't looked at em? They ain't eyes in my head? This looks like a bullet hole.

That's cause it is a bullet hole.

It's a bullet hole?

Yeah, you dumb shit, it's a bullet hole. You ever seen a bullet hole before? Pa looked down at Garrett and pointed at him. Hey you. Take Barbara back there to the back to see whatever she's goin on about.

Can I look at guns?

I don't care what you do. Go on.

We can't take these jeans back from you with a bullet hole in them, said the manager.

Will you shut up about the bullet hole?

The bullet hole's an important part of the issue.

Pa looked back to make sure Garrett was gone. The man that was wearin em got shot, he said. It wasn't none my fault.

He got shot?

Twiced.

Who was it?

That got shot?

That was wearing the pants.

It's the same thing, Pa said. The bastard that was wearin em got shot.

So who was it?

It was my cousin Coogar was who it was.

So these jeans aren't even yours?

I done told you, they're Floyd's. He pointed with an open frown at Floyd.

What about Coogar?

They never was Coogar's, Pa said. That was what Coogar didn't seem to understand. He thought he could take whatever the hell he wanted to. Pa lowered his head and narrowed his eyes. And what are yuns so nosy for? he asked, and when they didn't answer he kicked the counter with his boot and snarled, Say.

I'm just trying to ascertain the situation.

I'll give your damn situtation. You're gonna take these pants and get me a new pair, and then there won't be no situtation.

There's a *bullet hole* in the *leg*, said the manager. He sounded flustered.

I wouldn't have shot him in the leg, Pa said, but he ran so damn fast, I had to stop him before I could shoot anyplace else.

Garrett dragged Barbara through the sporting goods department until they found the glass case that held guns. He walked back and forth in front of it, touching the glass, and he tried to turn the lock. Looky there, he said. Barbara kicked her feet together as Garrett read aloud the names on tags.

My daddy had ten guns, he said.

Barbara shrugged.

Did you hear me? I'm talkin about my daddy.

I heard you.

He had ten guns.

I said I heard you.

He don't have em no more though.

What happened to them?

They got stole from him, back when he was killed.

Oh, said Barbara.

I'm gonna buy ten more to replace em. Then I'm gonna find out who shot him, and I'll shoot him in the nuts. He stuck his finger at Barbara's crotch. Pow! Barbara jumped at the noise. Garrett banged his body against the glass case and peeked around the corner to see if anyone was watching him. He found a flat-head screwdriver hanging on a rack and jammed it into the case's narrow keyhole and pressed until his cheeks turned red. When he gave up, he inserted the tool's head between the sheets of glass to jimmy the door.

You better be careful.

Shut up, Garrett said. I'm the one watchin you, not the other way.

No you ain't.

Yes I am. I'm the boy.

So?

Plus I ain't got a daddy no more.

So what?

That makes me more responsible than you.

Barbara rolled her eyes.

Say, was you there when my daddy got shot? said Garrett.

I done told you I wasn't.

Was Floyd there?

No.

Was your pa there?

I don't know a thing about it, Barbara said.

Garrett drew an imaginary gun and aimed it at Barbara. Tell the truth or I'll shoot, he said.

Leave me alone.

Your pa said for me to watch you.

No he didn't.

I'm a year and a half older than you, plus I'm a man. That means you've got to do what I say.

You ain't a man. You're fourteen.

I'm more of one than you are.

Barbara didn't know whether to feel bad for Garrett. She thought of her own father and imagined him dying, and it didn't make her sorry for herself, only thirsty. Pa wouldn't give her fifty cents for a Coke. She didn't like Garrett and never had. Now Garrett lived with them and used the same bathroom as her and dribbled piss on the floor sometimes and got hairs on her bar of soap. He loaded his imaginary gun and cocked it. Pow pow pow. Bang!

Be quiet.

Two for flinching, Garrett said, but Barbara hadn't reacted at all that time.

· · ·

It was Barbara who had screamed two weeks ago when Coogar
Cargill broke their bathroom window with a rock in the middle
of the night; she jumped at sudden noises. It was her scream and
not the rock that woke Floyd; his room was next to hers. She
zipped her mouth shut tight and hid beneath her covers as Floyd
yelled, Wake up, Pa. Get your gun. She prayed for God to help
her not make noise. She hoped the lump of her body beneath the
quilt looked like nothing but bumps in the foam mattress.

Coogar, is that you? her father had yelled. She heard a solid
thud.

Half a minute passed before she heard a gunshot. It was right
outside her window, and she curled into a ball to prepare for
God to whisk her out of herself. She was glad no one could see
her fear. A man screamed.

Goddammit, said Floyd, who sounded was also outside. You
shot him.

No I didn't.

Yes you did, Floyd yelled. Look at him.

Coogar's screams cut straight into Barbara's bones. The air
beneath her blankets had grown stale, it seemed, and she hoped
she wouldn't suffocate. You've got to shoot him again, Floyd
said. He'll kill you if you don't.

Barbara was scared, but she tried to concentrate on listening.
She exposed one ear to the air outside her shield and focused
hard, and Pa said, No, I cain't, and Floyd cursed. He grabbed
the gun from Pa and fired, and everything was silent. She wondered why the screams had stopped a good ten seconds prior to
the shot.

Doors slammed. She heard more muffled noises but didn't
know what they meant. It continued well into the night, and she
tossed and turned, too sleepy to identify the sounds, and fell in
and out of dreams. At four in the morning Pa came into her room
and stood above her and barked, They was some bats out there

causin a ruckus somethin fierce. I hope it didn't scare you too much.

She was still confused about how Coogar had been related to her. She knew Garrett was her third cousin. She didn't see why Thompson was his surname, which belonged to no one else she knew, not even Coogar.

Garrett was tired of waiting for an employee at the gun rack, so he took Barbara back to toys to look at soccer balls. She followed him through aisles of fishing rods, light switches, tire cleaners beneath a ceiling twenty feet above her, like four of herself stacked up on shoulders. Garrett said he could jump up and touch it if he wanted to.

No you couldn't.

I just don't want to, he sneered. He was ugly and had one eye lower than the other and a nose bent sideways. His ears were small and high and his hair and freckles red-blond, and he said, Your daddy's stupid, and laughed. Barbara was mad but didn't speak as they turned a corner toward the toy department. Say, said Garrett, pushing Barbara's shoulder.

What?

Your daddy's dumb, Garrett said. He waited for Barbara to answer, but he hadn't asked a question so Barbara said nothing until he added, And them jeans is fucked.

Your pa was the one that got em that way, Barbara said.

Listen to me. Don't you talk about my daddy. He's dead. He weren't stupid the way yours is.

I can talk about whatever I want to.

You listen, he said again. You ain't even the earl. It's Floyd gets to be the earl.

There ain't no earl.

Your daddy told me all about it. He must of told me five

times. He said if it weren't for Floyd bein oldern me he'd adopt
me, so I could be the earl.

He ain't adopting nobody, Barbara said.

He'd of give it to me before he'd give it to you.

Barbara's eyes were burning. Garrett whined just like his old
man, whose final gurgles Barbara had heard two weeks ago, from
her bed. She'd peeked out the window. He'd bled from underneath his mullet cut and coughed and died. Garrett had been
away on a Scouts trip and didn't know till Tuesday, when Pa
first took him in and fed him. Garrett didn't say a word that
night or all day Wednesday. On Thursday he started talking but
wouldn't say anything other than the Boy Scouts' creed. A scout
is trustworthy, loyal, helpful, friendly, courteous, kind, obedient,
cheerful, thrifty, brave, clean, and reverent, but Pa was nervous.
He asked Garrett if he was okay.

Always be prepared, said Garrett.

The police done took care of it while you was gone, Pa told
him. You don't need to be botherin them none about it.

Garrett didn't answer.

Did you hear me? Pa said.

Garrett barely moved his head.

How do you feel about what I just told you?

Thrifty.

Cut this bullshit out, now.

Brave, said Garrett. Loyal.

Two well-dressed girls giggled as they passed Barbara and Garrett in the aisle near the toy department. They were eleven or
twelve years old, and Garrett scowled. I hate girls, he said. Come
here and watch this. He pulled Barbara by her hand around a
corner to a shelf of dolls.

Look at this shit, he said.

Barbara shrugged.

I bet you wish you could buy ever one of these dolls.

She shook her head.

Yes you do.

No I don't, she said. She was getting mad at him.

You listen.

She didn't like the sound of Garrett's voice. She thought of telling him what Floyd had done; she didn't like his voice either. They both yelled when they talked, just like Pa. It made her jumpy. Garrett was unzipping the fly of his ragged jean shorts. What are you doing? Barbara asked him, and he laughed as she scanned her eyes along the ugly rows of pink-boxed Barbie dolls and cars and Barbie houses, Barbie dresses, Barbie shoes.

Garrett doused the dolls with a steady stream of piss. He knocked some down behind the stacks. With one hand on his hip he turned from side to side and soaked the entire shelf and the one below it. Plastic rippled loudly when the stream hit it, and Barbara watched, amazed, as shallow puddles formed on the beige modular shelves.

Watch this, said Garrett. He pointed his penis straight up and sent a fountain of his urine arcing toward the shelf top, which was four feet high, but the stream fell short. He drenched a row of Kens and dribbled several drops on the floor when he was done, and Barbara heard footsteps. She was scared. You smell that? said Garrett, grinning, and stood and pointed at the wide cascade of drips, and Barbara laughed. She thought it was about the most worthwhile thing he'd ever done.

We'd better get out of here, she said.

You're chicken shit, he said.

We'll get in trouble.

Speak for yourself, chicken shit. I didn't do nothing.

A woman in a red uniform stood at the end of the aisle, and

Barbara's heart caught. Her tag said assistant manager, and she cried, What the hell is going on? What is this? Oh my God.

Garrett giggled.

You. You nasty little pig. Oh my God.

She did it, said Garrett, pointing at Barbara.

The woman looked at the dolls and back at Garrett. Where are your parents? she demanded.

I swear it was her.

That's impossible, she hissed.

You should have seen it.

Where are your parents? she asked again.

I ain't got none.

What's that supposed to mean?

A bad man came and shot my daddy, Garrett said.

Who are you here with?

I live with my daddy's cousin now. They went and shot my daddy down.

Is he here with you?

No, he's up front.

The woman hung her mouth open. Garrett looked down at his penis peeking out from his shorts, and he zipped the fly up with both hands and pulled hard, biting his lip. Piss dripped down from doll boxes onto the floor. You're a disgusting boy, the woman said. She didn't seem to know what to do; briefly she looked at Barbara and shook her head. I'm gonna find your parents and make them pay for all this, the woman said finally.

I ain't got no parents, Garrett said. I done told you.

Where's your mother?

I never did have no mother. I got cousins, though.

Here with you?

Some of em is.

Where?

I just told you, they're up front, where the manager's yellin. Cain't you hear it?

She turned her fat head as if it might help her hear better. Large hoops of silver dangled from her ears. As soon as Garrett stopped talking, the woman heard a husky voice yelling, coughing, and cursing on the other side of the store.

He's one of those men that's no good from the day they're born, Pa was saying to the manager, his flustered face bright red. That bastard had another thing comin. He thought he could take whatever the hell he wanted.

The men behind the counter looked at each other.

Say, Pa said.

We're going to have to ask you to leave, said the manager in a nasal whine. He looked like he was worried.

I ain't leavin till I get my pants.

Like I said before—

I know what you said before, goddammit.

If you want new pants, sir, you'll have to pay for them.

I've got a *lifetime guarantee,* Pa snarled. He held the jeans up in the air with his fist. They didn't tell me nothin about no bullet holes, and they didn't say nothin about mud. It was forever. It was a lifetime guarantee.

Like for your whole life, Floyd said.

The clerk searched below the counter for a pamphlet. He located it and scanned the pages, mumbling. Pa squinted as the clerk read aloud.

Personal wear and tear, he said carefully, is not included.

They goddamn told me it *was.* Pa was standing on his tiptoes, his fists on the counter, yelling loudly. They said I could plug my septic tank with it if I wanted to. Rub it in blood.

It looks like you've done that already.

Pa squinted his eyes. You're startin to piss me off, he said.

We've got a sale on jeans this week. A pair like these is just thirteen ninety-nine.

Are you makin fun of me? Cause I'll kick your ass. So will my boy Floyd.

Do the police know about this man you shot?

Do they know, Pa repeated. You bet your ass they know.

How long ago did it happen?

Sunday week.

I don't remember reading about it, the clerk said.

Well, you wouldn't, would you.

I don't know why not. I read the papers every night.

Pa huffed loud, fast breaths. Floyd put a hand on his shoulder to calm him down and said, Don't lose your temper. You're doin good. Pa sniffed snot that gurgled in his nostrils. A woman on the intercom called someone to the toy department, and when the speaker clicked back off, Granny began to stutter. Everyone turned to look at her. It was a few seconds before words formed.

Tell them who you are, she said to Pa.

They don't give a shit who I am.

Tell them.

Leave me to do the talkin.

She leaned against the counter and pressed its glass top with her withered fingers, lifting one to point at Pa. He's the Earl of Crediton, she told the men behind the counter, slowly nodding her head.

Huh? said the clerk.

He's the Earl of Crediton, she said again. Has been must be thirty some odd years now.

What's that mean? asked the manager, and Pa's face turned redder.

Has been ever since my Floyd passed, said Granny.

Will you hush about it? Pa said.

I thought you was Floyd, said the clerk, pointing at Floyd.

I am.

But you just said Floyd's dead, he said to Granny.

She nodded. Must of been twenty years.

Pa looked like he was going to explode. Goddammit, he said, I'm Floyd. He's Floyd, my dead Papaw was Floyd, they're all Floyds.

Who's all Floyds?

The earls. He pushed Granny away from the counter. That's how it works. They're all Floyds.

Calm down, sir.

Are you tryin to shame me front of my family?

No, sir.

I'm the Earl of Crediton. Pa turned around to Granny and said, I wish you'd quit your blabbin all the time about that. He turned back to the counter. It's a direct descendancy all the way back to England, he told the clerk, and now here you are, tryin to shame me.

You're from England?

No, I ain't from England, you dipshit, I'm from Happy Valley.

Granny stepped up to the counter again and said with a shaky voice, He's connected straight to the queen.

For once and for all, Pa shouted at her, will you hush your mouth?

I just wanted them to know.

I ain't here to brag about my title, he yelled. I'm here to get my new pants.

The manager sighed. Floyd leaned to whisper in Pa's ear but never got to, because the assistant manager appeared at the shelf of jewelry they faced, blocking the display. She was dragging Garrett by his collar; Barbara followed behind them. The woman held most of Garrett's weight so that he barely even stood on his own. She stopped in front of Pa and Mama and Sheila and Rhonda and Floyd and Granny and let loose of Garrett, who nearly fell. Is this kid yours? she said with her hands on her hips.

Pa stepped forward. What's it to you? he said.

Why don't you answer my question.

Pa raised his voice and said in her same tone, Why don't you answer mine.

He just, she said and paused and began again—*urinated* on a bunch of Barbie dolls.

Pa squinted and looked at Garrett and pointed at him. Him? he questioned the woman.

Yes, she said indignantly. *Him.*

What about that one? Pa said, gesturing at Barbara.

What about her?

What was she doin when it happened.

Well, I don't know; I don't guess she was doing anything.

Pa glared at Barbara, who shivered.

You're gonna have to pay for what he did back there. He's ruined a whole lot of toys.

Pa stared at the woman until she looked away.

Kevin, she said to the manager, you better come look at this.

Oh no, Pa said. No you better not. He shook a finger at the woman and then at the manager and said, You ain't goin nowhere till I get my new pants.

The manager raised his voice for the first time. For the last time, you're not getting any new pants.

What's going on up here? the assistant manager asked.

You better step your fat ass back out of my business, Pa said to her.

Rhonda giggled as she sucked her thumb, and Mama kicked her with the heel of her shoe. The manager held the pants up for the assistant manager to see. This man wants to exchange these

jeans for a new pair, he said. The woman lifted her eyes incred-
ulously when she saw the rips and stains. The clerk burst out
laughing.

There's a lifetime guarantee, Pa shouted.

He shot the man that owned them, the manager explained,
so now there's a bullet hole in the leg.

I didn't shoot nobody, Pa said. You little son of a bitch.

You said you did.

You hush up.

You just got through telling me—

Garrett, Pa yelled, take the kids outside to ride the pony.

But—

Now. Go on, git. He pushed Sheila away from his legs, and
Mama nudged Rhonda. They headed for the door. Barbara was
mad that Garrett was in charge of her again; she wanted to stay
inside but knew she couldn't argue when Pa's cheeks twitched
like that, when his lips were that tight.

They went outside into the heat so Rhonda could ride the
pony. Barbara shuddered at the blast of heat. The pony had an
out-of-order sign taped to its saddle. Put me on it, said Rhonda.

You cain't ride it, Garrett told her.

Yes I can. My pa just said.

Look at the sign, dummy. It's broke.

Put me on the *pony*, she said angrily, stomping her foot.

Cain't you read?

Of course she can't read, Barbara said. She's four.

So?

The pony's out of order, Barbara said to Rhonda, kneeling
to the level of her height. Maybe next time you can ride the pony.

I'm hot, Rhonda said.

I'm hot too, said Barbara. Don't cry.

My daddy could read when he was two years old, said Garrett. But he was smarter than all of you.

Will you shut up for once about your daddy? Barbara yelled at him. There's a lot you don't know nothing about.

Like what?

Like your daddy.

You can't talk about my daddy.

I can talk about him all I want to.

Rhonda was beating her fists against the plastic of the pony's neck. She tried to climb atop it unassisted, but she was too small; she fell on the concrete and scraped her wrist and cried. I'm gonna tell your pa you said that, Garrett said.

Tell him then, Barbara yelled. She thought his threat was pitiful, and she couldn't look at him anymore. She took him by surprise when she pushed his chest with both her hands and yelled, Pa didn't like your daddy any more than he likes you, and Garrett fell backwards onto the curb beside Rhonda.

He don't like you either.

She faced Garrett again.

He don't think you act right.

You don't know shit, Garrett Thompson.

Your pa wasn't never gonna buy you no soccer ball, he answered, laughing. He might of bought you a Barbie, though, if I hadn't pissed on em all.

Barbara ran around the store to find some shade. Cars roared past her on the highway, and a cloud of bugs surrounded her and matched her pace as fast as she could run. She felt like an overheated engine as she hid behind a fenced-in compressor bigger than her bedroom. She wished she could throw Garrett inside it and compress him, and she prayed that he would cry at what she'd said, so Rhonda and Sheila could see what a sissy he was. She hadn't lied to him, because Thursday night at dinner Pa had said, I don't like him any more than I liked his old man. They were eating pork chops and mashed potatoes, and Garrett was down at the pond digging worms. Pa talked with his mouth full of gravied meat. Bastard always was jealous of me, he said, on account of the rulty.

The what? asked Barbara.

The rulty. He held it against me.

What's rulty?

Floyd rolled his eyes at her. That's what a earl is, dipshit, he said and laughed. When Barbara hit his arm across the table, he hit hers harder. Pa watched her rub her reddened skin.

You're probly jealous of Floyd, too, Pa said to her.

For what? she asked, surprised. She looked at Floyd, who smirked at her and stroked his greasy hair.

For the same as Coogar was. The rulty. A girl cain't never get it.

She looked down at her food.

Floyd's gonna get it when I die.

I don't care, she said as Garrett came inside through the back door, his hands muddy and his fingernails brown.

He might even get it sooner, if I decide to advocate it to him.

Pa nodded as he chewed his food. Where you been? Floyd asked Garrett.

Kind.

How's the worms today?

Clean, Garrett said. Above all, reverent.

Barbara could almost see the library over the hill from where she stood outside the store. She wasn't any cooler in the shade, so she walked up front and watched Garrett from a distance; he was talking to her sisters. They didn't see her. A security guard pushed Pa out the front door and thrust the ragged jeans at him. Floyd pulled Granny by the hand and Mama followed close behind. She smiled wearily at the guard, then her face reverted to the same as always, just like Rhonda's, and Sheila's too, a sad, blank frown. Barbara was the only one with a scowl.

The horse ain't got no order, Rhonda cried as Barbara slowly walked to rejoin them. Mama. Mama.

Hush.

When's it gonna get some more order?

I done told you to hush.

Rhonda tugged on Mama's shorts. Mama, she said, it ain't got no *order*. When's it gonna get more?

Mama picked Rhonda up and shook her. She turned herself so Rhonda's body blocked the sun, and she was shaking; she hadn't eaten all day. She hated being called Mama, because she wasn't Mama; her name was Mabel Watson. She looked as if her blood hurt as it raced inside her legs and through her guts, and sometimes Barbara thought that Mama wanted all her children to crawl back up inside her, to shrink until she couldn't hear them anymore.

Mama took a deep breath and spoke softly. That ain't a real pony, anyway, she said. It don't matter.

Pa was walking up behind her. That's right, he said. It's a goddamn lie.

I didn't say it was a lie, Mama said.

Everything in that whole store is a goddamn lie.

So is it ever gonna get any more order? said Rhonda.

No. It's lies.

Rhonda sucked her thumb. She walked behind Sheila, who sucked hers, too.

A woman walking into the store approached Mama and smiled. What a beautiful baby, she cried.

Mama stopped to let the woman see the baby. People were always stopping to see her babies. It was the only reason anybody ever spoke to her.

What's its name? the woman asked.

Mama with a glance deferred to Pa, who said, We don't know right yet.

You don't know? How old is that baby? What do you mean you don't know?

We just can't tell yet, Pa said, louder.

What is it that you can't tell? she asked. Is it a boy?

Pa grunted yes.

The woman didn't hear him, and her eyes got bigger. Oh my God, is *that* what you can't tell?

Why hell, woman, of course I can tell that.

She looked embarrassed. I'm sorry.

I just don't know if he's gonna have to be the earl yet.

You're gonna name him Earl?

No, Pa said, irritated to have to explain it. He might have to be earl after me, he said, if Floyd goes to prison. The woman stared at him, and Floyd nudged Pa's shoulder to get him to be quiet. Floyd, Pa yelled, get your grubby hands off me. He turned back to the woman. All the earls have got to have the same name, he said. Otherwise it don't work.

The woman nodded her head.

Ever single one's been a Floyd, Pa said, all the way back to the first one, or the roll privlege wouldn't keep on.

She nodded again, slowly, squinting at the sun. She looked nervous. As she smiled at the baby boy, he began to cry. You sweet little thing, she said to him before she hurried away. Her heel caught a snag in the pavement, and she nearly fell. She looked around herself, embarrassed; Pa was staring at her. He didn't turn away until Floyd threatened him: I orta punch your face.

Pa laughed at him. Go on, he said.

Floyd made a fist.

Free shot. Why, I wisht to hell you'd do it. I'd turn you in quick as a greased pig.

Floyd scowled. He jerked Rhonda's arm so that she fell from the sidewalk into his grasp, dangling there by bent shoulder, and he dragged her toward the car. Garrett followed with his imaginary gun, pointing it at Barbara and at the bright sky when he said, Pow, pow, proud of the invisible weapon he clutched with both hands to his chest. I'll shoot everything, he said. I'm gonna shoot deer and bears and squirrels and rats and possums.

You shoot all the possums and rats you want, Pa said.

Hey Floyd, Garrett said.

Huh?

Why would you go to prison?

Ain't nobody goin to prison.

But your pa said—

Never mind what Pa said. It don't matter none what people say. It ain't important.

Garrett thought about it and nodded. I wish you could shoot people, he said. Without goin to jail. Not just all those stupid squirrels and deer. I want to shoot people.

You can, Barbara said.

Floyd stopped walking right in front of Barbara and said, What's that supposed to mean?

Garrett pointed his gun at an old woman across the parking lot. I wish I could shoot her till she was dead, he said, ahead of them already.

Pow.

Floyd's head blocked the sun as Barbara squinted up at him. She thought about speaking. Floyd pushed her shoulders and growled, You'd better watch it. He turned away. No one else had stopped, so Floyd ran to catch up, his knife bulging in the tight back pocket of his shorts. Barbara stayed ten feet back from everyone and slowed as she approached the truck. Pa was still mad, his head red like a blown bubble. I hope you've learned yuns a good lesson over this, he said as he turned the ignition.

The truck shook and cracked and rumbled. Granny put her hand over her mouth until the noise died and faded into the engine's softer drone.

I'm cold, she said.

You're what?

She placed her hands on their opposite shoulders and shivered.

Floyd handed her the jeans through the window. Here, he said. Use these.

Granny looked at them.

Go on, take it.

What am I spose to do?

Cover up.

Floyd tossed them in her lap, and she stared at them uncertainly. Go on, he said. She put her timid hands into the holes in the knees and shivered. Floyd sighed and reached through the window and pulled the legs up her arms until they reached her sleeves. Her lip quivered, and Floyd sat back down in the bed.

Pa shook his head. There's got to be somethin bad wrong with you, old woman.

Barbara burned her hand on the bumper's chrome as she climbed in, sweating. Sheila sat down across from her with no expression on her face, and Barbara realized they hadn't bought her anything. She wondered if it was her fault. Her cheeks were burning, so she turned her face away. She wished Sheila would quit looking at her. She watched people load their cars with bags and didn't realize Mama was crying until Pa yelled, What in the tarnation is wrong now? The thunder of his roar caused Mama to sob out loud. What? he demanded a second time. I can't see what you're thinkin, he yelled at her. I ain't got eyes in my brain.

Mama's voice sounded like a mouse's squeak compared to Pa's. What *are* we gonna name him? she said through her tears. If he don't end up to have to be another Floyd?

Pa stopped to think. I don't have the first notion what to call
him, he said.

Can we name him James? asked Mama. After my father?

Pa didn't answer for a minute. Hell, he said eventually, I'll
probly just call him Floyd anyway. He scratched his chin with
the index finger of his fist and nodded. It's as good a name as
any other.

They drove home south on the bypass. Barbara sat on a different side of the truck so she saw the same things this time, but
backwards. The hot breeze dried her sweat but didn't cool her
down. Rhonda didn't cry on the way home. She waved at a
brand-new Toyota station wagon that followed them past the
mall and onto Highway 411. At Red Food the car switched lanes
and at the red light stopped beside them, to the left. A woman
rolled down the passenger window. You can't have children in
the back of a truck like that, she yelled angrily at Pa. It's against
the law.

Barbara sat up to hear her father's answer but missed it.

The woman had expensive clothes on, like the ones in JCPen-
ney's catalog. Do you know what will happen if you get in a
wreck? she said. They'll fly right onto the road. Their heads will
crack right open like eggs.

I'll crack *her* head open, Floyd muttered.

Sshhh.

Shush yourself.

Barbara couldn't tell what anyone up front said. She heard
her father cackling. Granny's head bobbed up and down. The
woman had two boys of her own in the backseat of the wagon,
alert, near Barbara's age, their belts buckled. One had a soccer
ball on his T-shirt. He looked scared. I should report your license
plate number to the police, the woman said. Barbara couldn't
hear Pa's answer. She watched the boys sitting in their cool, up-
holstered seat and wished they'd choke each other to death. Or

that Pa would wreck so she could soar across the sunrays like a cannonball, shadowing the pavement far below herself as she waited for the collision of her body with her shadow.

The woman got out of her car. Cover up the plates, Dad yelled, so Floyd put Rhonda down and took the old jeans by their ragged kneehole, dangling them behind the truck. He grinned at the woman contemptuously. Her teeth were white and straight, and her skin was fair. Barbara wanted to yell the license number to her, but she'd turned away already.

Bitch, Floyd yelled. Barbara heard laughter in the cab. Her neck burned.

The woman got into her car and slammed the door. The light turned green, and her husband propelled them south along the highway. They vanished quickly for Barbara, because she never moved, nor did anyone; Pa had stalled them at the light. Traffic sped around them, and horns honked. Eventually the signal changed to red again, and they had to wait through a whole new cycle.

THE FACE OF THE MOON

The first thing the old magician did when he arrived in a new village was buy a good map, one that showed the topography and all the trails. At one time he had traveled by rail, by moonlight, along the smooth, unearthly beams, but then trains had fallen out of favor in the magician's land, and someday they would vanish from his language entirely.

Do they replace a word when it vanishes?

In our world we do, yes. But in the magician's world? The magician's world is a sad, dying world. The town criers have fallen silent there. The magician wants trains to remain part of his language, but he has let himself grow very old. The words of his spells are dissolving into each other; and now ivy is creeping along the rails that carry him hopelessly and without end through the forests of Castolon.

And Wayman would have said so much more, but it had
floated away, until the crickets and owls were his boy's only
night, and trains; yes, the magician loved the distant whistlings
of the engines, but now, Wayman feared, the magician would be
departing their lives forever.

Is he asleep? Kip whispered from the hall.

I don't know, Wayman whispered back.

He's not answering us, Kip whispered.

Wayman grabbed his son's wrist and felt for a pulse. He
could measure a pulse in three seconds now. He went to Kip and
held him tight, because although Kip was the one dying, his lover
and son were both equally fragile to him. He would need his boy
to carry him into the future.

The storms are coming again, said Wayman. Look at the
west.

Maybe we'll explode out into fire and be nothing.

Kip didn't have any spirituality at all. It saddened Wayman.

That doesn't sound like a thing you'd believe, he replied.

I read that the poles are shifting again, said Kip. The mole-
cules will switch direction all over earth, within us and around,
every twenty thousand years, so everything we're doing will be
futile.

Wayman wasn't a real atheist himself, but he loved his partner, and it was a terrible time to think of hurting him. You won't
even be at the ceremony, he'd tried to tell Kip, but Kip assumed
his look and stared north until Wayman gave up, shuddering at
what would be thought of him if there were no funeral, and what
their son would think.

I suppose we'll soldier on somehow, said Kip.

In India, the atheists float their dead away on burning funeral
pyres, down the rivers and out to sea.

But he could see he was beginning to terrify Kip.

Why don't you go ask Cobby if that's what he wants.

Maybe in the morning, after the sunrise, said Wayman.

But Kip had exposed Wayman's hypocrisy; even asking would be painful for Cobby. A funeral itself would be absurd. There was still a chance Cobby loved neither of them and wouldn't care, because they kept him hidden from society in the woods in their cottage under the sweetgum tree to which the storms lowered themselves, causing great explosions. Wayman hoped Kip wouldn't believe he'd ripped their cottage walls apart with the decisions he'd made. When they held each other, they were scared together. It was one of the promises Wayman had made to hold Kip when Kip was unhappy, sitting alone with him those years ago in the savage green valley when the feeling he'd never felt before would put him cold in the grave before he could ever live a life alone. Now Kip said they'd be electrocuted by the billowing waters. He knew what he was doing. He believed in science. The tree might live for years to come, even ripped as it was from its root system.

Kip's voice was high and whispery and lonesome on the phone to their ancient landlady. Yes I know it's storming, he said to her. But a tree has crushed our house. The whole house, and the car. Wayman hated to disappoint people, but Kip had gone straight to the phone, so assertive and strong as he repeated Virginia, Virginia, but Virginia just wasn't there.

It was probably a bad connection, said Wayman.

Old people can't take bad news the way we can.

It must be nice to be old.

She's had some kind of heart attack, said Kip. He tried to call back. Any minute now, the windows of heaven would make them move. Wayman liked this place where no one knew him, but they had Cobby to care for, and so Kip bade him go forth into the storm's world where the magician floated down the train tracks, eating old blackberries that had never blackened, shortening his stride to match the ties that led him straight as a gun barrel through the piney woods. The sapling trees reached above themselves and chose what stars could stay, what stars went cold. There were three ways having a dying lover was like falling in love in the first place. He couldn't think about anything else; also he hadn't been able to enjoy any moment of it; also it frightened him so much to change into what he'd never been. If there were more ways, they were secrets, and he didn't care to learn them. The Bible said to walk the earth, open his eyes to it, so he'd hoped to go farther. At first the white-haired demon on the tracks was just another sapling. Wayman knew when men said *Open up your eyes* they meant that life was getting worse. Whatever it was, it folded its arms across its clothes, and Wayman could barely see eyes between the wrinkles.

You stop where you're going and get here.

Are you Virginia's boy? said Wayman.

But English wasn't spoken where he'd walked to. Had he crossed the state line into Georgia? It was Wayman who had brought his family here, because country people were good people and they wouldn't have to worry, as long as they stayed off unpaved roads and went to the general store one at a time.

First help me out, then go where you were gonna.

Is your name Forbus? said Wayman.

That's one name, said the man.

I have some news for your mother.

Can you tell if somebody's dead or not?

Most people I know are alive.

But if you see folks, you know if they're dead?

Wayman hid why he was uncomfortable with these questions. The funeral wasn't all that tormented him, but it was a central thing he could work his feelings around. Kip wanted so much that didn't work in the world. It made Wayman want to split himself in two. He supposed this would kill him. He didn't

believe in Western science, and he didn't believe in the principles
of things.

You don't want to be going that way none, said Forbus. You
ain't going nowhere that way. I think you've got yourself lost.
Those tracks just peter out to nothing. Suddenly Forbus seemed
as scared as Wayman was scared, and he began to cackle. You'll
die if you keep going that way. That is not a good way.

The train bore down the tracks and between them and
blocked each man's view of the other. Wayman thought how Kip
was being filled with wafts of fuel, too, a mile west. Together
they lost themselves in the clackety rhythm. One way not to look
at Kip was to pretend he was crying. Wayman couldn't go
through the old photographs anymore. Cobby didn't remember
those times. On the magician's world, the dying only disappeared
like wisps of dust that floated out of sunbeams, and Cobby would
agree and nod off so Wayman could write down what he'd
learned from the progenitor of his fantasies.

Well you stuck around for me, said Forbus when the train
had passed.

Do you see why I'm not scared of the men here? he dis-
patched to Kip across their rain-washed mile. They trust in me;
your fears are mythological. Forbus held the catalpa branches off
the trail for Wayman. In the magician's world, youths still hid
their love, because Wayman questioned his own trust too much
to nurture it into Cobby, who should experience just enough
torment in these years, no more. Wayman's mother hadn't died
until Wayman was eighteen, and now he couldn't give his son
the same childhood. Kids who didn't love their parents were so
free, running off to the wicked cities never to be seen again, so
he prayed for Cobby not to consider himself as part of the same
blood.

This is a seventy-three, Forbus said of his trailer home at the
edge of a clearing.

You ain't going nowhere that way. Wayman wasn't scared to follow Forbus into a musty room, even if it was a trap. He thought he would have met their landlady's son before, but he and Kip were renegades who'd erased themselves from the map, so when Virginia told stories of growing up in their cottage, of planting the sweetgum tree on her brother's grave in the year 1930, they were ashamed of themselves and paid little attention, focusing instead on the threat she presented, although Wayman felt he and Kip were the threat in allowing themselves not to listen, thinking instead of their own welfare as unwanted settlers on enemy soil.

She's lying down in there, said Forbus.

It was me who called, said Wayman.

I suppose we ought to give her a look.

Wayman followed Forbus into a dark yellow room and climbed a gentle slope to the bed. She's under there, barked Forbus, pointing at a quilt.

If she's alive, she'll need air to get through.

Forbus inhaled a breath for ten straight seconds. There's air, he said.

You think it can get through all those covers?

She sewed it herself. I reckon she knew what she was doing.

Wayman shrugged. Pull them off then, he said.

Oh, no, said Forbus, drawing back. It's my mama under there.

One tendril of kudzu had reached the window from the trees beyond. The phone was off the hook at the woman's bedside.

That's how it is when it's your mama. You were inside her, dead in her, and then you lived. If I breathe her air into my body, she'll get inside of me instead, and that's backwards. Lord I hope she's okay. I don't even know how she mixes up the ice tea.

Wayman looked at the quilt and wished everyone would live

exactly as long as their mothers and die on the very same day. And if there was no mother? Kip was the one who needed to live, so Wayman would be the father, but Wayman, of the two of them, was not the man, and had no idea how his body could be made to feel that way.

The ghost world is three feet higher than ours, said Forbus. That's why a ghost is always floating, instead of on the ground. If a ghost stands inside you, its feet are always kicking at your stomach.

Wayman shut his eyes and pulled the quilt from the bed. Virginia's skin was white and shriveled. Her eyes were wide like she was falling off a cliff.

Her name's Virginia. Never called her by it, though.

She's dead, said Wayman. Good Lord.

Forbus shook his head. You got to use the mirra, he said.

Wayman felt sick to his stomach, for Kip had done this to her with the phone call.

You got to use the mirra. Last time I nearly had her in the ground.

Wayman sighed. Where is one, then?

Ain't you got one yourself?

Who carries a mirror around?

I thought maybe you had one of them knifes.

Wayman shook his head. All my knife is is a knife.

There was a dresser mirror, four feet wide, circular, and framed. Forbus pushed his mother's jewelry box to the floor. Even in these moments Wayman was incapacitated by the same old feelings. He wanted to do something new with grieving. Virginia's ghost was kicking at his stomach, because he could believe at this moment what Forbus had said. The logic that had made him love Kip came geographically closer to him. A mile was too far for Kip to walk! These thoughts as they wrenched the frame back and forth proved little besides his control of nothing, and when the wood snapped, he caught the mirror just before it would have shattered.

Help me hold this, he said.

Forbus put a finger to his lips.

I'll drop it, Wayman threatened.

Shhh. I heard her breathing.

You didn't hear any breathing.

I might have, if you'd have got quiet.

The image of the room behind him dizzied him until Forbus took the other side of the mirror. They covered Virginia's corpse with its round shadow. Dust in the air grew thicker until Wayman finally sneezed, showering the brown paper of the mirror's back side with all the droplets of his spit.

Look at that, said Forbus, she's alive!

That was me, said Wayman. I did that.

Tears began to form in the old man's eyes. He was trying not to move his jittery hands, but then his arms jerked back so that the glass hit a bedpost and shattered, causing Wayman's image to disperse into the four corners of the room.

Forbus gasped. It's all gone. That was all the mirra we had.

Wayman extracted a small triangle of glass from his forearm. I'm sorry, he said as Forbus sank to sort through the motley fragments. Forbus turned the pieces over and over, and his left foot nudged the jewelry box aside. On its lid Wayman saw a small mirror.

We've got to find the ones she breathed on.

I don't think you'll find any like that.

Hurry, Forbus said, his voice shaking. The frost will fade away.

There were three ways, the magician told his apprentice boy, that having a dead mother was like falling in love for the first time: he wouldn't think about anything else anymore; it would frighten him to change his every feeling—but Cobby had never been in love, his mother wasn't a mother at all, and Virginia might have been the only woman he knew, cordoned off as he was from the world, his one grandmother dead and his other having disowned Kip when Kip was fifteen, a common thing really, they said when Cobby asked why, so there were no women in the magician's world save the witches and dryads who mined elixirs from the forest floor.

I think I might know why she died, said Wayman.

She didn't die till we find the frost.

She looks kind of dead, though.

Forbus's hands were beginning to bleed.

I'm sorry. I know she's important to you.

But Wayman had to find a new place for his family. This storm would kill Kip too soon, and Wayman clutched Kip's chest to a chest in his mind. It was the drugs giving him the disease in the first place. He didn't believe in the theory of evolution. He rammed trains together head-on as he waited on the porch for the thunderstorm to end.

We got to put her in the dirt, said Forbus.

Wayman shook his head. I can't help you with that.

That's alright. I've got just the one shovel, anyhow.

He'd been telling Cobby the same stories over and over, because he'd never create again. He understood why dying men killed their families. It was a selfish act, but the selfishness sprang from a deep pool of love. A story he desired to tell Cobby was of a lonely boy whose father made him work long hours in the tobacco fields. The tobacco would always dry up and rot, because the father would stay gone for months at a time. To stifle his desires, the boy imagined each body part with which he might express his longings severed: his tongue, if he would speak to the saddler's son, his hand if he would touch the tanned skin of the saddler's son. The story went on for many years and even now

wasn't quite over, but Cobby wouldn't feel it from within, because he had no loneliness save what their lifestyles had given
him. In six months God would cleave their inadequacy in half
again. Poor Cobby! thought Wayman, and Cobby appeared from
the trees with Kip in hand in thunder so near it was concurrent
with the lightning.

You got to carry her yourself, said Forbus sadly.

You don't want to wait for somebody? said Wayman.

Won't nobody come, said Forbus. It's lucky you showed up
or I would have had to get the engineer.

How would you have done that?

I reckon I'd just stood there till they stopped.

Is this a funeral? said Cobby.

The rain hit Forbus broadside when he turned to see who'd
joined them in the yard. The grave had grown quickly, thanks to
the softening effects of the rain, so Cobby stood as high as Forbus.

Mr. Forbus's mother just passed away.

You were right, Cobby said to Kip.

What was he right about? said Wayman.

She loved the sweetgum tree, said Cobby. She told us all
about it.

I guess I wasn't paying attention, said Wayman. The strang-
est things could cause his waves of sadness. He and Kip were
sterile forces upon the earth. They were the ends of their lines,
and they were death. He averted his eyes from Cobby and
thought of being a mother. Everyone was a girl in his mother's
womb until the third month, but Wayman had taken a wrong
turn, which was affecting everyone. Forbus drove his weapon
spade into a tree root and began to cry again. Wayman, who
wept a lot himself, knew how his son would react, and he moved
around the grave and held the boy.

You asked him about the funeral, said Kip.

No, I want what you want. I said nothing.

How would he even know the word? said Kip.

Cobby seemed to want to answer, but could not, and Wayman knelt.

Isn't it rude to argue while someone is crying? his son whispered.

It seemed Forbus would never be able to go on.

Let me dig, said Wayman.

It has to be at least three feet deep.

Why did you come here? said Wayman.

Why three feet? said Cobby.

The water was almost up to the sockets, said Kip.

The ghost world is three feet higher than the real world.

He needed to be saving Kip from the diseases of the driving rain. He wished he weren't a fool! He wished he were living in the middle of the Great Depression, kicking into dusty towns whose names he didn't know. He asked his son to remain with Forbus while he led Kip inside the trailer, where he wrapped Kip's shivering body in green quilts. Call Cobby in, said Kip, who was still afraid. Instead they sat together clinging until Kip was asleep and all Wayman wanted on earth was to sleep, too, because they dreamed each other's dreams sometimes, and Kip saw Wayman's apparitions but remained an atheist, and Wayman woke from the miserable visions of the one man who'd promised never to leave him and found himself squeezed tight and lay awake hours that way, till all his earthly thoughts had disappeared.

He needs you now in the grave, said Cobby.

Wayman opened his eyes. I'm sorry we've brought you here.

It's okay. She was so old.

What were you talking about out there?

Dad, you have to carry her outside now.

Why? said Wayman.

He can't touch her.

I don't see why not.

He just *can't,* said Cobby. Wayman knew Cobby was fearful he'd refuse. Cobby understood how strangers could hurt him, and Wayman hoped his boy was glad they lived the way they did. That he liked to experience life vicariously through his books, through Wayman's stories; there'd be plenty of time to suffer later, when they were too old to be a family anymore. The whole time Wayman lay thinking of his son's precocity, he wasn't sad about Kip. The reprieve continued for twenty seconds, until Wayman, to ease his boy's fears, brushed ghost white forelocks from Virginia's eyes and took her like a baby in his arms.

The rain had stopped. A train was screeching past. Wayman tried not to slide in the mud as he knelt in the grave and bunched folds of Virginia's dress beneath her body.

Is this okay? he asked.

Forbus peered into the grave. I don't know.

I mean, in these clothes, and all?

Forbus looked at the treetops. Things can get wrinkled, he said.

He walked around the perimeter of the grave. Wayman leaned against the mud wall, averting his eyes from the corpse, smearing his jeans with earth.

Will we have the ceremony now? said Cobby.

What kind of a ceremony? said Wayman.

Where we fill in the dirt and stuff.

That's not a ceremony.

Cobby leaned into the grave. Dad, he whispered.

Wayman's eyes welled up. What's the matter? he said.

Don't say those things. Can't you see how sad he is?

Wayman considered that Forbus had a disease of the mind. It would be nice to forget things. He'd been standing in the hole too long, having forgotten the need to move away from the corpse.

Do you want to hear a riddle? Forbus asked.

Kip appeared on the porch.

Brothers and sisters have I none, said Forbus.

Kip walked out into the drizzle.

This man's mother is my brother's son.

We should cover her up, Wayman suggested.

It doesn't make sense, said Cobby.

Forbus scrunched his face up. I was just trying to think of what to say, he told Cobby. People are always telling each other things, so I figured I'd see how that goes.

Where are we going to live? said Wayman.

Stop it, Dad, said Cobby.

My partner is ill. We have to be dry.

How tall are you? said Cobby.

Cobby, will you leave me alone?

Was it at least up to your waist?

What in the world?

It has to be three feet!

Stop sounding so desperate!

Cobby was breathing erratically as if to induce a panic attack. Kip was lowering himself into the grave, shrouded in green, hovering like a specter, feigning calm, outdoing Wayman, who could try to list these things that made his love seem illusory, and he breathed normally again, if only out of impotence to induce a different thing from what was happening. That's my mother's quilt, said Forbus. It's not yours. I see how it is with you. Who are you and what are you doing with that boy? Where are you taking him down that track? But Forbus was backing up. He was trudging away toward the trees and he was gone, and Kip measured the grave against the inseam of his jeans. It's three and a half feet. What is it about Cobby you can't answer him? said Kip. Why are you the only one who gets to be illogical? Why can't anyone else be illogical? If Cobby doesn't want her ghost to escape from the ground, why can't that be enough?

He doesn't want your ghost to escape from the ground either.

You want the community to come together and know us?

We'll take this trailer as our own, thought Wayman.

What if it were Cobby dying? Why are you in love with your own destruction?

He's just saying it for my sake, said Cobby. You should do what you want.

You know we love you more than anything.

But you've been together longer. It's more important to you.

Wayman embraced Kip. I don't want you to be a ghost.

I don't want to be a ghost either.

But he should have hugged Cobby first, because Cobby had come up with an excuse for Wayman's terrible feelings, and other things. They clung together at the grave's edge until Virginia's pale light rose through them skyward so it was too late to fill the hole again, except to hide the coming stench of death. And because Wayman was inextricably joined to his family, they fell with him when he slipped in the mud. Each man had to pick another never to abandon; if not one, none; and Wayman chose, covered as he was in the aftermath of the storm, which felt good to him, so that he was moved to take off his shirt and dig into the pile of mud.

This man's mother is my father's son, said Cobby.

That's not even what he said, said Kip.

But it's like us, said Wayman.

When will he come back? said Cobby.

He may have departed our lives forever.

Should we do something? It's getting dark.

But it's clearing up, said Wayman. Look at the moon. He

was glad it stood watch above them as they scooped mud into the hole. Its face was white and furrowed like Virginia's, which darkened as they covered it, but the moon's grew only brighter when Wayman saw it ever-higher above the hills. People were lucky to have it buoying them. The magician's world was a moonless world where the blood of the folk knew no tides. It was lonely walking the tracks endlessly without moonlight, but it was a great thing to see new hills, and how they rose, and not to fear them. The crickets cried for mates at sunset, cloaking distant blows of engine steam so he would think he was alone. The wind hit him, but he didn't know it howled. The air was dry, but he was never thirsty, because if he was immortal, it didn't matter how long he went without soothing his parched throat: he'd continue to live.

OLD TIMERS' DAY

This was Lonzoe's papaw, he was dead when I was born. They built the national park because they wanted Clayton off his land, most everybody knew it. He got hisself some brand new land, he got a Colt, he got a side-by-side.

If I shot every ranger just one gun I'd get awful bored with that one gun.

His boys was big enough to farm, he didn't farm no more. He'd just turned sixty-five when Lonzoe's daddy come, he laughed just like a hoot owl off the mountains. He rocked his chair and thought on what they'd took, the more he thought the more he couldn't stand it, same as Lonzoe. Park starts up the Old Time Days they wrote to Clayton asked him would he come. The fuckin nerve. Now Pa. They want me up there at that mill and play my banjo for the tourists. Well don't do it. Well I ain't. He sits and whittles corn like it was wood. He gets this grin from ear to ear, he grins so hard he might of been an ape. Never told nobody what he'd grinned. Old Time Day it come along and Clayton got inside his Dodge and headed up the cove and gave his daddy's grave some corn and drove around to Cable's Mill.

I come for the Old Time Day.

They told him what was goin on, it must of been a hundred ten degrees, they was a crowd and they was Esau Tipton. Everyone this here's my buddy Clayton. Clayton got that grin but then his mouth went straight and Esau finished up the fiddle, shady grove I'm gone away from here. Clayton sits beside him on the porch. Everybody's watchin when he tells em how you hunt a deer and how you farm and how you hunt a bear. How to build a cabin with your hands. How lightnin hit him up on Parsons Bald, it took a day across the hills to get to town and his own pa made him run the thorns without no clothes on when he said he'd seen a plane.

If you'd of been there you'd of thought that someone else was in that chair but him.

Clayton talks and talks and Esau Tipton says has the old fart had a stroke. Clayton waves his hands and shouts his hair's on end, the babies that was bawlin all shut up. His cheeks was like a steak was up inside of it, just talkin on and on. It wouldn't end, but then he stops and spits a wad of juice down on the wood, it smacked down on the boards just smack.

Everyone was real uncomfortable.

Fuck shit ass bitch cunt, Clayton yells.

Come again, says Esau Tipton.

Dick suck fuck twat, whore cock ass. Cunt lick cock suck pussy.

His voice went off Rich Mountain, folks was all confused, it was a sight. These folks was from all walks of life, all kinds of states, you couldn't tell. They covered up their babies' eyes, you didn't hear those words as much back then. They tried to shut him up but was they supposed to cover up his mouth? Tit cock twat, he'd slowed it down but every little bit you heard another shit and folks stayed quiet till he shot that gun up in the air, he laughed that laugh like groundhogs in his guts. Get out of my cove. Go home and suck your daddy's dick. You ain't shit, says Clayton, all yuns ain't.

Esau walks up front. Put down that revolver, go back home. I am home you old fuck. Home to Laurel Valley. Your mama died up here you buried Clara out behind your house. Clayton that was forty years ago. Esau I bet you give it up for free, I bet you told em rape your daughters too.

I hope you rot in hell.

Folks knew Clayton wasn't gonna shoot no one, they headed toward their cars but Clayton throws the gun at Esau's head, they turn around and Esau's right to sleep. This little bitty ranger grabs the gun. Clayton stick your hands up in the air. You put em up. No you put em up. You got my gun you peckerwood.

Clayton goes and spits tobacco in his face they just stare.

Shit bitch kike prick gook ass nigger twat fuck.

Ain't nobody knows what Clayton said to that head ranger with the carrot hair but Clayton put the fear in him I'd say.

Esau stands, I guess he wasn't hurt so bad. They wasn't no arrest, it pissed off Esau good. Clayton stops at Townsend Store for five fried pies, he ate em all. They still put on the Old Time Days but Clayton he don't go no more, he had a stroke and then he couldn't talk period. He got a cane he busted Lonzoe's pa upside the head most every day. He ate potatoes breakfast lunch and dinner. He died out in the rows of corn. He never fell, he only stood there dead, just grinnin at the birds like a beat-up scarecrow.

AURORA

Sam, his father said to him on the way home from Christmas, we're gonna stop up here real quick at the grocery and get some more money, okay?

Okay, Sam said, and he checked the battery in his new walkie-talkie to make sure it was pointed the right way, so they could communicate while his father was getting the money. His father said Sam was the best sidekick since Tonto. Back at the Gulf station in Soddy-Daisy Sam had been Ground Control, his father Major Tom, and Sam had watched out the Chevette's rear windshield for blue lights while his father was inside. Ground Control. Come in, over.

Sam held the red button down and spoke into the circular receiver. This is Ground Control.

Tell your mother not to hold her breath anymore.

Why'd you close the blinds inside the gas station?

Say over.

Over.

Tell her we're good.

We're good, Sam said.

I heard, said his mother in the front.

But it's not much, over.

What's that sound behind you, over.

Nothing, over.

Over and out, and Sam heard static and then silence. His father ran from the station with a brown bag to the car and climbed inside and turned the key and shouted like a cowboy in a rodeo and pointed them north on empty Highway 27. He leaned to kiss Sam's mother, who was shaking, and Sam wondered if it was his baby brother inside her making her breathe so loud. When she was finally calm again they pulled into the parking lot of Sparky's Spirits, and then she wasn't calm at all. There weren't any blinds this time to close. The lights inside the liquor store went off, and Sam's mother began to whisper to herself. Sam couldn't hear what she was whispering. Maybe she was talking to the baby; maybe she was counting in another language. She'd taught Sam how to count in four languages, plus backwards language. There was a language for every year of his life. Stop whispering, his father said to her when he was back in the car. He kissed her on the cheek. He rubbed dust from his hands onto his jeans and started the car and buckled his seat belt as he backed up and drove them away. That just feels so good, he said. Like jumping from a plane.

It doesn't feel good to me, Sam's mother said.

It would if you did.

It wouldn't, and I have.

That's because you're German, said Sam's father. He rolled his sleeve up high and patted his coat-of-arms tattoo, its yellow griffins winking at a crescent moon on the escutcheon. I feel the highway blood, he said and blew the horn and swerved into the left lane of the road.

Please don't, Sam's mother said.

This is how we do it back in Ireland.

You've never been to Ireland.

I'm practicing for when I go.

He gave Sam a handful of bills to put in the Gulf bag, and he moved into the right again, the tires crackling from a coat of rock salt spread onto the road for the coming storm, although the skies were mostly clear. Sam had been awake two hundred miles, ever since Alabama, and he let himself fall in and out of sleep. Clocks went faster when he dreamed, and it scared him for time to move so fast; he didn't want to miss the rest of 1982. He woke up when his carnation pink crayon fell from behind his ear. What if the heat's gone off? his mother was saying. That was today.

We'll go somewhere else, Sam's father said.

Eventually there won't be any more country to go to, and we'll be in the ocean.

I like the ocean.

I like it too, she said, and she craned her neck to look up at the stars. The sky was bleak and empty like the highway. Sam's mother squinted her eyes. What's wrong with the sky? she said and rolled her window down and shivered, because everything outside the car was frozen. The sky had begun to ripple with pink-and-purple light above the ground fog.

There's a problem with the sky, she said.

What kind of problem?

Am I the only one who even sees it?

I see the sky, Sam's father said.

The light.

Holy shit. They drifted into the other lane when he craned

his neck to see the pink shimmers floating there like headless ghosts. They faced a hilly sweep of wilderness, and Sam shuddered at his father's worry. The clouds were made of ruby-colored flesh like unpeeled plums. The night was dark in spite of so much liquid pinkness in the sky, and Sam couldn't make out the horizon. He remembered the veil from the murder song, how it might have blustered in a midnight wind like these clouds that trembled above the knobs and granges and a distant concrete shaft of the Watts Bar nuclear reactor with its shining smoke that rose into the light and made it brighter.

Oh, my God, Sam's mother whispered, that's what it is.

What? Sam's father said as Sam's arms broke out in bumps from her fear.

Radiation.

He looked at her.

The plant, she said and pointed at the twin pillars looming to the east.

It looks okay to me.

That doesn't matter with radiation, she said.

The road now curved in closer to the bulging gray reactors on the river's shore. Sam caught a glimpse of water. We'd hear about it on the radio.

Not if it was a war, Sam's mother said.

Of course we would if it was war.

It's getting bigger.

The blight upon the sky had spread out like a photo-negative sunrise from the foothills of the Smokies to the Cumberland Plateau. The brightest stars shone through it down to earth, but the dim ones died inside it, leaving gaps in all the constellations. The Chevette didn't have an FM radio. Sam's father twisted the knob across the AM band from six to fourteen hundred twice and finally found a woman's crackly voice and turned the volume high.

The children need a tangible experience, the woman said. When they bake their birthday cake for Jesus they learn that he was real, that he was one of us.

Goddamn Jesus, said Sam's father, and turned the radio off.

Sam's mother turned it back on, but the station had gone to static, and the woman sounded like she was speaking a harsh foreign language.

His birthday wasn't really even Christmas. It was in the spring.

Sam had heard his father explain this once before. It had to do with Saturn, he remembered. The sky got low like it was wrapping itself around the car to choke them the way a snake would, and Sam held in his breath to practice suffocating. Ten seconds was all he could manage. His mother was breathing hard; the baby was struggling. I want to know what's happening, she said. There's not a car on the road. There's not a single station on the radio.

You're nervous because of what we did, Sam's father said.

What we did, she repeated and shook her head. What you did.

We as in me and Sam.

You leave him out of this.

He's my sidekick.

You're not a hero. You don't have a sidekick.

You're jealous cause you don't have one.

Does the air smell funny to you?

He's the dispatcher, his father said. Sam clenched the walkie-talkie and hoped his baby brother would be his mother's sidekick once he was born.

What if there's been an accident at Oak Ridge? she said and pointed to the north, where the sky was as deep as a bruise. It would be a target for the Soviets, she said, because we make the bombs there.

Do they hate us? said Sam.

We've got so many children over here, his father said. They hate children.

But they have children too.

They send their little boys off to war.

Sam felt cold when his father grinned at him through the rearview.

But really Ronald Reagan hates children more than Russians do.

Ronald Reagan doesn't hate children, Sam's mother said.

It's right there in his eyes, Sam's father said, sounding more serious. How can you not see it in the bastard's eyes?

Sam tried to picture Ronald Reagan's eyes but saw only black holes.

He's jealous because he's so old, Sam's father said. He'll be dead soon, but all the children will live to be a hundred.

Sam thought about whether or not it might be true.

With all the new medicine, that is, his father added.

Will you live to be a hundred too, with all the medicine? Sam asked.

Maybe ninety-five, his father said. If this bomb's not too bad.

Sam knew about radiation poisoning because of a movie they'd seen the week before. He'd lain between his parents on the queen-size motel bed and watched a mother try to raise her children in a nuclear holocaust. The youngest ones died first. The twelve-year-old helped his mother bury them in the backyard, but then he wasn't strong enough to dig holes anymore. It was the saddest movie Sam's mother had ever seen. Sam had almost cried too just watching her. She'd sobbed long after it was over, when Sam's father was asleep and all the lights were out and even truckers on the highway had gone to bed so there was nothing to distract Sam from her sobbing, not even shadows on the ceiling.

We should turn around and go the other way, she said.

And then what? he said.

Keep driving, she said.

To where? he said.

South, so we won't breathe the radiation.

Once it's happened it's happened.

It's cumulative, she said.

You think south's the answer to everything.

Put the air on recirculate.

It's too late, he said.

Maybe the car will filter out the fallout.

That's not what cars are made to filter.

At least we can try, Sam's mother said.

Recirculate gives you cancer, he said.

Fallout gives you cancer, she said.

No, it just kills you.

I'm scared of how my stomach hurts. My tonsils feel like fingernails.

We shouldn't talk about this in front of Sam, he said.

Don't look at me, she said. Look at the road.

That's a stupid thing to say, said Sam's father.

Why is it a stupid thing to say? said Sam.

Your mother knows what makes it stupid.

Of all the days to act this way, she said.

Christmas isn't supposed to be happy. It's to make us feel like shit.

Sam's mother put her fingers to her forehead. Sam's father sped the car up every time he finished talking. Why would Jesus lie about his own birthday? he said.

Why would Jesus drop a bomb on us? she said.

Jesus is very mysterious, he said, laughing. Sam, what if I told you your birthday's the first of May, and you thought it was December.

But it is December, said Sam.

You can fake a birth certificate, said his father.

Don't worry, said his mother. Your birth certificate's real.

It's just a piece of paper with some ink, his father said.

Sam looked out the window. He liked his birthday, and he didn't want a new one.

If it was May he'd be a Taurus, said his mother. You can't fake that.

Maybe he is one, said his father.

He's way too smart to be a Taurus.

She turned and rubbed Sam's pant leg with her hand. Sam loved his mother's voice, how she spoke so calmly and how she taught him so many different things. His Gemini was moving out of Jupiter, so his life was going to change. He'd figured it meant his brother, but maybe it was the sky, which looked like his Nehi grape would have looked if it were melted to the glass. He thought about nuclear war, how it could shut things down so he and the baby would never have to go to school, and he drew sevens with his pink crayon on the paper sack that held the money. Seven was the best number. He drew it seven times and seven more, and when he ran out of brown space on the bag he drew new sevens on top of the other sevens.

Sam, said his mother, I don't want you to be scared just because I'm scared.

Her face looked wet as she smiled at him and stroked his knee. I'm not scared, said Sam.

It's okay to be scared, but you don't need to be.

Okay, he said, still drawing. It made him sad the way she smiled, but then she turned to the front again and whispered in his father's ear, and he wasn't sad anymore. Disasters were exciting; they brought everyone together, and everybody had to think about the same thing. Now the sky was his crayon's color, pale pink like dogwood blossoms, and he drew thick, furious sevens as he watched it grow.

Sam, his mother said.

What?

You've still got that crayon in your ear.

No, he said, it's in my hand.

His mother turned to the window and put her head against it and sighed.

Just let him draw the sevens, said his father.

It's not that they're sevens, she said, and she turned to Sam and added, You'll be starting kindergarten soon. You should think about getting a new favorite color.

Where do you get one? said Sam.

You just think of one, she said.

Why can't pink be my favorite color?

This is a different place. People are different here.

You don't know that they'll be different, said Sam's father.

His mother cleared her throat. I think we can assume.

That's just you. You're fostering an environment.

That principal could barely talk, she said.

But we'll have the money for the Montessori school now.

That money's not even enough for the baby.

How much does the baby cost? said Sam.

His mother swallowed. Different things, she said. Depending.

Sam's father picked up the walkie-talkie and said, Come in, Ground Control.

I'm in, said Sam.

Over.

Over.

Count the money, over.

It's too dark, his mother said.

Sam can see fine in the dark, his father said.

He'll hurt his eyes, she said.

It's one of his special powers.

I'll never understand what it is about you and powers.

He squinted at her and mumbled something Sam couldn't hear.

Shut up about it, she said. My family was here since the eighteen hundreds.

Once a German, always a German, he said.

You get to be the good guy, and I'm the big bad voice of reason.

It's the German blood, he said.

You're undermining me.

You're fostering an environment.

Sam, she said, I think pink's a very pretty color.

He continued drawing, because they'd talked about it several times before.

If the world were just us, she said, I'd never say a thing.

What's your favorite color? he asked his mother.

Ground control, said his father. Over.

It was blue, she said.

Did they make fun of you for it? said Sam.

Is your mission complete, over.

Not for that, his mother said.

I'm working on it. Over.

I know there's not enough, said his mother.

There's always more, his father said.

No, she said, there's not going to be any more.

The money was mostly tens and twenties, with some ones mixed in, and Sam counted it carefully to make it be enough. It was fun to add the figures in his head. Numbers were his favorite thing. When cars passed on the highway, he did the squares and square roots of the license plates, but tonight the road was empty.

His parents' license plate was seven cubed, three hundred forty-three and several letters, until his father stopped to switch it at a wayside. He got a Mississippi plate from the hatchback and crouched behind the car with a flathead screwdriver in his fist. Sam opened the door to see what the new number was, but his mother stopped him.

I want you to stay in the car and keep me company, she said.

Why? he said.

It's cold.

I'll be okay.

You're safer here.

I'm hot, he said.

Take off your sweater.

His father heard them talking and yelled, Come out if you want to.

Stay right here, his mother told him quietly.

Can't I get out for just a second?

Can't you please just stay?

Sam wondered if he should disobey her. He never had before, but he needed to know the license number. Sometimes his mother didn't understand things like that. His father rapped a finger on her window; when she waved him away he rapped again. She rolled it down a half an inch, and he growled something into her ear. He opened Sam's door and pulled him out into the night. The trickly flux lines made triangles, and he knew which ones were scalene, which were isosceles, acute, obtuse, and they stretched to the horizon like a range of upside-down mountains suffering a slow, endless earthquake.

We don't know what it does to breathe this air, his mother said.

Sam's father ignored her and shut the door and stood very still until he walked behind the car. Your mother's having a hard time right now, he said. I need to remember that.

Sam nodded. The number had no sevens, no matter what kind of math he did to it.

You left your walkie-talkie in the car, his father said. You're incommunicado.

But we're right next to each other, said Sam.

Never leave your post. That's so important.

He twisted two rusty screws into their holes. When he lifted the old plate up to pitch it away, Sam opened his mouth and grabbed his father's arm. He wanted to keep the plate, but the air was too cold for him to talk. He wondered if fallout could keep his throat from making words. His father offered him the dirty piece of metal, but he didn't let go when Sam tried to take it. You'll be responsible, he said. You can't let them see it.

I won't, said Sam.

Dead or alive, his father said. Keep it out of sight.

Sam tucked the plate beneath his shirt. Its cold chill bumps rubbed against his own chill bumps. When he was in the car again, he hid the plate beneath the rug at his feet.

What's it like in Mississippi? he asked when they were driving again.

It's brown, his father said. It smells bad.

What smells bad?

The land. The open space.

But why? Sam said.

If everybody's evil in a place, and they're always thinking evil things about how to take stuff away from people, then it starts to smell bad.

The land does?

Uh-huh.

Like the grass and the dirt and things?

Pretty much the same things as here, said his father.

Why did we move up here then?

There are things you can't do down in Mississippi.

Let's just be quiet for a few minutes and enjoy the scenery, said his mother.

Sam wondered if his eyes would begin to hurt from the glow. You couldn't mix things with black, but shivery streaks of pink were lighting the sky like frozen fire, even though black wasn't a color. It was happening in the north, above the tree line where they were headed, and the ribbons of it looked to Sam like sevens. A great many of them had formed now toward Oak Ridge, all manner of sevens, streaks of lavender on a bed of darker pink.

Can I tell you how much money's in the bag?

Of course you can, his mother said.

Because you said not to talk.

She turned and touched his leg and said, I meant about Mississippi.

It's three hundred twelve dollars, said Sam.

His parents looked at each other and didn't say anything.

Is that enough? said Sam.

Enough for what?

For what you need it for, said Sam.

When his mother turned to the window, Sam watched her to make sure she wasn't going to cry, but then he looked away. You couldn't just sit and watch your mother cry. He wondered if she'd cried this much when she was pregnant with him. He knew he'd counted the money right, but he counted again anyway, because he wanted her to like the number.

Let's play a car game, his father said. I Spy, or Riddle Me, or what do you call it.

Don't look at me while you drive, his mother said. We'll wreck.

I'm not looking at you.

Good, she said.

That's good? he said.

Don't get sensitive if you know what I mean.

Sam could feel his father's anger as they raced around the curves. He was gripping the wheel with callused thumbs. All the other cars had disappeared from the planet; their Chevette was the last one. It made Sam feel lucky, because there were so many people. He felt his fingers preparing for the radiation. If he grew an extra one, he wanted it on his left hand. His mother giggled and then coughed and said, I didn't mean to do that, so don't go basing anything on it, and Sam imagined her locked in an asylum, saw the whiteness of its walls and felt how hot he was and rolled his window down and pushed his head outside into the wind and felt the frigid world breathing and choking with him as he breathed.

Get back in here, his mother said. You'll smash your head on a road sign.

Sam felt like he'd been sitting in the car for all his memory. He started counting as he rebuckled his safety belt, and he decided to count until everything ended. If he counted to death he'd reach two billion, unless the fallout killed them early. His brother would count with him when he learned to count. His father was turning his head away from the road, and Sam wished he would quit turning his head, but his mother didn't notice; she wasn't moving. What if she was counting too; what if she'd been counting since he was born? What number was she on? It scared him as they sped along the highway. He wanted to be the one to have built those sharp curves. The drivers would wonder who'd built them, and he'd feel their wonder. His ears popped as he sputtered through the darkness like a season that was gone and so much shadowed space spread out beneath the fallout cloud, and his mother shuddered; maybe she was dying. In the movie the children had been first to die, but grown-ups had died too, and no babies had been born.

He wished his parents spoke another language, so he would

never know what they were fighting about. He drew with his
crayon to slow his breathing. The bag was already covered with
sevens, and he looked inside it at the repeated ones and zeroes
and serial numbers. There needed to be a seven-dollar bill. Seven
was less than ten, but the money would be luckier after he re-
numbered it. It would buy lucky things.

Money will get devalued, his father was saying. After the war
in Germany they had to fill a wheelbarrow full of money to buy
a jug of milk.

Where'd they get enough money to fill wheelbarrows? said
Sam.

Ask your mother. She's the Nazi.

Sam wished she knew his father was just teasing her, and he
wished his father would tease him instead. Her ears were twitching as she told him about school. How he should look forward
to it, how it had a playground and a library. Just try to act like
everybody else, she said. The way you walk. Your handwriting.

What about my handwriting? said Sam.

It looks too neat, she said.

But I want it to look right, he said.

The other kids won't even know how to write yet, Sam's
father said.

They've got eyes, said his mother. They can see it.

Sam wasn't supposed to want things to look neat or pretty.
Mountains from a distance, weeping willow trees. His mother
said I'm sorry and stretched back and pinched the skin on his
lower back with her hands as she hugged him tight. If I weren't
scared of what would happen, I'd shoot them, she said, but it
would only make things worse. They'd make fun of you because
of me.

Mama, said Sam, you're not making any sense.

I didn't even want to have a baby, because the world is so
terrible. I knew the baby would grow up and hate the world too.

But I don't hate the world, said Sam.

I know. I'm just telling you a story about what I thought.

Your mother likes to try to talk herself out of things, said his father.

What are you trying to talk yourself out of? said Sam.

Nothing, said his mother, and the force of the word made Sam shudder. He wondered if his brother would hate the world when he was born. He'd probably be a Pisces, and his mother was worried about that. Sam hoped she could hold him inside long enough for Aries to begin. He imagined his brother's mind changing inside her like the numbers and pictures on a slot machine until she finally picked the right month.

I didn't want to be this way, she said. That's why people stay confused their whole lives, because the parents say confusing things the whole time they're a kid.

I'm not confused, said Sam's father. I know exactly why I hate the world.

You want this to be a bomb?

It doesn't matter what I want.

Sam, your father wants us all to die.

As opposed to just one of us.

Sam hoped it was sarcasm, but he didn't know how to tell. As he changed the money into sevens, he drew crooked lines and pointed them different ways and different sizes like clouds. The rosy shadows in the sky weren't really clouds, because clouds were made of rain.

Dad?

What?

What's an APB?

All Points Bulletin.

Can it blow up if there's a bomb?

Everything can blow up if there's a bomb.

The sky was growing. Sam drew the last seven on the last bill and everything was done.

Sam, what are you doing to the money?

His father kept the car completely straight as he reached back for the bag. He took it from Sam, who held his breath as his father filtered through the seven-dollar bills. He watched his father's face in the rearview's narrow band. The old face was curious, but Sam couldn't tell whether the new face was angry or sad or both or what until he heard words.

Do you realize what you just did?

Sam thought he did until he said, No.

This was really stupid, Ground Control.

Don't tell him he's stupid, Sam's mother said, although she sounded hesitant.

I'm telling him the thing he did was stupid.

You told him to keep on. You fostered the environment.

Sam's father's words came out so twisted up in his teeth that Sam could barely make them out. Do you want me locked away? Is that why you cry so much? The car went back and forth with his shaking hands, and Sam wondered if he'd be mad forever, if his face would never get smooth.

We'll get the markings off with wax or something, said his mother.

That's what a crayon already is, said his father.

It doesn't matter, because of the sky.

It's not going to make the sky any better for you to sit there and scream about the sky, the sky, the sky, like we forgot it's there.

We should ask somebody, she said.

You know what they'll say, he said.

This isn't about us. The sky isn't pink just for us.

Sam waited for them to look at each other. They hadn't

looked at each other for the whole conversation, and he wished he had a blindfold. Holding his breath conserved energy. He wondered if they'd used up all the oxygen inside the car, and that was why his mother looked so tense. Thinking about oxygen made him feel like fainting. He imagined flying over cliffs. Other planets were pink and had no air, and maybe that was happening now to earth. It might have been a sunrise, but the time was just three-thirty in the morning, and Sam's father moved too late to block Sam's mother's arm from turning the wheel left toward the pulloff, trusting him to brake before the guardrail at the cliff's edge. The Dumpsters were green, the sky was pink and black; it was so peaceful. He held his mother's hand and watched it burn.

There's gonna be a roadblock, she said.

Prove there is one, said Sam's father.

Prove there's not.

You'd be fine anyway.

She nodded. I'd keep getting finer and finer until it was too late.

Sam wondered if he knew what she meant; he could hear two voices in her voice. His baby brother was very strong to make her think with both their brains like that. Someday he'd be wonderful. Fallout made mutations. It was probably too late for Sam, but the baby could grow an extra arm. Its rosy skin would glow like the sky. It would have the three arms, but Sam would have the power, because he'd always know the story of why.

You have to name the baby soon, he said, because fallout might make her forget names. It could change the shape of people's hair. It bent everyone's knees up so they could hide beneath the furniture. It probably did ten times as many things as he knew about.

I don't want you talking to the kids at school about this, his mother said.

Why would I want them to name the baby?

Don't talk to them about babies.

There won't be any school anymore.

She shook her head. That's the problem. There wouldn't be anything.

There'd still be things, said Sam, but all he could think of was Dumpsters. All the dark trees were bent like they were whipping one another. He thought of them too.

The doctors would all be closed, or dead.

We never get sick anyway, he said.

I can't tell you. I'm just gonna let you watch.

They don't let people watch, his father said.

Not with his eyes, she said. Not right there at a specific time.

Why are we stopped? said Sam.

We have to think about ourselves, she said. We don't want to starve.

Sam wondered if radiation did anything to the food. If someone had to die, he hoped it would be the policemen who were out somewhere in the night searching, and he kicked the money beneath his father's bucket seat. A skunk walked by with its tail raised and didn't spray a thing. The air made Sam light-headed, but only because he knew it could, and he looked out at the twinkling lines like grain elevators carrying bits of the black hills up to hidden stars. His mother was fiddling with the revolver. She didn't quite know where to point it. The sky, the Dumpsters, her waist, the sky, her belly again. She was laughing, running a hand nervously down her long brown hair, and it scared him, because what was funny about the gun?

This would be the cheap way, she said.

Cheap for you, said his father. Might cost me and Sam some money though.

Sam hoped his brother wouldn't get the gene that had said that. The two sides of the pink light tugged each other like magnet powder. He could feel it pulling him like it was the moon and he was the ocean. He tried to levitate above his seat but made it only an inch. Magnets were dangerous; what if they melted him right out of the car? He'd never find his family again, because he wouldn't be allowed to tell what his father had done. He'd ask for his mother instead, because she hadn't done anything, but she wasn't talking to him anymore.

Maybe she was still counting. By now she was probably above a million.

Sam held her freckly wrist tightly with his hand. She looked happy and sad and alive and dead, all at once, because she was two people. He wondered what her knowing frown was knowing as she stared at wisps of light caressing the plateau. He waited for it to explode; it was just a matter of time until there'd be nothing to get out of the car for. They'd move forever. His little brother would feel the highway blood too. When he came to life, they'd be moving.

Why are we still stopped? said Sam.

They were still mad at him about the marked bills, because they were blocking him from their minds. His mother didn't need money if everything was dead. Maybe he could use it all on batteries, so the walkie-talkies could last forever. He punched Morse code with his toy's red beeper. Dash dash dot dot dot, seven times. His mother kept opening her mouth to talk to him, but she wasn't ready yet. The sky was getting darker. She closed her mouth and opened it. He couldn't wait to hear what she would say. He wanted to be driving again. She opened her mouth wider, like she was using it to decide something. He handed her a walkie-talkie to help her talk, and he looked out at the fingery lights that had shriveled like mimosa blossoms groomed for dusk. He hoped he wouldn't forget what they looked like as soon as the next unlucky thing happened.

A FLOCK OF BLUEBIRDS

Froggy wore tight jeans in which a wallet with his newly issued learner's permit bulged. Let's go for a drive, he said to Ben. I could shit, I'm so bored. He twirled the keys on his finger as they snuck out of the rental cottage and downstairs to a driveway made of oyster shells. Shut the door real soft, he told Ben when they got inside the Buick, even though the engine roared when Froggy revved it, and he yelled with excitement now, which made Ben happy. Shells shot into the sea oats. Ben wondered what he'd be excited about when he reached his brother's age. Cars, cigarettes. Froggy lit one, and Ben warned him that their great-aunt Celeste might smell it later, but Froggy just laughed. Old people can't smell, he said. Didn't you know that? Your smell dries up when you get old.

He rolled his window down and thrust his hand into the

humid air, accelerating quickly. He swerved around a cyclist. The car lurched forward violently when he shifted into fourth. Don't worry, Froggy said, that don't mean nothing, and Ben tried to match his slouching posture. He decided not to be nervous. Above the tops of stunted pines he saw the bay; across the dunes an amber sun rose on the gulf. I had another dream that Mama died, he said.

So? said Froggy.

What do you mean, *so*? She was dead. That's what's so.

I don't care about your dreams. They're boring.

Froggy drove faster. Ben wanted to tell Froggy that it wasn't boring at all, but terrible, and they were lucky to be awake. They drove down to the gated community whose guard refused them entry. Froggy made a three-point turn and honked the horn and loudly screeched away. Hell, yeah, he yelled, and he blew a sphere of cherry-colored gum and flipped another driver off. We could cross the bridge to town, he said, and he hit two orange traffic cones on purpose, knocking them on their sides. When Ben laughed, Froggy said, That wasn't funny. It's a very serious thing. The cars they passed shrank quickly in the side view mirror, on whose glass a moth had landed, and then they were alone on the road when Froggy swerved and shouted, Shit.

What's wrong? said Ben.

Take the wheel, yelled Froggy, grabbing at his eye. I can't see.

Don't joke like that.

I'm not joking, Froggy shouted as they drifted into the wrong lane. Take the wheel. He blinked his watering eye and felt his shirt in a panicked hurry, and then his lap, and Ben obeyed; the car's left tires had crossed the shoulder line when he steered them back onto the road, jerking the wheel left and right to try to keep control. It was too heavy. They moved too fast.

Tell me what's wrong, he yelled again as Froggy scoured his clothing frantically.

I lost my contact.

I don't know how to drive, Ben yelled. Put on the brake.

I can't *see.*

You don't have to see, Ben said. Just step on the brake.

I can't.

We're speeding up.

No we're not, Froggy shouted, breathing fast.

I can't find it.

Just stop the car.

Shit. Oh shit.

The trees shot by like bolts of grounded lightning. The road was going to end. Ben pushed at Froggy's leg to move it off the gas, and their speed finally began to fall. Keep us on the pavement, Froggy cried, his eyes shut desperately, and he screamed when they hit a bump, which was a dove, dead beneath their tire.

Ben steered them onto a pulloff made of sand as Froggy pressed the brake and found his contact lens and placed it back against his eyeball. The bird they'd killed looked like a pirate's skullcap in the mirror. Ain't that a bitch, said Froggy, grinning now, already calm. He drove them back to the rental house with the parking brake on. He just wanted to see if the car would still move that way, he said. He liked the smell of burning rubber.

You got any cash for gas? he said.

Ben shook his head, which made him dizzy, and he shut his eyes.

That's too bad, Froggy said. I was gonna drive you to Mexico and sell you to the taxidermists, so they could stuff you full of cocaine.

. . .

They were on the panhandle. Their great-aunt Celeste had paid for a beachfront house with a private boardwalk for an entire month. She sat in her rocking chair on the screened porch, talking to Mama, when Froggy and Ben got home. You kids sleep too late, Celeste said, watching the girls from next door float in the gulf in pink inner tubes. You miss the sunrise.

There'll be plenty sunrises left to see when I'm as old as you, said Froggy.

Celeste smiled at him as Mama said, You take that back.

Okay, I take it back, said Froggy. There won't be any sunrises left at all.

You won't be able to see them through the wrinkles, Celeste said.

Mama sighed, and said to Celeste, You don't have many wrinkles for your age.

I've got at least three hundred, said Celeste.

Mama shook her head, said, Well. She cracked a boiled peanut open and tossed its oily shell aside. Froggy sat down in a wooden rocker and drank RC Cola and played his Game Boy, and Ben sat down beside him, and Celeste crocheted and watched the girls drift down-sea in their inner tubes. Ben read his book until Froggy stood up and said, That's *our* ocean. Get back where you belong.

The ocean belongs to everybody, Mama said without looking up from her novel.

They're right in front of our house, said Froggy, and he turned to Celeste and added, Aren't they, and she nodded. See? he said to Mama, who continued reading as the wind picked up and rippled the checkered tablecloth. The air began to smell more like the bay. The girls floated like dolls beneath expanding clouds, riding bigger waves now, never moving independently of their tubes.

I hope they get struck by lightning, Froggy said.

Celeste smiled again. Ben tried to think of how to make her smile himself, but maybe she couldn't see him. The sky grew darker as the sun got higher. Ben sat still and waited for someone to speak to him, and every half a minute he turned a page to make it look like he was reading. He hated his book. He wished he weren't already thirty pages into it, because now he had to finish it before he could start the next one. There's a cloud hanging over us, Celeste said somberly, and Ben looked up. It squatted above the gulf like a mass of coal, and Mama nodded. There it is, said Celeste.

Hmm, Mama murmured into her orange juice. We ought to go inside soon.

We are inside, Ben said.

The screened porch isn't inside, Mama and Celeste said at the same time, and then Celeste said, It's one of the long ones. They have a name.

Storm clouds, Mama said.

Have you ever heard of anvil-shaped clouds?

Mama shook her head.

They're scientific.

I guess you could have any shape of cloud.

Celeste nodded. But I mean something that's been named before.

Anchors dropped from it, too short to hit the water. The anvils changed into a horse's heart that palpitated wildly, its shadow threatening the water. Sand blew up into the air as the sun's last rays were blocked, and the girls floated beneath a sky charred black as chimney soot. Celeste sipped lemonade. It looks like Central America, she said. If there was just a volcano.

Have you been there? Ben asked her.

There's a war, she said, looking at Froggy. Nobody goes there, because of the war.

But there hasn't always been a war, Ben said.

I don't have the slightest idea how long there's been a war, she said. But there have always been mosquitos.

You talk so much I can't hear the birds, said Mama, looking at her book.

They're perpetual, said Celeste to Froggy. The mosquitoes, not the birds.

Birds are perpetual too, Mama said.

Of course they are, Celeste muttered.

You said they weren't, said Mama, so I'm just saying that they are.

So are a million things, said Celeste. So are bird droppings. All over your car, forever.

Mama turned the page of her book.

Maybe they don't have legs, said Froggy.

The birds? Mama said.

Those girls.

Birds have legs.

In that direction, Celeste said as she pointed across the gulf with her glass in her hand, is a war. Straight past that storm.

How close? said Ben.

I certainly don't know.

Can't you estimate?

Good Lord, she said and finished her lemonade. Too far for a mosquito. The girls' tubes no longer shone as bright a pink, because the sun was gone. Ben wondered where their mother was. Celeste's fat cocker spaniel trotted out onto the porch, and Celeste reached down to pet her. Ginger's a good dog, she said, patting Ginger's head and neck as lightning flashed, and Ben flinched for the trembling noise that shook his ears a second later. A funnel formed above the water, merging so its separate spirals called up water from the sea and formed a spout. Celeste gasped. Look, she said. It's spinning.

Mama had finished her juice, and she poured herself a drink from the Flor de Caña bottle on the table. Whitecaps, she said.

What?

Whitecaps.

Oh yes, said Celeste. How pretty. The cylinder of water widened, and the girls from next door finally emerged from the sea, whispering in each other's ears, their inner tubes around their waists as they walked unevenly across the sand to their wood-plank boardwalk. Ben looked to see if Froggy was watching them, but he was playing his video game. Last time I saw a spout, said Celeste, there weren't any houses. She rocked and tapped her foot upon the wood. The funnel whistled like a teapot, but maybe it was just the wind, or the swallows in their nests beneath the porch. At every clap of thunder Ginger cowered lower.

I hate that fat old bitch, Froggy whispered to Ben.

Celeste isn't fat.

Not her, stupid. The dog.

Froggy threw his shirt on the picnic table and felt the breeze against his chest. Behind the opaque shield of storms the sun was at its zenith, and Ben got sleepy. The storm didn't scare him. He drifted in and out of consciousness as the funnel dissipated. The sun came out at two o'clock and Mama read all afternoon. The girls came out to float again in water freshly calm, and sometime Froggy disappeared onto the beach; when Ben awoke at three his brother was gone, but the girls were still there. He wanted to go out and play with them but he didn't know how to swim, and he didn't want them to know. He stepped onto the boardwalk. Seagulls swooped into the sea for fish as smaller birds flew over Ben in droves. He was hot, and the sand was dry; the sky had never stormed. The sun had never sunk from its throne.

Why don't you go talk to those girls? Celeste asked Ben.

Huh? he said, although he'd heard her.

You heard me.

He shook his head. No I didn't, he said. She was supposed to believe him, whatever the truth was. Your family was supposed to trust your lies.

I said, why don't you go talk to those girls. She spoke very slowly.

Oh.

Did you hear me that time?

He nodded.

Do you want to answer me?

I don't know.

You don't know if you want to answer me?

No, he said. That's not what I meant. That's the answer.

Go on out there, she said. They're right there. They've been there all week.

I don't want to, he said.

I'll bet Froggy's spoken to them.

Ben shrugged.

They look your age, not his.

I'd rather read my book, Ben said.

Do you like being young?

He shrugged.

Celeste's gray hair shook as she repeated herself: Do you like it?

I don't know, Ben said. I guess so.

You guess so.

Yeah, he said.

But you don't know.

He shrugged.

When I was a kid we didn't just guess so.

Ben looked out the window and thought about going down to the beach.

How old are you now?

Thirteen.

I can't keep up, she said, and Ben hoped she wouldn't talk anymore, but after a minute she said, Do you like it? Does it feel good to be thirteen?

I said I don't know.

She threw her hands into the air. Which part of it don't you know? Ben stood up and started to walk away. He didn't understand why she was attacking him. Can't you feel things? she continued. Can't you tell if a thing feels good or bad? As Ben slammed the screened porch door to go inside she said, Might as well be a wrinkled old man.

Froggy stayed away all afternoon. Celeste wanted to eat out, so they got dressed and Mama went to freshen up. Celeste sent Ben downstairs to latch the storm doors. She made him fetch the rafts from where they'd blown into the dunes.

She wanted to eat at the cafe by the shell shop.

Not that old place again, said Mama. Couldn't we go somewhere else?

Celeste looked down at her lap.

The tavern on the shore, or the seafood place that's over on the bay.

It's my money, you know, Celeste said quietly. Of course I don't like to hold that over your head.

I know you don't.

I don't want to be the bossy old lady nobody likes, she said, her left cheek twitching.

Of course you're not.

I've got a few pleasures, here and there, and I want them to stay. They're the only ones.

Mama patted her aunt's shoulder. Put your shoes on, she told Ben.

They're already on.

Well, go wash your face or something.

Ben sighed and went out to the car, and eventually they followed. Mama drove them three miles down the beach to the cafe, where Celeste asked for a sarsaparilla. When the waiter said they didn't have it she asked for cottage cheese. The waiter shook his head, and Celeste trembled. She asked for fried tomatoes.

Just bring her a tuna sandwich, Mama said.

I don't want a tuna sandwich, said Celeste.

The waiter looked at Mama, who nodded at him. When Celeste saw it she said, Don't do that to me.

It's the only thing you like on the whole menu, Aunt Celeste.

I want a bowl of cottage cheese, she told the waiter. It's my money, and that's what I should get.

We'll get you a whole carton of cottage cheese at the Piggly Wiggly.

I don't want the grocery store kind.

They've got lots of different kinds.

They're all the same kind. They all taste like a goddamn grocery store.

Ben felt sorry for old people. He imagined a cafe fifty years ago, full of young men sipping sarsaparilla, women spooning cottage cheese. The food they liked had vanished long ago. They were always looking for things that weren't there.

I want to leave, said Celeste. The waiter still stood awkwardly beside the table.

Mama took Celeste's hand in hers. You feel this way because your blood sugar's low, she said. You need to eat something.

Celeste shook her head. It's my money, she said through tears. Now take me to my car and drive me home.

As they drove three miles back east each house was different from the others, like a fingerprint, but bigger. Cannibals had held the island once and eaten each other's flesh but now you couldn't buy a sarsaparilla, and the bay was empty of its shrimp boats. Ben shut his eyes. He felt a pimple on his face, and he hoped his acne wouldn't spread like Froggy's had once, down his back, all the way to his ass.

Froggy was sitting shirtless on the porch when they got back. I was just heading out the door, he said; I met some girls. I'm going to their place for dinner. Grains of sand encrusted on his legs began to crumble to the ground and Ben looked at his brother's whole body at once and wondered how he had attracted friends so fast, with the beach always so empty.

Won't you have some tea? Celeste said, sitting down to face the ocean.

Froggy thought about it. No, he said, I won't.

She smiled at him and returned to staring at the sea, and Froggy went inside. Ben waited a few minutes before he followed his brother into the cottage. He didn't want to seem nosy, so he walked slowly to the corner, appearing quietly in the doorway of their bedroom, where Froggy dug into his suitcase for a shirt. His silver necklace hung below his chin. I know you're there, he said to Ben. You breathe as loud as farts.

Ben turned red.

I hate all these clothes, said Froggy. I can't find a single thing to wear.

Where are you going? he asked.

I wish you'd hurry and grow up, so your clothes would fit me.

Where are you going? he asked again.

I'd like you a lot better if you didn't ask me things like that.

Ben looked away uncomfortably.

I'm going out.

Where?

Froggy pointed east, toward town.

How come you always meet people? Ben said. It happens everywhere we go.

I don't know. It's predetermined.

That's not true.

I'm a Gemini, so I'll meet people.

Ben shook his head like he was disappointed in the answer.

You're a Scorpio, so you'll be depressed and lonely.

I'm not depressed and lonely.

You'll pry into other people's lives, wishing they were yours to live.

Ben turned and faced the other way, trying to breathe quietly. He didn't want Froggy listening to his breaths. He didn't want to be in the room with Froggy, or beneath a roof at all; he thought of walking to the beach and wading in the water, but the girls would be there. He thought of crabs that ran so rampant on the beach, scuttling across dead skin that fell from all the people's bodies.

Hey, Froggy said.

What?

I wasn't trying to be mean. Ben didn't answer. Really, Froggy said. I wasn't.

I know.

It's not my fault Dad screwed Mama when he did. If he'd waited a few more days, you'd be a Sagittarius, and you could travel all over the world. People would flock to you like seagulls.

If his father had waited a few days, Ben thought, he wouldn't be himself at all. It made him nervous. Froggy fixed his bangs so they stood out from his forehead, ending at his eyebrows. He put a T-shirt on and looked in the mirror and took it back off and

flexed his muscles. You know what? he said to Ben. You haven't
seen me naked in three years.

Ben didn't answer.

Look at my muscles. I can bench-press a hundred fifty pounds
now.

Ben shrugged.

Froggy had a glassy glint in his eye that faced the light. That's
just six months, he said. Imagine in another whole year. He bent
to touch his toes. He sat on the carpet and did butterfly stretches.
Ben closed his eyes again; he couldn't imagine another whole
year. He had a hard time believing one would come at all. I
wonder if Scorpios can get strong muscles, Froggy said. I can't
even remember. Ben thought back to last year and tried to recall
his vision of the current one but couldn't. The number had
sounded strange. He remembered that much.

When Froggy was dressed and ready, he went out the swinging
door and drank from Celeste's tall glass of lemonade as he passed
her and assumed his shades and ran his fingers through his hair.
What's in that bag? Celeste asked him, as he slung his backpack
onto his right shoulder.

Drugs, he said.

She smiled at him.

And rum. Drugs and rum.

You're just like your uncle, she said.

Except I'm still alive, said Froggy.

Celeste looked at him with amusement. Ice clinked against
the side of her glass. Don't stay out too late, she said; you've got
to come home and spend some time with me, too.

I've spent my whole life with you, Aunt Celeste. Why don't
you spend some time with Ben for once, instead.

You know, she said, you're the kind of boy I would have liked. Water was glistening on his smooth, hairless arms.

As a son?

As a lover.

He gazed at her intently.

When I was your age, she added.

People don't have lovers at Froggy's age, Mama said. He's fifteen years old. Barely even that.

You've got exactly what I looked for, said Celeste, ignoring Mama. How old are you?

Fifteen.

Fifteen, she repeated, smiling into a shaft of sunlight that brightened her henna dye to orange. You would have liked me when I was fifteen, she said. I was something to look at.

Celeste, said Mama, stop it.

I don't mind bragging about it, since I'm so ugly now.

You're not ugly.

When you're my age, Celeste told Froggy, you can brag too. You can say you were the prettiest boy in all of Florida. If anyone will listen.

Boys aren't pretty, Mama said. They're handsome. Her finger moved across the page of her book as Froggy rolled his eyes. He folded his arms and stood there starkly fleshed between his shadow and the sun and walked away down the boardwalk.

Mama read faster than Ben did. He shuffled restlessly in his chair and stood and stretched and paced the porch. This beach is boring, he said. Ginger licked his leg, and he kicked her away, making sure Celeste didn't see. She was probably almost blind anyway.

It's only as boring as you make it, Mama said.

I didn't make it, Ben said. It would be a lot more fun than this if I had.

Mama didn't answer. He went out to the beach an hour after Froggy and he turned left when he reached the sand and left his sandals on a mound of crushed-up cockle shells. He kicked sand at the crabs that ran away to sink into their chutes below the earth. He kicked plain-patterned shells. He hadn't seen a sand dollar all week; he would walk until he found one, he decided, even if it got dark. He took off his shirt and left it with his sandals and decided to get a tan. Sunscreen was a lie, like toothpaste, designed to make his life more complicated.

He walked for half an hour counting his steps, ducking beneath a row of propped-up fishing rods with lines that stretched into the surf. He stepped on slimy seaweed washed ashore. He stepped on a beached jellyfish to see if its dead body could still sting him or make him bleed, but it didn't, and he looked at every face on the beach to see if it was Froggy. He watched the birds. Mama liked birds, and Ben was supposed to like them too. They were interesting.

He took note of their number and their size. Some of them were everywhere, like blackbirds. A large black creature stood upon the sand in front of Ben but it was different. He approached it with a mechanical precision, expecting it to fly away. He wanted to identify it in the bird book when he got home, but it hobbled down the beach when he approached, holding an injured leg up as it walked. Birds were fast but not if they were crippled, and maybe he could catch it. He began to run.

I just want to look at you, he told it. He wanted to know its genus and its species. Froggy would just return to playing his Game Boy, but Ben would return with the name of a new kind of bird. He ran and ran but couldn't catch the bird; it stayed always the same distance out of reach. Goddamn you, he said.

He stabbed its forked and narrow footprints with his toes, erad-icating them.

People watched him as he ran, plain-faced men and familes on the sand. The bird still hobbled east along the sparsely pop-ulated beach. When Ben got tired of running the bird slowed too; this was an ugly, stubborn bird, and he wished its leg would give out so he could quit walking. He kicked up sand again but none of it reached the bird. He couldn't tell how old birds were; maybe this one was about to die. Maybe the others didn't like it.

Certain men on the beach sent waves of chills across his body when he passed them, and boys, too; they did it with their eyes. He knew it meant they hated him, that they wished he were dead. It happened every day. The injured bird rocked back and forth as it progressed along the breaking waves. He tried to blast it with all his energy, but his eyes emitted nothing. Fuck, he said aloud, and it sounded strange inside his mouth, and the bird had ruffled feathers sticking up like a carrot from its ass.

Ben hurt the callus of his foot on the sharp end of a crab shell. His elbows itched where biting flies had tasted him, and sand was in his shorts. He hated beaches. He hoped the bird he chased belonged to an endangered species. He hated the men around him on the sand. He tried to think of one thing in the world he didn't hate. He waded through tidal pools of stagnant water. The bird would have to stop eventually, because beaches didn't stretch on forever; they all ended if you walked far enough.

He reached the stretch of beach that fronted condos where lifeguards sat watch every several hundred feet on towering wooden chairs; they sported heavy tans. The beach was crowded here. Ben weaved his way between the bodies in the footsteps of the bird. He knew its color pattern now by heart; he'd watched it so long he could close his eyes and draw it with acrylics on his eyelids. These people looked good. He was thin and white and lanky, and he stumbled on a crab hole. He wished he'd worn his shirt. Topless boys played volleyball and Ben looked among them for his brother, who was laughing, holding hands with girls, telling dirty jokes to every unfamiliar face.

I'm gonna twist your neck, he told the bird. Just you wait.

Beyond the condos the beach was undeveloped; few houses stood, then none, and he entered the state park. His feet were being sculpted by the sand. Here birdie, he whispered thirstily and chased it onto a spit of sand and made it wade through minnowy water to rejoin land.

He cupped his hands and wet his hair with the frothy surf and washed his sweat away. He couldn't see the sun for all the clouds. He didn't know the timing of the tides. He couldn't tell how far he'd walked when the bird collapsed on the sand ahead of him. Suddenly he was on top of its wounded breaths and its one upturned eye that shone like a melted bullet. He caught his breath, but the bird didn't. He couldn't see anything on its body he hadn't seen already from a distance. It twitched its left leg and tried to flap a wing.

He counted to five hundred. As far as he could remember, it was the highest number he'd ever counted to, incrementally, adding just a unit at a time, but the bird still didn't move. He didn't even stop at five hundred, but kept going, all the way to five fifty-six.

The island stretched on ahead of him for miles. He didn't see a human body anywhere as he continued walking east. Mosquitoes would bite him while he slept on the beach but the Indians had withstood the pain of insect bites, had focused on greater things. He tried to walk so lightly as to leave no footprints, and then he saw another set. His feet fit easily inside them. His legs ached a while, but then they stopped.

The tracks led into a tide pool and then emerged from its shallow water toward the dunes. Ben climbed the beach's slope

and followed them. His stomach growled. The footprints led into
the dunes but not back out. He approached a crop of sea oats,
avoiding sandspurs. He saw an orange flower. He saw a mass of
tanned skin lying facedown in the sand with one hand on the
ground and one beneath its crotch, shorts around its ankles. Ben's
heart jumped so hard it hurt. He coughed. Suddenly the naked
body was on its feet and was his brother struggling to pull his
shorts up, sand across his naked front, his eyes full of fear.

You don't know me, Froggy said.

What—

Go away, he yelled. Get the hell out of here.

Ben just stared at him.

Get the hell away. You didn't see me. You saw someone else.

Ben turned and fled down the beach as fast as he could go.
His heels hammered sand into itself like sawdust into wood. He
ran past the dying bird that still breathed fast and ruffled its
feathers as Ben leapt over it and thought of how his newborn
muscles might throb tomorrow if today he ran forever, blinded
by sweat in his eyes.

He ran until he reached the crowded stretch of beach in front
of the condos, where he slowed to a brisk walk. He didn't look
at faces anymore. He blinked his burning eyes. He wanted to
blink all the bodies into hell. He came closer and closer to a tall
wooden chair. The lifeguard was around eighteen with navy
trunks and pointed his finger at Ben and spoke from deep within
his sun-browned chest. Hey, you, he said, and Ben kept walking,
and the lifeguard jumped down from his chair, bending his knees
for impact with the sand. Hey. You. Ben turned to see the lifeguard staring at him, and he walked faster. You'd better stop
right there, the lifeguard said. Two women turned to watch.
Ben's cheeks burned as he slowed his walk, stood still and turned
around. The waves crept back into the sea so steadily his ears no
longer knew it was even happening.

Why did you chase that bird down the beach? the lifeguard demanded with curt, soft-spoken anger. He had short blond hair and his skin was deeply bronzed; he had a full, handsome face, a silver necklace, a navy blue tattoo on his upper arm, and stood a full head taller than Ben, towering over him like a cross-armed golden giant.

Ben shrank into himself. I don't know, he said.

It's from the Caribbean. It stopped here so its broken wing could heal.

Ben shut his eyes. He turned his head down to the sand and hoped he'd sink through. The women sunbathing beside them turned their heads to listen.

They let it out of the veterinary hospital yesterday, because it was almost better.

I'm sorry, Ben said.

They thought it might be happier on the beach. They hoped out here it wouldn't be as scared.

I didn't know.

What the hell did you think? the lifeguard said. That it just didn't want to fly? That it enjoyed running away from you?

Ben shook his head. Tears welled in his eyes as he remembered the bird's unmoving body when it had finally stopped. I just wasn't thinking, he said as his voice cracked. I'm really sorry.

Don't apologize to me, said the lifeguard.

I just wanted to know what kind of bird it was, Ben said.

The lifeguard narrowed his eyes at Ben. You probably kept it from healing in time to fly south again for winter. Maybe it'll freeze to death, because you wanted to know what kind of bird it was.

Ben couldn't hold back his tears anymore, and the lifeguard stood in front of him and watched him cry, listened to him breathe and choke back mucus, rub his eyes, stare at the sand.

It was a cormorant, the lifeguard said. It was from Trinidad. He turned away to climb back into his chair.

Ben cried as he walked down the beach. He made his way among the crowd and stopped at the edge of it and sat and dug his feet into the sand. He covered his legs. His skin began to burn from bugs inside the sand. He felt like they were covering his body. He ran into the sea and shuddered as the water rose up his legs and soaked his crotch, his stomach. He dove into a wave head-long and tumbled over and lost his sense of gravity. The ocean burned inside his nostrils as he held himself beneath the water, counting all the breaths he couldn't breathe, and when the waves flipped him over on his back he pressed his head beneath the surface again and opened his eyes to be stung by the brine. He tried to force his entire body under, struggling, sending spouts of water skyward. He waited to be rescued, but the lifeguard never came.

He forced his way ashore through the weight of the ocean. When he got out of the water four boys his age were tossing a yellow Frisbee by the shore. He knew they'd watched him flailing, but they threw their Frisbee and never said a word, and he walked straight through their playing field silently, his shoulders shivering, his arms crossed so they couldn't see his nipples.

He walked until he couldn't remember if he was walking the right way at all, or if he'd ever seen this stretch of beach before, or if his brain was waterlogged, damaged, so that everything he remembered now was wrong.

Pelicans surged toward the water, three twisted razors, ridiculous and sharp; Ben laughed at them. He found a skinny driftwood quill and scribbled on the sand beneath him. When he sat down to rest, his legs collapsed beneath him. The tide was coming in. Its raspy waves assaulted him and stole his etchings piece by piece, smoothed them, and the words were borne up by the sea where seagulls perched on the gawking beaks of the three poor, hungry pelicans, waiting to steal fish from the caverns of their mouths.

The house smelled like hamburgers when he walked up the boardwalk at the start of sunset and crept inside. It's just that I'm not in situations where I meet people, Mama was saying when Ben walked into the house. I always stay at home. She was sitting with Celeste in the overstuffed chairs by the window looking out at the water. Ben hadn't noticed until he got inside that the girls next door were still in their inner tubes.

You like to stay at home, said Celeste. You told me so.

Mama nodded. Ben got an Orange Crush from the refrigerator and popped it open and sat at the kitchen counter on a barstool. He wondered if his eyes were still red from crying. You hated your job, Celeste said to Mama. I know you did.

I'm just saying that's why I don't make a lot of friends. Because I haven't had a job for so long.

You don't even want my money. All I do is make things worse.

I'm grateful for the money. You know that.

I'm not trying to control your life.

Of course you're not. Of course you're not.

Celeste began to cry. I try so many ways to help you, she said. It's all I want to do. Mama patted Celeste's shoulder and dried her first few tears with a scented yellow Kleenex. I thought if you didn't work, Celeste said and trailed off. Mama opened her book to a dog-eared page and fanned herself and held Celeste's hand. Eventually she let go and began to read. Celeste quit crying. Who knows if you'd even make friends at work anyway, she said. Ben goes to school every day, and he's pretty much the same as you.

Mama turned her head to look at Ben like she hadn't known he sat there, and then she turned away again. I saw a cormorant today, Ben said.

A what? said Celeste.

A cormorant. It's a bird.

She knows what a cormorant is, Mama said. Everyone knows. She continued reading *Waiting for the Potato Digger* and asked the color of the bird, her eyes still focused on her book.

It was black.

It was probably just a blackbird, Mama said.

It was a cormorant, Ben insisted. I know it was.

They don't come this far north.

This one did.

I guess you just know everything about it, she said.

I know what I saw.

She rolled her eyes and said, You might as well have seen a toucan.

Ben sighed.

Did you see a toucan?

No, I saw a cormorant.

Well, I doubt you saw either one. She went back to her book, and Ben stood by the window, staring at the sea. Celeste petted Ginger, who was fat like she was pregnant with ten puppies, and Ben imagined sitting on the dog like a beanbag chair, molding her to the shape of a seat. Light outside was swiftly fading. Ginger limped away to her bowl of food, and Celeste picked up a dead Game Boy battery from the table and stroked it. This is only three days old, she said. I'll see if I can fix it.

That boy plays it constantly, said Mama. Three days is pretty good for one battery.

Celeste rubbed it.

I don't see how that could help, said Mama.

We'll see, Celeste said quietly.

Mama stared at her. Ben saw before she even yelled how the speed of her breaths accelerated evenly, for nearly half a minute, until they were twice as fast as before. She drank the remainder of her cocktail and spat an ice cube back into the glass as her eyes grew wide. What's wrong with you people? she cried out suddenly. It's a dead battery. There aren't any cormorants in north Florida. There isn't any sarsaparilla at restaurants.

Celeste stared at her with an open mouth.

A dead battery stays dead. You don't go to the beach for a goddamn month.

Nobody answered her.

It's like that flock of bluebirds, she said to Celeste. That time at my old house, before you sold it. You swore you saw a flock of bluebirds. I've never heard of anything so absurd. Celeste sighed and squinted her eyes and looked at Mama, who said, You probably can't even remember.

I remember it with my own eyes, said Celeste. They were swarming on the red honeysuckle.

No, Mama said, you didn't.

Two dozen of them.

It was blue jays, probably.

It was bluebirds.

They don't even like red honeysuckle. I planted that honeysuckle for the hummingbirds.

It was bluebirds I saw. Celeste's voice quavered. I was the one that taught you about birds. I bought you a hummingbird feeder when you were six years old.

Bluebirds don't flock, Aunt Celeste. You can look it up.

I taught you how to mix the nectar.

Mama turned another page of her book. That was a long

time ago, she said. You've probably confused it with something else.

I will not listen to you anymore, Celeste declared.

It was probably just spots in your eyes, from looking at the sun.

Celeste continued to rub the battery. She petted the smooth surface of the cylinder and stroked its opposite ends, humming softly as she massaged the silver metal, too old to understand it. As Ben formed that thought she turned to stare at him, and he shivered. You know, she said, people always told me it was terrible to be old. They said it was the worst thing that could ever happen to a person. Die early, they said, while you still can.

Mama turned a page of her book.

I didn't listen to them. I never listened to anything old people said, but you know what? They were absolutely right. It's terrible. Most of the time I'd rather just be dead.

You said you still had pleasures in your life, said Mama. Just earlier today you said so.

Name one. I wish somebody would name me just one.

You were the one that said it.

Celeste shook her head. I don't think I would have said any such thing. Her head fell to one side as she sniffed her nose and shut her eyes, keeping them closed when they heard a sonic boom from the air force base several miles to the west, and Froggy came through the door. Celeste looked up and smiled weakly at him. I'm glad you're back, she said quietly.

I got us some dinner, he said.

Well that was nice of you, Celeste said, looking out toward the girls' pink tubes in the water.

We already ate dinner, Mama said into her book, but then she glanced up. With what money—she began and stopped short. The bird when Froggy slapped it down by its legs upon the table bounced like it was hollow. It was black, just as Ben had said, except on its neck, and Froggy turned it so one eye was pointing at Celeste, the other one at Ben and at the ceiling. Mama opened her mouth like she might scream. The sun had fully set now, and the sky outside was a deep, glorious orange.

Fire up the grill, said Froggy.

Mama shut her book without even inserting a tissue to mark her page. Get it outside, she said. Get it outside.

Froggy shook his head. Then it wouldn't be inside anymore, he said.

Mama hurried to the kitchen sink and unrolled a long length of paper towels and bunched them up. It wasn't dead enough to smell bad, but she picked the bird up by its neck and ran with it outside and flung it down on the porch and violently shook her hand. The bird landed half atop the towel so that its stomach pointed up. Mama breathed hard. She caught her breath in the doorway and said, Why would you do that? Why would you do that?

I thought we could take it to the bird hospital, he said. But only if there's leftovers.

I'm going to throw up, Mama said.

People don't just throw up, said Froggy.

That's a cormorant, said Ben.

So now there's just cormorants everywhere, said Mama, all over the state.

That's the cormorant I saw.

It's not a cormorant, Froggy said. It's a ruby-throated argus.

There's no such thing, Ben and Mama said together, and Mama looked annoyedly at Ben and said again, There's no such bird.

Of course there is, said Froggy. Tell her, Celeste.

There is, Celeste said.

It doesn't even have a ruby throat, said Mama. It's all the same damn color.

It's too young to have its ruby yet, said Froggy.

Then it's probably good you killed it, said Celeste as Mama stood and walked toward her bedroom.

I didn't kill it. Ben did.

I bet it's no more fun to be an old bird than an old woman.

I didn't kill it, Ben said. How could I have killed it?

Celeste stared straight past him and said, Of course you didn't kill it, and Ben shivered. Mama emerged from her bedroom with the bird guide, flipping through the index. You're spelling it wrong, said Froggy. It starts with R.

It doesn't start with R, she said.

Look it up! he screamed, startling everyone.

It's not here, said Mama, and then she whispered, It's here.

Froggy laughed. I don't know what kind of piece of shit bird guide wouldn't list an argus.

It is here, she said.

It can't be, said Froggy, cause I made it up.

It's noted for its watchfulness, said Mama.

Look up cormorants, Ben said.

I already know what a cormorant is, Mama said.

Anyway, said Froggy, it's not a cormorant. It's an argus.

Ben was careful to wait two whole minutes before he followed Froggy out to the porch, where lavender was fading fast to black and far out on the ocean ships had gathered. Ben wondered if they had binoculars or telescopes to watch him, if they had seen him chase the bird, and if they had a telephone, if they'd call him if he held the number up, and Ben tiptoed across the porch to Froggy's standing place against the screen and said, Are you mad at me?

Only when you pout like one of them, said Froggy, gesturing with his whole head toward the house. I wish she'd just leave me the fuck alone. She's like a girl.

Mama?

Froggy stared at him and laughed and said, You're a dumb-ass.

I thought you liked her.

You can have her, Froggy said.

I don't want her, Ben said.

Froggy laughed.

That's not what I mean, said Ben. I meant we should both want her. I mean—

You're a pervert, Froggy said.

No I'm not.

I know why you don't go in the water.

I go in the water.

Queers can't swim. They fill up with water through their asshole and then they drown.

Ben watched Froggy hit him on the shoulder.

I know why Mama and Celeste don't go in the water, too.

No you don't.

Froggy shrugged. Okay, I don't.

Why?

Froggy turned his mouth and nose up like he smelled shit on someone's shoes. You want me to gossip about our own mother, he said. Now how do you think that would make her feel?

Ben shrugged and kicked the dead bird off the porch through a hole in the screen and watched it land on sandspurs on a dune below and tumble beneath the porch and out of sight. He wondered if Froggy might have caught a fatal illness from the bird when he had carried it to the house. There were still diseases down in the Caribbean that had no cures. He didn't know their names, but they were there.

Froggy laughed as he went inside the house. Ben hung his shorts on the deck rail to dry and walked up and down the boardwalk, counting the number of times he turned around. He decided he was bored and went inside, where Froggy had sprawled himself across the couch, playing his Game Boy. Celeste was eating a saltine cracker spread thick with butter, nibbling tiny bites and chewing each one for minutes at a time.

Can we play a two-player game? said Ben, even though he didn't want to.

When I'm finished, Froggy said.

When will that be?

The hell if I know.

You're never finished, Ben said.

Froggy loudly sighed and turned around. I'll be finished when I'm finished, he said. Leave me alone. The animated boy he controlled on-screen leapt over bottomless chasms, swung on vines, and ran across the grayscale pixels. Stop looking over my shoulder, he yelled, and Ben backed away, and Froggy raised his voice further. I'm in the middle of this game, he cried out, and I'm not finished with it. Or with any of the others I haven't started. Suddenly Mama choked on spit caught in her throat, and Froggy shut his mouth to listen. Are you okay? he asked her nervously.

Please stop it, she begged him. I just can't live through all this ugliness.

She closed her book and thumbed its pages. Froggy paused his game and walked across the room to stand behind her chair, whispering in her ear as he softly massaged her shoulders. Ben tried to hear what he was saying. She let her head fall over until her chin came to rest against her chest. Froggy guided her hand to a cocktail glass that sat on the end table, and she lifted it and drank.

I'm sorry, she said.

It's okay.

I shouldn't have yelled like that, she said, taking a big sip. It hurts my voice.

I'm sorry too, said Froggy.

It's all right, she said, her voice distorted by the soreness in her throat. I know it's natural for boys to yell. She wiped her forehead with her left hand, wet from the glass, and shut her eyes and reached across her shoulder to hold Froggy's hand. Celeste was at the table, staring with wistful eyes at the darkened sea, where the girls next door still bobbed in the surf, their backs toward the shore.

By the time they're done, said Celeste, they'll be as wrinkled as I am.

You know why they stay out there so long? said Froggy.

When no one answered him he stretched his arm to nudge Celeste so she said, Why?

They can't get out, because I fucked them so hard.

Mama stood so his hands fell from her shoulders to his side, and she walked to the picture window and leaned against it with her forehead.

For God's sake, Froggy said, I'm only joking. Celeste smiled at his voice and leaned her head back delicately against her chair. You know, she said to him. You're going to need a car soon. You'll be sixteen in June.

He looked up at her. You don't drive the Lincoln anymore.

Celeste shook her head. You don't want to drive that old piece of junk, she said, and ran her finger along a wrinkle that curved across her cheek to the top of her nose. A boy like you needs a sports car, she said.

Yeah, said Froggy, and an airplane, and a gun.

I think I'll buy you a sports car, said Celeste.

Mama shook her head and said, You're not buying anyone a sports car.

Celeste's eyes grew thoughtful as she traced a facial trench with her little finger like she was sculpting the car in her mind, painting it a shiny red and firing up the pistons. Sports cars went two hundred miles an hour. Ben wondered if Froggy would be one of the kids who die in wrecks at age sixteen. He'd seen a dead boy in the newspaper whose hair looked a lot like Froggy's, although not as dark.

Will you take me on a drive in it? Celeste asked Froggy. She smiled into the lamp. It's been a long time since I've ridden in a sports car.

Froggy didn't answer. Ben wanted to tell her about their drive that morning to see how widely she would smile, how many false teeth he'd be able to count at once. He knew from television commercials that they were all connected, that they came out, but maybe Celeste's were glued onto her gums.

I can be the very first girl you take for a ride.

He won't be taking anybody for any rides, said Mama.

It's my money.

Mama sighed.

You're just waiting for when I'm dead. If it was up to you, I wouldn't get to spend a penny. I'd never get to leave the house.

That's ridiculous, Aunt Celeste.

You'd lock us all up, she continued, her voice jittery and low. You'd make us live on beans and applesauce.

Ben wished they didn't have to stay at the beach for so much more time, but he knew if it were shorter the rest of his life would just be longer. He imagined himself in the middle of a nightmare where Mama was stockpiling cans of beans and jars of applesauce, her face writhing like a scorpion; she was a Scorpio, like Ben. He shut his eyes to make it go away. When he opened them, Froggy was staring at his game screen. The night's first stars began to shine as a ship blinked red on the horizon, and Ben saw the girls next door floating as always in shallow water, their pink tubes milky from reflected moonlight. He looked across the room at Froggy, who pressed two buttons with his thumb repeatedly, his feet propped on the hassock and a drink between his legs, breathing like a moth in a cocoon. His eyes glowed as he sucked a cola-darkened ice cube.

Ben's skin was already flaming into red. He stood and scratched his burnt back against drywall and rubbed his itching legs on the edge of a cardboard box. He looked up at Celeste and wondered what kind of sports car she had ridden in, but he didn't ask her; he didn't see why she'd remember.

C O W R I E

Sina can't remember how many Iraqis he shot as a boy during the war. For three years he patrolled the Iranian desert while meanwhile in the States I smoked pot, stole tapes from the mall, thirteen years old. Now we're twenty-four. Mist on the Pacific dissolved in summer air. You're lucky to be American, he said. You can go anywhere you want.

I was holding his left hand while he drove with his right.

I spent three years in jail for painting a giraffe, he said.

We were living off the cash I got from selling my return ticket. My visa had expired two months ago, and Sina knew a nightclub up in Auckland where I could get a fake one. I needed a legal job; you can't pick kiwifruit until autumn.

The last town we passed before the car broke down was Wharekaka.

Perfect, Sina said when the engine died. I'll bet there's a beach right through those trees. He leapt across a grassy ditch on the road's left shoulder. Don't look at me, he said, look where we are. His long black hair blew in the wind as I took note of all the hooking clouds like swaths of crinoline. This was in the early afternoon.

We shouldn't be leaving cars across the island like slime trails, I said.

I'm hungry, he said. Are you hungry?

They'll have your registration, I said, but I had to follow him off the road into a virgin grove for him to hear me. Striding beneath those trees he looked like silver muscles, antlers that hadn't grown yet. He threw his sleeveless T-shirt down onto a rock when we reached the beach, where there wasn't much sand but trees grew crazily.

What happens if they send you home to Iran? I asked as we walked downshore.

I'll go to prison.

How long?

A year for every illegal month abroad.

How many months have you been gone?

He thought about it. Fifty, he guessed. Sixty.

Blue sky, red blossoms fought above the sea. We climbed into a vast pohutukawa tree, its branches an inverted dome where we swung our legs above the rhythm of waves. Avocados! Sina cried, and he dug through his backpack and stood up on the rough bark with three and juggled them. When he staggered backwards, I thought he'd surely fall and split his head on a rock, but for seven rounds he never faltered. He peeled his avocado in a swift, unbroken curl and reassembled its skin upon the bark. Together we bit into ripe, green flesh that melted when we mashed it in our mouths. Was that your last dollar? I asked, pointing to the fruit. He turned his empty pocket inside out and took my hand and stroked it.

What would happen if we did that in your country? I asked him.

It depends, he said. They'd probably put us to death.

The wind nearly blew me backwards from my perch. I thrust out my hand to right myself and lost my avocado to the sea. Sina offered me a piece of his, and we bit it together. He wiped its green pulp from my nose. When I'd eaten the last bite he licked the pit clean and pitched it into the water.

We rode to the next town in the back of a police car. Sina had been grinning on the roadside with his thumb out when it came. Get back, I'd shouted, but he shrugged and said, They can't do a thing to me. We stood in the car's shadow when it stopped. How you fellows doing? he said, and we got in. Where you from? said the cop after introductions.

States.

You?

Papua New Guinea, Sina said.

I would have guessed the Middle East, said the cop. He had an untrimmed mustache, and I wondered what New Zealand called its FBI, if this was how their cars looked. What language do they speak in New Guinea? he asked.

I don't remember, Sina said. I've been away from home for quite a while.

Where are you from? I asked the man.

Here, he said.

He quickly rounded curves and overtook a van. We passed brown earth stained green, burnt stumps, hills like beached whales, wild grass that bowed in unison to the sea. Shadows all fell backwards in the southern hemisphere. Let me see your passport, the policeman said to Sina. I've never seen one from there before.

It's hard to get to.

It's against the law not to carry your passport.

It's deep in the bowels of my bag, Sina said, and I laughed uneasily. I had a blossom in my pocket that I crushed and tore. The cop looked in his rearview mirror: he hated me, and his yellow eyes shone like glass.

I could pull this car over now.

I've got it, Sina said.

Let me see it then, the cop said, shouting now. As he swerved around a bird, I shut my eyes and wished for Sina not to have said New Guinea. I loved him and we needed for this cop to die. I tried to make it happen with my mind.

Who's the leader of New Guinea right now? the cop demanded with narrow eyes. What's the capital? He slowed the car down as he said, What city did you live in? What's the currency? We were coming into a sad wooden town. Red roofs and a stormy sky, an empty store, a square foundation in a grassy field. Sina coughed. What's the national anthem? sneered the cop. I was ready for him to disappear. He was turning the landscape grayer than the sky could ever light it. I saw the old roadbed by the highway, the sheep, the furrows on the hills below a sword-shaped cloud. I knew it was risky to whisper *let's kill him* in Sina's ear. I saw a perfect cliff to drive the car off.

You don't even swat flies, Sina said to me aloud.

Please, my head cried.

The cop had stopped his car by a derelict stone bank. He turned his head around. Port Moresby, Sina said.

Are you threatening me?

My hands and forehead sweated. I don't know which I wiped on what.

Sina held my sweating hand. Port Moresby was the capital of Papua New Guinea, he said. Bill Skate was the prime minister. Sina had lived in Lae, on the Huon Gulf. A kina equaled a dollar ten. I jumped when his palm began to vibrate from the deep, rich notes of the anthem he hummed. He sang a few words. I never learned the rest, he said. There's so many different languages. The policeman tapped a finger on the wheel as Sina's voice carried out into an empty ghost town: thousands of languages.

The cop shook his head. You've got a good voice, he told Sina. He apologized. When Sina opened the car door, I saw the ocean gleaming across a field of yellow flowers. I felt like a chain of powerchords. It was wonderful to be walking. My legs knew the air was clean; it reeked of brine. I wanted to play those moments over and over.

Let's work on our tans, Sina said, although his was already a deep brown.

We've got to get rid of that car, I said.

He scanned the sky and laughed into my eyes and said, You think they'll come in choppers?

We could both go to jail.

My father spent twelve years in jail for owning Bob Dylan tapes, he said, and he ran ahead of me and jumped up and down, capturing energy from the sun. It made me want to be a good person. He did cartwheels. The whole town was three blocks square; electric lines petered out into the hills. Chalky cliffs rose like glaciers from the water, trees greening them like moss. When we got to the rummage sale where two old native women smiled at a table piled with bright, flowery clothes, I could see the whole ocean.

The women wore pale blue skirts that sagged on the ground, and I couldn't help but stare at them. Kia ora, they said together.

Hello, Sina said.

Sorry, said the left one, her eyes pointed somewhere between the two of us. All we've got is women's clothes.

Sina sorted through the dresses and held one up beside him. This is my size, he said. In the sunlight it was deep blue, studded with ivory rosebuds. The women watched us from within their wrinkles as Sina turned to me and said, Do you want to take me to America?

That's impossible, I said.

He pressed the fabric to his body. I think this might fit me perfectly, he said softly to the women as they stared. I watched the sea. Wind blew a silk scarf off the top of the clothes pile, and I replaced it on the table. The dress cost two dollars.

Are you ready? I said to Sina, but he didn't answer me.

Do you have any lipstick? he said to the woman who had taken his money.

She nodded.

Can you sell me some?

You'll need to go to the chemist for that.

Give me your wallet again, Sina said to me. He took a twenty-dollar note from it and listed what he wanted: lipstick, eye shadow, fingernail polish. Rouge would be good.

We were on the bleached East Cape, unpopulated, fifty miles from any city. He found a slender pair of women's shoes beneath the dresses and squeezed his right foot into one and asked, How much are these?

Those were my daughter's, said the woman.

What size does she wear? asked Sina.

She drowned in them.

The woman's empty smile never changed. Sina held one shoe to the sun: it bore no sign of water. He knew just how to touch the woman's shoulder when he asked, How old was she?

Forty-two.

I'll give you whatever you want for them, Sina said.

You really want this junk?

If you're selling it.

The woman went inside. Her friend said nothing as we watched the clouds and waited, gazing beyond the trees to the calm ocean. When the woman limped back outside, the sunlight caught her jewelry. Her white shirt bore five Maori words. This was hers, she said, presenting a box inlaid with cowrie shells to Sina.

I can't take that from you.

It'll only rot, she said.

A dozen different kinds of makeup filled her reliquary. Her friend smiled straight through me like I wasn't there. Can makeup rot? I wondered. Sina found a white bracelet on the table to match his dress's flowers. He fitted it onto his left wrist for my approval. We're headed up to the cape, Sina told the women. We're going to be the first people in the world to see the sun.

They stared back at us. Suddenly I couldn't tell if they were smiling anymore, or if they'd smiled even once since we met them.

You can come with us, said Sina. We're hitching to the sunrise. The older, shorter woman glanced at her friend, who held a pebble and stared at the ground. We've got lots of food, Sina said, which wasn't true.

It was hard to tell how old they were. Their wrinkles said they'd smoked for many years. The cape is where my daughter drowned, the woman said. She smiled apologetically, like it was her fault, and she turned her head back down, submissive to the earth, humming and rearranging trinkets on her table. Sod was rising between her toes. Later at the beach Sina cried over what he'd mentioned, and the empty dresses, the box of moments she had known, her face against the sun. He gave her twenty dollars, which was all the cash we had. My mouth was dry. Just from breathing the town's air I had swallowed enough salt water to sink ships.

We walked past several houses, a church, a school, weedy yards of lemon trees. Dark-skinned children giggled on a tilted porch; cars rusted along the road. I was happy for the houses

crumbling in the sun; I wanted to meet all the town's old women
and stroke their hair like it was Sina's, let the sunlight dance upon
their tangles. Sina stashed his purchases beneath a fern and we
took our clothes off on the empty beach and swam naked. Sina
splashed my face with water. We must have floated there for
hours. When the Maori boys got home from school mid-
afternoon, they ran to the beach and played rugby across a tidal
pool. Clouds moved like sambas across the mountain shadows.
A boy dove into a dune and spoke in Polynesian as he grabbed
the ball, his voice like a xylophone, his eyes drenched sixteen
years by light. For a moment everyone looked like that.

The boy ran toward the game. He never caught the ball but
only watched his friends and brothers. Sand fell from their chests.
Starfish, Sina whispered, and when I blinked the sky turned
black. Palm trees blew like jungle warriors, boys kicking across
the beach. Do you really want to go to the cape? I asked him. It
was at least twenty miles out of the way. Across the dunes the
rusted town's marae shone with the iridescent eyes of paua shells.

We've got to do it now, he said as sunlight shone on trees.
For the drowned girl.

If we don't get to Auckland soon, they'll freeze my bank
account.

But I've got a new plan, he said as we came ashore and
dressed. The boys didn't seem to notice us.

What's your plan?

To go to the cape.

So we hitched out to the lighthouse, two separate rides. A
hops farmer from the south island picked us up at the town's
edge and took us north to Hicks Bay, then at sunset some kids
from the backpackers hostel picked us up and drove us to the
road's end half an hour out the gravel. They were German; they
were camping on the shore. We waved off and hiked uptrail to
a cliffside meadow. It was dark now. I'll never understand how

clouds could disappear like that each night to show so many stars. The tree trunks grunted at us while we climbed the trail. These are poison trees, said Sina. They'll kill us if they touch our ears. Up top we stood on a grassy shelf above the ocean, and I wondered if the water would show green tomorrow. It made my teeth feel dirty. I couldn't remember if I'd brushed them the last night, or at all since we left the capital.

Where's the toothbrush?

In the front of my bag, said Sina.

I searched for it by the light of two matches. Rocks and pebbles were collected in a pocket. A folded letter bore New Zealand Post's embossings. It was hard to read with so little light. A note to all employees—it flickered like a vampire candle. If this man comes to collect a letter poste restante, phone the police immediately.

What is this? I said. How did you get this?

Sina was lying on his back in the tall grass, counting stars. The bloke that worked there liked me, he said.

You never told me. This makes everything worse.

It's no different than before.

They're out looking for you.

His name was Martin, Sina said. The postal clerk. He said the cops are always sending letters like that.

He liked you in what sense?

The same sense as anybody, Sina said.

Not everybody likes you in the same sense, I said.

Sina shrugged.

Answer me, I said.

You didn't ask a question.

The country was so small. If we were just in Australia, I said. It's as big as the sky. We could go our whole lives. Sina hummed the ocean's song. What a cunning rhythm bearing down on us, the smell of every bird that had ever flown above that spit of land. I didn't really want to go to Australia or anywhere, ever, but the dark cliff where we lay that night. A morepork owl cried *quorquo, quorquo.* I couldn't tell which diamond was the Southern Cross. We slept on wildflowers, the whole night. I dreamt I touched the end of the earth. It was the largest, brightest emerald I'd ever seen.

A family's voices woke me up at dawn. They stood across the field by the lighthouse, waiting for the sun. Sina's eyes were already open. I untangled myself from him and saw him staring at the boy, who edged away from his parents toward the cliffside and followed it around to where we sat. He was sixteen, seventeen. Hi, he said. He was from Adelaide. Together we saw horizons in a circle, land and water, white and green.

I'm sorry to stare, said Sina. I just want to look at you for a minute.

The boy leaned back against the black-and-white seismometer, facing the Pacific. His skin got lighter as the sun rose over Whangakeno Island. Sina didn't turn to face me when he said, Did we eat yesterday?

We ate avocados, I said.

We should do that again today, he said. We watched the sun sneak up behind a cumulus of gray. Every cloud was racing toward us. The boy's mother clicked her camera, and now in a rectangle of color in Oceania I'm forever watching Sina watch a nameless boy with a pale, chiseled face.

Come with us, Sina said to him. We can go down the steep side, through the gorse. We'll leave on a boat.

We're not going to leave on any boat, I said as the boy gazed uneasily at the shipless sea that brewed no waves.

The three of us, said Sina.

No, not the three of us, I said. We stood on the easternmost point of land in the world, where a hundred miles out to sea it was the day before and Sina held three fingers up—we'd been the last three people in the world to see darkness.

The boy's parents drove us out to the highway. We waited at their little car at the bottom of the hill looking helpless, and they squeezed us into the back. At the highway they dropped us by a creek where a single sheep had wandered to the water. The boy's head bobbed above the back seat as they sputtered away toward Napier. The sheep bleated. When the family was gone, Sina declothed right beside the road.

What are you doing?

Juat give me a minute, he said.

A car will come. We've got to get a ride. Sina was pulling his belongings from his bag. He stretched his arms up to the blue tuft above his head that fell across him and became his dress, and he knelt to a deep pool between two rocks in the creek and dipped his head beneath the water. His hair now touched his shoulders with its added weight of liquid, and he toweled it there with his old shirt.

What do I look like?

You look like a boy in a dress, I said.

That's not what you really think, he said. He brushed his hair with his fingers, and he leashed a string of silver around his neck. I was walking up and down the ditch. You're uncomfortable, he said.

It makes me nervous.

You don't think I'm pretty? he asked, his face awash in sunlight, and I wondered if it even mattered to him whether I said yes or no.

I think we'll have some explaining to do.

We'll get more rides, anyway. Men stop for a girl. He laughed as he applied his ruby lipstick, and he spread his arms and shrugged. When I was fourteen I was at war, he said as I kicked at fern leaves. He padded his chest with toilet paper and slid his slender shoes onto his feet. He knew how to balance on the raised black heels, and we stood on the highway beneath the sun, clouds, the sun again.

Wait, he cried, I forgot my eyeliner.

He rummaged through his rucksack for the pen. I don't have a mirror, he said when he found it. You'll have to do it for me.

I can't.

He tossed the pen to me and said, It's easy. Just draw a straight line.

I hesitated.

Hurry, he said, before a ride comes.

He presented me with his eyelids. They were shut, but it felt like he was staring at my own eyes, and I decorated him to match the bright, faded land. I wondered if it tickled. You know, he said, I never get thirsty here, not once, and he was bejeweled, a gypsy princess, his olive skin now cindery with rouge. His earrings were gold inlaid with turquoise; they glistened when he turned them to the sun. He kissed me, and my face filled up with blood.

You should have painted your nails last night, I said as he brushed the ruby color on. They'll take forever to dry.

It won't matter.

What if you have to shake somebody's hand? I said. My stomach churned when we heard an engine coming right then, as if I'd placed it in our distance with my words.

Two men stopped their dirty old ute on the sandy pull-off by the bridge. The passenger rolled down his window and grinned at us, revealing chipped teeth. There's a pretty picture, he said, and Sina stroked his eyebrows once apiece.

Climb in, the driver called to us. He wore an All-Blacks jersey. Their truck had an extended cab, and their voices were difficult to understand. I was sweating. I'm Logan, said the driver. This is Gass.

Sina introduced us. Where are you going? he asked the men.

The quarters.

Where's that?

The shearin quarters. Got to open er back up.

Logan took an uphill bend too fast and I said, Holy shit.

I've done these curves a thousand times, Logan said to me. Your lady friend ain't scared there.

I'm not scared, I said.

If you're not now, you will be.

Gass burst into laughter and turned to Sina and said, We'll take you on a wild ride.

Where you from? asked Logan.

America.

I wasn't asking you. I can tell a Yank when I see one.

Iran, Sina said, softening his voice. I remembered I could hold his hand now, so I squeezed it. The wind played with his hair.

Iran, said Logan. What in the hell are you doin down here? How'd you two meet?

At a bar, said Sina.

You ever shear a sheep?

I looked at Sina, who didn't answer. Logan snorted and said, You think I'm talkin to her, Yank?

Huh?

Shearin's man's work. They sensed things about me subconsciously, as I did about them, a smell or the shapes of their cheeks and noses in the sunlight. I felt behind myself for a seat-belt but didn't find one.

No, I said, I've never sheared a sheep.

Gass took Logan's can of Speight's and chugged it. Logan spat on the windshield and then turned around to Sina while he drove. You want you a man that can shear you a sheep, he said, and Sina smiled politely.

Why don't we drop this poofter off in Raukokore, and I'll take you back to the quarters, Logan said. He and Gass looked at each other and burst into laughter as I held Sina's hand. Logan twisted his arm around his seat and slapped me on the knee. I must be awful drunk to say that shit out loud, he shouted, cracking up again. We were all over the road. Cheers to that! he cried, clicking cans with Gass, who whispered in his friend's ear, and they laughed harder.

Should we give them a beer?

We ain't got no pink drinks.

I've sheared a sheep, said Sina. Oh God, I thought. Sina's smile was childlike as Logan and Gass fell silent, turned around. I was in the war, said Sina. Gently he brushed his bangs away from his eyebrows.

What war? Logan sneered.

She said she's from Iran, Gass said, drawing out the hard *I*. They've got heaps of wars.

There aren't girls in those wars.

I was in it, Sina said.

Bullshit you were, said Logan.

Everyone was in it, said Sina. It was a terrible war.

Air soared through the truck and blew the sleeves of his flowery dress, the land beyond him crisp and green. His moons of ruby lipstick stretched apart. For six months I picked up bodies, he said. When the battles were over we burned them in a heap. The dead soldiers weren't too heavy; they were my age—fifteen or sixteen. Sometimes they still seemed to move.

Two kereru scurried across the road to disappear beneath a crop of ferns. We skidded along the gravel by the sea, causing dust to billow up behind us. Logan had been in some fights before. In admiration he recounted them, and Sina listened, smiling. In pubs in Nelson, Gore, Dunedin. They had all ended the same way.

Once we were without water for three days and nights, Sina

said. I used my knife to dig for toads. We squeezed the liquid out.

Do you know how many people you killed?

Twenty-two, said Sina. His voice didn't sound like a girl's to me, but Gass and Logan didn't seem to notice; they wanted him. They did it with their eyes. I could tell from watching them, how Logan pushed the gas pedal with his whole body.

With what?

Guns, said Sina.

Gass opened the glove box and pulled a revolver out and said, Like this?

They both laughed out loud.

No, Sina said, assault rifles.

Those are illegal here, said Gass.

So is this, Logan said, hitting the gun with his finger.

I was the only one who lived of all my brothers, Sina said, the first I'd heard him speak of it. I was the youngest. It was the perfect year to be born in.

I touched the azure nucleus of his bracelet. What an experience to have offered up those corpses in the desert, his ash-streaked face aglow with oil. He had obtained a visa to Kuwait where he'd fled to Greece and then to Vietnam on a false Italian passport. The jails were very comfortable, he told our drivers, moving his hands more and more as he talked. There was a library and a television. Logan nodded and blew smoke out the window as we passed a native village, a hilltop pa, a field of unshorn sheep where rimu trees were mangled by the wind. The truck was spinning wildly. Sina perched on the edge of his seat and smiled.

Where you headed to? asked Logan.

Coromandel.

What for? he said.

To get married, I said.

The truck bounced with Logan's hearty laugh. The sky was barbed with cotton daggers. We cut across the matai shadows westward.

Let's see you kiss the bride, he slurred.

Gass twice clapped his hands and hollered, *Woooo.*

That's a real pretty girl you got there, said Logan.

I nodded.

So kiss her, he said.

Sina had his eyes shut; he was smiling. In the wind his black hair shimmered like a horse's mane. I slid my arm around his shoulder. Clouds turned the hills into volcanoes. The whole world rang.

You're awful young to get hitched, said Logan.

Sina released me so that I could say, It's the only way they'll let him into America.

Sina blinked his eyes. My brain twitched. Logan said, What?

Gass threw his beer can out the window and nailed a crooked road sign rising from the left ditch.

Iranians, I said. Only way they'll let 'em into the country.

You said him.

I said them.

Why would you say them? he said.

It's just the way I said it.

There's no them. There's just you and her.

There's different ways to talk, I said.

He narrowed his eyes into the mirror. Logan looked straight at Sina's Adam's apple working like a piston when he swallowed. He saw Sina's shoulders, their angles sharp and cuspidal, his necklace linked by tiny sailor's cutlasses, forged to match his neck: I felt those blades like they touched the skin of mine. There was no them. The dress didn't quite fit and Sina's feet were so long and skinny and Logan's head turned red, and I shut my eyes and listened for the car to stop.

Then Logan snorted. That's how all you Yanks talk, he said. Like your asshole's hummin the kazoo.

I said *them*. Really.

Get off it already. Pass me another beer from back in the bed.

When I turned to do it, a blue fire filled the landscape behind me and burned everything at once: my red cheeks with ice, my hand by way of the cold beer I now held.

She's only using you to get in, said Gass, so she can blow shit up.

Blow shit up, Logan repeated and laughed.

Gass shouted in an Arabic accent. I will explode you! Die Christian scum!

It was the funniest thing Logan had ever heard.

Answer me, kid, said Gass—have you thought about it?

I don't care what she blows up, I said.

Let me kiss her and I'll drive you all the way to Tauranga, Logan said as we skirted an island-studded bay.

That was a long way. Logan turned around and smelled like motor oil, and Gass couldn't steer at all. We had many miles to cover. I thought about the sky, how if it did this every day, I'd never sleep. Sina clawed his hands telling how he'd torn hearts out of corpses once, at a sixteen-year-old's command, how they'd reeked like raw butcher's beef. He spoke a Farsi sentence. Gass guffawed to Logan and they slurred in Kiwi brogue and Sina answered them. Every word was foreign. Clouds bolted across the sky. Suddenly Sina was holding a ponga frond, and he fanned me with it. That was the best moment of my life, I think. My ears couldn't catch a single word. I didn't even speak a language, except for the names of trees.

CADES COVE

Picking blackberries was the only way Clay could make money. Three cents a quart. His aunts bought them to use in cobblers; his mother had always made the best cobbler. What was up in the trees going rudy-rudy-rudy? he asked, and his sister Laura laughed, because it was jarflies. The ice cream melted quickly; Clay could taste the sawdust grains. Listen, listen, the cats are pissin. He played horseshoes with his uncles until late at night. The summer passed like fading ironweed. There wasn't anything to buy with his twenty-four cents. Laura wanted a nickel, but he kept it all; he'd picked the berries himself. She'd never even climbed a mountain. The moonshine jug was heavier than he'd imagined. He poured it onto his chest so that it dribbled down to his belly. By August all the corn had died. His uncles roasted the pig overnight in cinders and shot skeet while Clay's cousins played tag in the orchard. Fall was snake time; the sky was dark when he walked to school and dark when he got home. Kids built forts of snow, threw ice in one another's ears.

Hey kid, said Laura, I'm gonna kill that cat.

Stay the hell away from my cat, said Clay.

Say hell again I'll tell Aunt Lottie.

The snowflakes felt so cold against his face, and Piggott and the others watched Laura's pupils glinting. Kitty, kitty, right between the eyes.

She pointed to her own chin.

Free shot, she said.

Clay didn't know if it was a trick. Snow tickled when it melted on his tongue. He didn't take the shot, and Laura didn't hit him. She was learning how to crochet. When she slipped on algae on the gristmill's waterwheel, it made sense, because Clay couldn't picture her grown up. He knew what he'd look like; every night in his nightmares he became an ancient man, but Laura wasn't with him. The cat hissed when he tied its paws to the highboy with twine. After the blizzard it came home with frozen eyes. He sat by the oven talking to it, giving it milk; he didn't care. I'll saw your arms off, he told Laura at the viewing. It was harder to breathe on top of mountains. God bless all my aunts and uncles, everyone, please forgive me all my sins forever.

The redbud trees bloomed three days before the dogwoods, and Clay built a dam with rocks and watched blossoms filling the holes between the stones. The government men surveying the cove poisoned themselves on indianberries that had burst up among the dandelions.

That was a year.

DOG'S EGG

Isaac's father bought him a German shepherd for his seventh birthday, and Isaac named it Rocks. He called his father Jearold, not Daddy, because that was his name. They lived together in a trailer on Jericho Road at the foot of Chilhowee Mountain. Isaac had never had a dog before, except the one that had died before he was born. His mother hated dogs, but she was dead now too, so one day in October Jearold came home from jail with a puppy, and it grew fast; by December they had to tie it to the gum tree to make it mean. Jearold stood at the back door and shot at it with the BB gun.

Stop it, Isaac said.

He ain't mean enough to hunt yet, said Jearold. Look at the little faggot.

The dog looked up at him with scared but angry eyes and panted.

He's my dog, said Isaac.

That's where he gets the fag part from.

But Jearold was only joking when he said things like that. Isaac knew his father loved him because they spent so much time together. Jearold had taught Isaac how to play horseshoes. They played it every evening when Jearold got home from his job at the airport in town. They laughed and chased each other through the mud. Afterwards Jearold took Isaac with him to his friends' houses where the men drank whiskey in lawn chairs until two or even three o'clock in the morning. No one else at Isaac's school got to stay awake that late.

Load up your gun and you whistle that dog, sang Jearold, rounding the words out drunkenly in baritone. We're off to the woods to hunt groundhog.

Winter came early that year, and the dog got tough fast; it was already a lot tougher than Isaac was. He hoped his father wouldn't shoot at him too. He flinched whenever Jearold picked the gun up. Jearold was drinking more and more. The dog wasn't fun to play with now—it just growled. Isaac wondered if it would ever break its chain and pin him to the dirt, its foul breath warm on his skin as it ate his flesh. He saw ribs pressing through different shades of brown on its stomach.

He's hungry, Isaac said.

The hell he is, said Jearold. Dumb shit's done eat a deer this week whole.

That's not true, said Isaac. You and Diesel and them ate most of it.

Jearold ignored him. Don't you feed my dog, he said. We ain't rich. He sparked a match on a round rock and lit a small, red cylinder and pitched it overhanded at the dog and clapped his hands. Isaac cried out at the sound of gunfire. The dog bolted to the end of its chain and yelped and snarled and dropped strings of drool to the mud.

You said you weren't gonna do that anymore, Isaac said.

Gotta learn to fend for hisself, said Jearold.

Isaac felt bad for the dog, but he wanted to seem grateful for the long hours his father worked every day; eventually they wouldn't be poor anymore. Jearold was a deliveryman for Delta. He'd wanted to be a trucker, but then he failed the tests; that was where the hole in the bedroom wall came from. Now he drove lost luggage to people's houses and took Isaac with him on the longer trips sometimes, which made Isaac happy. He got to see far-off towns and cities: Bristol, Corbin, Coalfield. He learned how freeway exit numbers worked. He didn't know what *lay of the land* meant, but he figured if he rode around enough he'd understand that soon too. He closed his eyes and dreamt of bridges, lodes of limestone late at night, deep caves to blindness. His car dreams were the only ones that weren't nightmares.

Goddamn cunt birds, Jearold muttered when he failed to crush a vulture gutting some roadkill.

It startled Isaac. He looked at pine trees' shadows to see if he was awake; it was hard sometimes for him to tell. All his nightmares were of mothers—his mother, for the most part, but sometimes the nightmare mother was many selves at once: Shontelle, which had been his mother's name, and her own dead mother, and the maggots that had lived inside Shontelle's sinuses but couldn't speak. They had no mouths but only holes for ink. The words they wrote were baneful, and they loved each other, the maggots; they writhed and embraced.

This was Isaac's first Christmas without his mother. The holiday was cold and dark, and Jearold had a load to deliver across the mountains to Cullowhee that night. Isaac liked to cross the Smokies. He liked the views. Jearold bought them Christmas dinner from the Hardee's drive-thru, and they headed up the curves toward Deals Gap. Jearold waved to all the motorcyclists at the Calderwood gorge, so Isaac did too, even though they frightened him. They yelled like railroad bandits in black leather. Harley people hated Honda people, and the other way around. Isaac didn't know much about it.

I need to pee, he said.

Piss, said Jearold. Don't talk sissy talk.

I need to piss, said Isaac.

Jearold stopped on a pull-off at a sharp curve, and Isaac got out. He urinated on dead leaves in a ditch below a wood cross marking the location of a biker's fatal crash. He hoped no cars would pass. The air was crisp and wintry; he could see a moonlit finger of the lake downhill, far through the woods. When he sat back down in the car, his father handed him a small, black silk bag with a drawstring and said, Merry Christmas.

Isaac took it and said, Thank you.

Open it up, said Jearold.

Isaac reached inside and pulled out a pair of Oakley sunglasses.

Them's expensive shades, said Jearold. Isaac put them on, but they were too big for him. They were made for a grown-up. He took them off and tried to smile.

Thank you, he said again, quietly.

Ain't this Christmas? said Jearold, looking at him. Did I screw up the days?

It's Christmas, Isaac said.

Durn act like it, then.

Isaac nodded. When he put the shades over his eyes a second time, the scratches on the lenses marred his vision. From what was written on the bag he learned that they were made of plutonite, and the frames were graphite. He turned around and saw an open pocket on the suitcase they were delivering. A sock was hanging out. Where did you get these? he asked Jearold, who was driving quickly through steep-angled curves.

Store, Jearold said.

Which store? said Isaac.

I don't fucken know which store, said Jearold, irritated, so he blew the horn and added, I never would of asked my daddy where he got me my present. Goddamn. Jearold had stolen things before—money, mainly, and some vodka bottles from the bar on Airport Highway. He stole a car once but he didn't get to keep it, and now they had their own car anyway.

I was just curious, Isaac said.

What if I told you I took it out of that bag there? said Jearold. What would you do then?

Isaac looked back again at the open pocket. His mother had told him never to steal. She was a Christian. Before she died she'd given him a yellow book of Bible stories that told why bad things were bad, and Isaac knew it was wrong to steal anyway, because then the other people wouldn't have the stolen things anymore, and they'd be unhappy.

I'd put them back, he said.

What the hell for? said Jearold.

Because I'm a Christian, Isaac said.

Jearold laughed. A Christian, he repeated. Well I'll be.

Isaac looked away. His cheeks went red, and he realized he had spoken loudly. He knew he couldn't return the Oakleys to the suitcase; Jearold would just take them back out and keep them for himself. Jearold didn't own any sunglasses. He never went to church, so Isaac didn't either, which meant he wasn't really a Christian at all. He didn't want to be different from his father anyway; it embarrassed him. He wished he hadn't said anything about the glasses.

How come we don't bring Rocks on trips? he said to make Jearold forget.

That durn mutt'd shit all through my car.

But it's cold at home, said Isaac.

It's cold here, Jearold said.

But we've got heat, said Isaac.

Heat takes gas, said Jearold. I ain't rich.

But the heat was on in the car, although it didn't warm them up. Isaac didn't like it when Jearold said things that didn't make sense. The route was steep and twisted, and he watched the stripes of moonlight on the road and tried to count them, but Jearold accelerated fast beyond a waterfall of icicles on a man-made cliff the road cut through. He picked his nose and snorted. The amber clock was brown in Isaac's Oakleys right when midnight hit, and they were nowhere: Knoxville's stations drowned like Asheville's in the static. Jearold said he hated music anyhow. It made his lips itch. He liked AM better—it was talk shows, preachers, NASCAR races.

Jearold drove forty miles an hour even on the gravel road they finally turned onto. Isaac read him the directions. Jearold's writing looked like pine twigs. Get them things off your head, he ordered Isaac when they arrived at a log cabin atop a ridge and gave an old, fat Cherokee his Gladstone bag and golf clubs. The man gave Jearold a wadded-up bill and smiled and waved to Isaac, and Jearold screeched down the driveway in reverse and grumbled, Mother, mother, motherfucker.

What's the matter? Isaac said.

Jearold threw the dollar at him and said, There's the matter.

Isaac examined it and said, Is it not real?

I'd as soon get nothin as a damn dollar.

That doesn't make sense, Isaac said. He wished his father would be more logical. Jearold's eyes were red and bleary when a pickup's headlights shone at them, and Isaac didn't know if Jearold was drunk or tired. He hadn't seen Jearold drink since three o'clock, but he wasn't sure how long a drink could make you drunk for; sometimes Jearold acted drunk for eight days straight. Isaac wanted to get drunk too so he could figure it out, but he was scared to try, and anyway that wasn't what Christians did.

You sound like a three-legged dog, said Jearold when the cold made Isaac shiver, but he gave Isaac the dollar anyway, just to be nice.

Isaac tried to sit still. He wished his dog had a heated place to rest. Christians were nice to each other; they were even nice to animals. When he got home, he decided, he'd go out back and rub his hands across its fur to warm it up, but then he fell asleep against the window. They crossed the Appalachian spine; Isaac dreamt they swerved along the slopes like boulders in an avalanche, their car suffused with amniotic fluid so he drowned in it but lived to wake again, to tremble across the hoarfrost to his bedroom where he dreamt his mother dealt out hands of rummy in a circle around the dog but it was dead, and she was living, and that was wrong. The dog was barely grown; it was still a puppy. Isaac's mother sat upon the hulk of its carcass and displaced hordes of flies; she cackled at their flight and with the dog's limp tail she bludgeoned flies and laughed, her head thrown back; she snatched them with her six-inch tongue and screamed them out her mouth. Isaac cried when he saw her cheeks contoured by starlight, living. When he awoke, his mother and the dog were dead together. He carried a candlestick into the yard at home and cupped its flame from the breeze he made by walking. It blackened the terrain so his only light was flickers galloping across his palm like leprosy. The moon and stars were clouded, deeply black. Isaac stumbled across a gully and burned his middle finger with the flame. The dog was dead at his wet feet.

Rocks, he cried. Rocks. Rocks.

Name it Rocks, said Jearold behind him with a horseshoe in his hand, that's just what it's gonna be, and the horseshoe mashed the flame out.

But—

But nuthen, Jearold said.

Isaac's eyes adjusted to the darkness, and he balled his fist up. He hated his father's voice sometimes. He wished it would freeze so his throat would stick forever between the same two words.

It was a pansy dog, said Jearold. It was weak.

It wasn't weak.

Jearold laughed and said, It's dead, is what weak is.

We didn't feed it enough, said Isaac.

We fed it plenty, Jearold said.

What if it didn't have water? Isaac said.

How could it not of had water? There's water everywhere.

No there's not, said Isaac.

There's water in the goddamn dirt, said Jearold.

But you can't drink dirt.

Jearold took a moment to think about it. It sure don't matter now, he said. It's dead.

Isaac didn't want to cry. He wasn't sad, he told himself; he just felt sorry for the dog. It hadn't been much fun to play with lately, only showing its teeth. Isaac didn't even like dogs; they were loud and ugly, and they smelled bad. The dog smelled worse and worse as time passed. It stayed tied up to its tree, prostrate two days on the ground, and the nighttime gave its skin to bugs and ants and blended it with mud. Isaac wanted to bury it, but he didn't know where to find a spade. He didn't want to touch its flesh and catch a disease. He stayed at home alone because school was out for Christmas break, and Jearold got called in to work all hours of the day and night. Be there fast as I can drive, he said into his cell phone, and, I don't give a shit what the hell the durn red nigger said, and other people too, and Isaac hoped his father didn't get himself in trouble; he didn't want foster parents. In a textbook at his school he'd seen a story where the orphans had to wear their shirts tucked in and eat brussels sprouts and broccoli, but Jearold never bought vegetables or any groceries from the store at all. The first full day the dog was dead was french fries, milk shakes. The second day was double-decker Moon Pies. Thank you, Isaac said.

Chocolate or banana? his father said.

Chocolate.

The stale cake crumbled to bits when Isaac ate it. He sat outside in the dark in his hunter orange coat and wondered if a Moon Pie had the vitamins his mother had said he needed. He wished he'd said banana. He wondered if he'd join her too from lack of vitamins and if the dog had died that way; it scared him. Jearold might live; he might have been eating healthy things while he delivered bags. Isaac didn't trust him anymore. His beard had grown out crooked. He drank each night with Diesel, and they smoked pot from a plastic bag sometimes, and Diesel charged into the driveway while half of Isaac's food was still uneaten; he parked his car and ruffled Isaac's hair and grabbed the Moon Pie from his hand and ate a bite and slobbered on the rest. He held a brown-bagged fifth of Captain Morgan's rum and barked to Isaac, Say.

Say what? said Isaac.

Say.

Isaac didn't know what to say. He looked away. Diesel was picking his nose when he saw the dog's corpse. Shit, he said and scratched his septum open with his fingernail so blood trickled out. It looked like it was painful. What the hell happened? Diesel said.

Died, said Jearold, who had stepped out of the trailer onto the gravel patio.

No shit, said Diesel.

Yeah shit, said Jearold.

Things like dogs, said Diesel, you gotta feed em, or look what happens.

Fed that thing like it was my mama, Jearold said, and Diesel walked into the yard and kicked the puppy's stomach with his snakeskin boot. A fly buzzed up from underneath, and Diesel jumped as if the dog had barked itself. Its coat was caked with the mud in which it lay. Its eyes were being eaten by gnats.

Did you poison it? said Diesel.

Jearold shook his head.

Did you give it chocolate? You know you can't give a dog no chocolate.

I didn't give it chocolate, said Jearold. It just died. That's just the way it was.

You got to bury it, said Diesel.

You bury it, said Jearold.

Ain't my dog.

I ain't a buryen no goddamn dog, said Jearold. You sound just like my boy. He coughed abruptly, propelling spit to his red chin. Might as well just shoot the sonofabitch.

It's already dead, you dumbass, Diesel said. What good would it do?

That ain't what I meant, said Jearold after pausing.

It's what you said, said Diesel.

Jearold stood up from his chair. Don't make fun of my intelligence, he said.

What intelligence? said Diesel, who laughed and tried to pass the rum, but Jearold knocked the bottle to the ground. It landed upright on the dog's gut.

Don't push me, said Jearold. I'm at the end of my rope.

Go ahead and hang yourself then, said Diesel.

He stooped to retrieve the bottle and wiped its mud on his coat. Isaac wondered if suicide was really what his father meant about the rope. The Bible said men who killed themselves were rooted to the ground in hell like trees, and Jearold wouldn't like that, Isaac thought. A fly perched on the dog where the rum had lain before, and Isaac watched it run its feelers across the ripe flesh. His heart beat fast to know whether the fly would choose to suck dog-blood. Or was there blood at all. Or was it frozen? he wondered, staring until the corpse's straight-up legs became its arms, the blurry firs and birch trees so the whole world was a dead dog.

I might have to do some driving tonight, said Jearold.

To where? said Diesel.

How should I know where? To where bags go.

Are you on-call? said Isaac.

Jearold ignored him and said, You want to come if there's trips?

Yeah, Isaac said.

Not you, Jearold said.

Sure, said Diesel. I just bought some shit.

Where? said Jearold.

Diesel mocked Jearold's deep voice and said, Where bags go, and Jearold punched him in the arm.

Why can't I go? Isaac said. He felt angry. He made a fist.

For Jesus' sake, said Jearold, I didn't say you couldn't go. I just said I wasn't talken to you right then. He set the bottle down and stood and lumbered toward Isaac and hugged him like a bear and messed around in his hair like Diesel had done. You're gonna go, said Jearold. You're gonna go everywhere I go. For good. He pushed Isaac back so they could see each other's eyes, and then he said, Look at me.

Isaac looked at him.

Look at me, Jearold said.

He's looken at you, Diesel said.

Shut the goddamn fuck up, slurred Jearold.

Isaac shivered when his father cursed. It made him sound angry even when he wasn't mad at all. Jearold reached for the bottle and forgot about Isaac for a while; instead he talked to Diesel. Isaac watched the dog, but it didn't change. Standing in the yard wasn't what he wanted to be doing. He was seven years old. There were people his age all over the earth, and dogs and maybe insects; they spanned continents. He didn't know if flies were even supposed to be alive at Christmastime.

Bottle's small, said Jearold.

You go buy one then, said Diesel.

I bought the last one, Jearold said.

And you drank it, too. Just then Jearold's phone rang; it was his boss telling him there wouldn't be any trips. Jearold twisted the phone like an Indian burn, but he couldn't break it that way. Diesel laughed at him, and he hit Diesel with the receiver, and then he pointed at the dog. That's what I wanna do, he said.

You wanna fuck the dog?

No, dumbass, that's what I wanna do to that faggot-ass boss of mine.

You wanna fuck your boss?

Jearold kicked Diesel and said, I want to kill him.

Diesel looked at the dead dog and then at Jearold and back at the dog.

Not fuck him, said Jearold, and he hit his palm with his left fist. *Fuck* him.

Diesel grinned. He'd hurt some folks himself; that was why his name was Diesel. He swigged out of the bottle and shone his face red like a blister inside out. He laughed and said, That there is a dog. That is sure one fucken dog.

Jearold laughed too. Isaac didn't see what was funny, but he didn't mind his father's laughing; Diesel was their guest, and they had to make him feel comfortable. They went inside so everyone was warmer, because bitter air was on its way and would come fast. Water froze like freezing wasn't anything at all, and the windows rattled. The whole trailer rocked when Jearold jumped. Isaac didn't know why he jumped. He watched the men pass a joint back and forth. It seemed to put them right to sleep, but

Isaac stayed awake and knew he'd have bad dreams. Please forgive me for the dog, he said to God amidst the blessings in his prayers, and he said them standing up, out loud, with the kitchen light on, because he'd never done it that way before. Jearold and Diesel were asleep, and he wanted to see if anything would be different.

Snow fell that night. The mercury dropped to ten below as Isaac watched the dog turn white outside his window, the flurries gathering like unguent on its rot. Snowflakes made no sound against the pane. Tears filled Isaac's eyes, and he wondered if he had loved the dog, if it had died for him. He didn't think so. He imagined his mother standing beside it, beneath the walnut tree. He was falling asleep. Flies were dying from the cold. They died on Diesel's body, on the metal kitchen table which was gray and shiny from its plating bath, and on every part of the dark, bare countertop; on an empty beer can and on the unmade single bed where Jearold now lay drunk and softly snoring, and they fell dead on the barren iris bed outside and on the frozen dog, on every rock that broke the grass's shield of worms and flies' dead eggs and on Diesel's sleek Camaro; on its shiny, living gloss.

*   *   *

Jearold didn't kill his boss at all. He stuck a knife in the backyard bones like Rocks was a voodoo dog, and he twisted it counterclockwise thrice and cried, Lord God. Several days passed. When the boss called, Jearold listened to the receiver and stared ahead and nodded; he said, Uh-huh, yeah. He wore new clothes that didn't fit him; Isaac didn't know where they'd come from. Jearold never shopped for clothes himself. He'd started taking a barbiturate; it was in the cabinet, dusty, with Isaac's mother's name typed on the bottle. It made Jearold sweat and cry now to drink alcohol, which seemed to embarrass him, but sometimes it made him scream. Don't you ever let on I cried to Diesel, he ordered

Isaac on Sunday, crying, and Isaac nodded. Or I'll do you like I done the dog, said Jearold. Isaac wished his school would hurry and start back up again. Jearold cracked the trash can lid with a fist that held a knife, and his boss gave him one last trip before he had to quit his job. I ain't got nobody else to work tonight, the boss said on speakerphone. I got my cousin's luggage here. It ain't airline-paid, but I won't get the police in all this if you do it.

For how much?

For free, said the boss. That's what I just got done telling you.

Jearold threw the phone across the room. He'd knew he'd have to give it back to Delta soon. It wouldn't break. He drove to the airport. An hour later he came back home with a full-grown Labrador retriever on a chain leash. This un can eat up the othern, he said, but he was just joking again; the dog was for delivery to Cumberland, Kentucky, which would have been an eighty-dollar trip. The joke was loud because Jearold spoke it loud. He didn't make jokes much anymore. The new dog couldn't have eaten the old one anyway, because the flies had fled already with its flesh and left behind a twisted infrastructure of knives all white like ivory and dirty rows of teeth, and Isaac stroked the spine with his tennis shoe, which had a hole in it. He shivered when bones touched his sock. He pissed on the tree because Jearold had locked the new dog inside the bathroom, where it clawed at the hollow door and startled Isaac. He was almost glad the old one had died so early in its life, but Jearold saw him staring at the bones and said, Stop feeling sorry for yourself. I'm the only one that loves you. That dog wouldn't never of loved you. But Isaac knew his mother would love him in his dream that night. She hugged him underneath his eyeballs, where she said, You're in a dream, wake up, so Isaac woke into another, deeper dream in which she said, Wake up, you're in a dream, but her eyes were dogs' eggs now, and he obeyed her infinitely down the quickfire spiral into dreams where her eggs were bigger, deader, bonier.

*   *   *

Jearold didn't need to make the new dog mean; it was already mean. It growled and bared its teeth each time he kicked it. He kept it on a short chain so it couldn't claw him back or slobber on his new black boots. They were a few sizes too big. My boss don't know where I live, he said. His eyes laughed at Isaac and everybody and the dog. I've had it up to my eyes in shit with that little ass-munch, he said.

The dog? said Isaac.

Old ass-munch, said Jearold.

Who owns that dog?

You do.

I don't want it, Isaac said, but then he stepped back and wished he hadn't spoken. In the other room the Labrador was snarling.

Somebody wants it, Jearold said and laughed. I'll bet somebody's just shittin his pants up a storm. Somebody's cousin, too.

We should deliver it, said Isaac.

They're gonna be sorry they ever hired me, said Jearold.

I bet they're already sorry, said Isaac.

Jearold looked at him and laughed and punched him gently on the shoulder. Hell, he said, grinning, I bet you're right. He was drunk. Diesel showed up, like always. You wanna go on a drive? Jearold asked him.

I just drove, Diesel said. I don't wanna drive no more.

You ain't gonna drive, said Jearold, you'll just get drove.

They loaded the car with whiskey and a six-pack of Pabst

and a Gerber jar of Diesel's marijuana. It had held squash once; the label was half–peeled off, and Diesel put it in the glove box and said, Where we goen?

That's for my boy to find out, said Jearold. He gave the cell phone to Isaac with a piece of paper with a phone number on it. Get us some directions, he said. Get em from Harlan.

What's Harlan? said Isaac.

It's a place.

What else do I say?

Tell him we got his dog, said Jearold. Tell him today's his lucky day.

Why can't you do it? said Isaac.

I got some shit to do. Don't bother me.

Jearold went out to the backyard as Isaac dialed the number. He'd never called another area code before. Diesel watched him dial. Isaac didn't see why Jearold couldn't make the call himself. The man on the other end of the line grunted when he answered, and Isaac introduced himself. I'm with Delta Airlines, he said, afraid his voice sounded too high and childish for the man to believe him. Don't hang up, he said, we've got your dog. I need directions from Harlan.

Harlan, the man barked.

The phone was on speaker; Isaac didn't know how to turn it off. Diesel stood behind him and poured whiskey into a glass over ice and listened. Yeah, said Isaac, Harlan. He hoped it was a real place, not a name his father had created to make a fool out of him.

You know where five lights is? the man said.

I don't know what you mean, said Isaac.

Red lights, he said.

Uh-huh, Isaac said.

You turn at them five lights, the man said.

Which way? Isaac asked.

At that corner there, the man said. Isaac watched his father through a break in the curtains; he was leaning over in the yard, lifting something. They's three turns, the man was saying. You turn at the first one. It's all gravel like.

Okay, Isaac said when the man paused.

Look for the pink toilet.

I don't know what you mean, Isaac said.

They's some shit on the left, the man said. Mine's got the biggest flag.

Big flag, Isaac wrote.

You be good to my dog, the man said.

We will, said Isaac.

Play him my radio show.

What's that?

I got that highway ministry, the man said. They play it every night.

Okay, Isaac said, I will, although he had no idea what the man meant. He wrote the directions down neatly on a paper napkin and gave them to his father, who had the dog carrier in his hand. He put it in the car. The Labrador was locked in Isaac's bedroom now, because they needed the bathroom.

You got the shit? Jearold said to Diesel.

Yeah.

All of it?

Where are we going? Diesel asked.

Let's just do some now.

Diesel pulled a plastic bag out of his pocket and poured about a tablespoon of powder on the dirty countertop. He cut chunks up with a potato-crusted butter knife as Jearold swigged a beer. This thing ain't shit, Diesel said and threw the knife at the sink. Isaac flinched as it clattered to the floor. Diesel split the powder up into four lines with his long, uneven fingernail and reached for his wallet, which was empty. Jearold turned his pockets inside out. They both turned to look at Isaac.

Hey kid, said Jearold.

What?

Gimme that dollar.

I don't have any money, said Isaac.

Don't lie to me.

I'm not lying, Isaac said, but then he remembered the tip from the man in North Carolina. He went to the bathroom and fetched the wadded dollar from the pocket of his dirty jeans. Jearold mashed it flat on the counter several times before he rolled it up, and they snorted two lines apiece through it, and Diesel watched Isaac the whole time through the edge of his eye.

Kid shouldn't watch us do this, he said.

Jearold shrugged and rubbed his nose.

They got that dare thing now, where you rat out your parents.

You ain't nobody's parents, Jearold said.

You are, Diesel said.

He ain't gonna remember none of it, said Jearold. Eventually, I mean.

Why not? said Diesel. He ain't drunk.

Of course he ain't drunk, said Jearold. He don't drink.

Then why won't he remember it?

Cause he's seven years old.

Isaac didn't understand where they were going if they weren't taking the dog. He sat between his father and Diesel in the front bench seat and meant to ask about it as soon as they finished smoking pot, but he was tired and fell right to sleep. Diesel was blowing smoke back at the dog carrier. Go fetch, he said, pointing at it.

Fetch what? said Jearold.

You're always so concerned with *what*, Diesel said. Roll

over, he told the dog carrier. Isaac felt like his head was rolling as they sped up Montvale Road around the curves. He liked closing his eyes in cars; it was comforting to have a conversation to fall asleep to. Maybe the man just wanted his empty carrier; maybe it had the wrong dog in it. Isaac knew there were still a lot of things he didn't understand.

How was jail? Diesel was saying when Isaac awoke.

I met some good guys there, Jearold said. I wouldn't mind hangen out with them again.

You just might get to, Diesel said.

Isaac drifted into sleep again and didn't dream at all; he woke back up from a solid slab of black. The clock on the dashboard said he'd slept an hour, and he didn't know the road he saw outside the car but there were signs. They shot through Tazewell, beating every red light. Jearold and Diesel were smoking again. They laughed so hard that Jearold could barely drive. I hate how coke always makes you feel like you have to shit, said Jearold. They went through the tunnel at the state line and raced through Middlesboro, and Jearold stopped in the middle of nowhere to piss. Isaac got out too, so he could stretch. It was so dark he couldn't even see his shoelaces. He didn't know who was pushing whom against the car until he heard Jearold say to Diesel, You think I'm strong enough to kick your ass?

Fuck you, you fuck.

Fight me, Jearold said with his hand pressed up against Diesel's chest. I need to practice.

You can't fight, said Diesel. You've got to drive.

Isaac couldn't see their faces yet, but he could see their eyes, and he couldn't tell what they reflected. Do me like you want me dead, said Jearold.

Maybe I do want you dead, said Diesel.

I'll fight the dog, said Jearold.

What dog? said Diesel.

Jearold pointed up at a hill. This is Kentucky, he said. They fight dogs here all the time.

That's with other dogs, said Diesel.

How would you know? said Jearold. You ain't done it. He opened the car's back door. Here boy, he said, here boy. Isaac didn't understand what was going on until he saw Rocks's bones inside the carrier. They lay curled up and motionless, but Diesel got so scared he laughed out loud. He kicked a hole in the dirt with his boot.

That ain't no dog, he said.

That's as much dog as anybody's gonna get.

Ain't any need to fight that dog.

I done it already, Jearold said. I won. He grunted and pointed out at the land. Suddenly Isaac could see their switchback and the craggy rocks that stretched downhill below their car, and it made his stomach sick to see how sharp the slope was. It was one-thirty in the morning. They had fifty more miles of mountains to drive.

Can we go home now? said Diesel. This is bringen me down.

Of course we can't, said Jearold, we've got to deliver a dog.

I doubt they want it now, said Diesel.

I don't really give a fuck who wants it.

It's not gonna go fetch little Susie's baseball anymore.

It's a joke, Jearold said, his voice strangely flat. It's not the real dog.

How much are they payen you for to drive all this way for a joke? said Diesel.

Jearold hesitated and said, A fair bit.

How much? said Diesel. Why don't we split it down the middle?

Why don't you get in the car.

I need money, Diesel said. I cut you a deal on that last bag you bought.

Get your ass in the car, Jearold yelled.

I am in the car, Diesel said, but then he opened the door and sat down. The dog was still and quiet and unafraid; the road was its entrails laid bare. Isaac sat in the backseat this time; he didn't like to be so close to people he didn't like. He'd rather sit beside the bones, he decided. He knew the dog was in heaven, so there was something about the bones; he wanted to be near them. They were the right color. Mountains glowered in the glass like sawed-off witches' hats. Jearold drank stale coffee. Clouds covered the stars. The telephone poles were shaped like Jesus.

What if it starts to smell? said Diesel.

It done smelled, said Jearold. That's all over with.

What if it had rabies?

You're acting like a little baby, Jearold said. Isaac didn't see what so was bad about that. His mother used to stroke his head and say, My little baby, and it was something good. He tried to imagine Diesel with a mother, but the face in Isaac's mind had pimples and a beard. He was tired and cold and sleepy and hungry, and he wished the heater worked right.

Diesel was shivering too. I'm cold, he said. This car's a piece of shit.

Jearold nodded. He'd put sixty thousand miles on it since he started the job; he'd driven all over east Tennessee and into North Carolina, Virginia, Georgia. The miles on the car didn't matter so much in summer, when it was only the air conditioner that didn't work.

You didn't tell me I should bring a damn coat, said Diesel.

Be a man, said Jearold. Isaac could see his father's breath and Diesel's mingling in the colder and colder air. Jearold's hands seemed frozen to the wheel. He rubbed them against each other.

A state map slid along the dashboard when they went around a sharp right curve. A stick shaped like an alligator crunched beneath the car's tires.

When I'm about to freeze for good, said Diesel, I'm gonna kill you, to stay warm.

Cover yourself up with the dog, said Jearold.

I ain't gonna touch that dog, said Diesel.

Skin him, said Jearold. Make a good coat.

It don't got fur.

Jearold stuck his hand into his pocket and pulled out an old switchblade. As it fell open he grinned.

You never had that before, said Diesel.

That's cause it was someone else's, said Jearold.

Whose is it? Diesel asked.

It's mine, said Jearold.

Why'd you bring it?

In case I need it, where we're going.

There was another hour to go, and three hours' drive back. Isaac was shivering, but he said nothing. The temperature was going to keep on falling. He wondered if his father felt bad for having brought him along, for making him so cold. He hoped it was bad for Jearold's heart condition; maybe he'd have a heart attack. Isaac hoped it happened while the car was stopped. The engine made as much noise as a radar detector, and the trees all clashed like midnight armies; branches fell from them, and leaves died on the windshield. Isaac saw a sign: Kingdom Come Parkway.

That's stupid, said Jearold.

What's stupid? said Diesel.

You, Jearold said, and your mama.

But he meant the sign, Isaac knew, and it irritated him that his father was making fun of heaven. The two-lane road carried them uphill into lonely, narrow woods, unlit. Jearold's face looked like a red throat. Stand back boys and let's be wise, he crooned, I think I see his beady eyes. They crossed into Harlan County and everything kicked in. Those people are gonna fuck us up, said Diesel. That dog's dead. That's a big, dead dog.

I know how big it is, said Jearold.

I can smell it, Diesel said. This is Harlan County.

I don't give a shit if it's goddamn wet twat county.

Didn't you see that movie? said Diesel. They'll fuck you up up here.

They're probably rich, said Jearold.

Nobody ain't rich here, Diesel said. They mine coal.

They flew on a plane, Jearold said. Coal miners don't fly on a plane.

Where'd they fly to? said Diesel.

Jearold turned the car light on and pulled the ticket from his sun visor and tossed it at Diesel. Read it, he said, and Diesel looked at the ticket like he couldn't read. The name, Jearold said.

Swope Swortzel.

Swope Swortzel?

Diesel nodded.

Swortzel comes first?

Swope comes first, Diesel said.

So it's Swortzel Swope, said Jearold.

Four, said Diesel, and Jearold turned the light back off.

Four what?

The number four.

Is it letters or numbers?

It's a four, Diesel said. It's a goddamn four.

Four spelled with numbers?

What the hell other kind of four is there?

The kind with a *V*, said Jearold. He flipped his lights from dim to bright and said, I guess he's the fourth, then.

The fourth what? Diesel said.

The fourth Swortzel Swope, Jearold said.

Swortzel Swope the fourth, said Diesel.

Jearold nodded. Diesel looked back at the dog and breathed hard. Stay on the road, he said when the car skirted the shoulder, and he turned the radio on and pressed the scan button to make it race across the frequencies. The green numbers slowed down sometimes but never stopped. Nothing, Diesel said. It was a valley, and the hills were high; it seemed to worry him. The empty stations made a song together. Isaac couldn't hear it very well.

What if they's all four there? said Diesel.

I should have left you home, said Jearold.

I bet they've got a dozen guns apiece, Diesel said.

They ain't no four Swopes, said Jearold.

It said it right there on the page, said Diesel.

That's four in a line, said Jearold. Some's surely dead by now.

Diesel shook his head.

Think about it, said Jearold. If you was the fourth, your great-grandpa would be first.

My great-grandpa's living.

Your great-great-grandpa, then, said Jearold.

That ain't it, though, Diesel said. That's the fifth.

But you're young, said Jearold.

Maybe Swortzel Swope's young too, said Diesel.

He flew on a plane, Jearold said. He's probably old. He's got an old dog.

We don't know how old that dog is, Diesel said.

It's old enough to be dead, said Jearold.

Isaac knew how old the dog was—it was a puppy. He was glad Diesel was scared; he wasn't as scared himself that way, and he didn't have to talk. He hoped his father would forget he was in the car at all. He was pretty sure Swortzel Swope wasn't a coal miner; the man was probably a doctor or a farmer, with a big house and a garden. If Jearold got in a fight with Swortzel

Swope, Isaac decided, he'd run and hide behind the four Swopes and watch Jearold get beat up, and he hoped Diesel felt the same way.

They're all up there, Diesel said. On their porch, way up a gravel driveway. Waiten for their dog.

You don't know about it, Jearold said. You don't know how it went.

We'll get up the mountain, Diesel said. They'll say, what are you doen on my property? Where's my damn dog? Diesel was shouting. Isaac was starting to picture it too. They were bald and short and scary-looking. The part of their heads that wasn't bald held long, white, stringy hair. Where's Rocks? demanded Diesel. That's my dog crate there in your car. How come they ain't no barken?

Cause it's dead, said Jearold. That's the fucken point.

This is Swope land, Diesel shouted. You best of got my dog to be a trespassen. He breathed hard, right in Jearold's ear. Answer my question, boy—where's my dog? Where's my dog?

It's right here, Jearold yelled to shut him up.

Give him here or I'll make you dead.

Shut up, Jearold screamed. He said it over and over until suddenly the radio stopped its scanning on a gospel song. The volume was up as loud as it would go, and Isaac hurried to turn it down, and they all breathed in synch with one another.

I better not get hurt, said Diesel.

I'll let you out of the car right now if you want it.

The song died down, and the radio went quiet. Isaac heard thick static crackle as they passed through a granite cut. Another gospel song began. They hadn't passed a car for many miles up and down the steep hills, through sliced stones of the earth's crust. It was twenty miles to Harlan by a shot-up sign whose paint was almost gone. The dog cage rolled over on its side and stretched the seat-belt to its limit, and Rocks's bones crashed

against the metal grid. Holy shit, Diesel whispered. Isaac hated
Diesel's voice as much as he hated Jearold's. The radio reminded
him how raw and red they were. He wondered if this program
was the highway ministry that Swortzel Swope's dog liked; he
hoped so. Gospel music sounded pretty, like something God
would want him to be listening to.

Just call and tell him, Diesel said. Drop the dog off at a
parken lot and tell him where you left it.

That ain't what we're up here for, said Jearold.

It won't matter what we're up here for once you're dead,
said Diesel. He reached across Jearold's body for the phone, and
Jearold swerved.

It's out of range, dumbass.

Stop at a pay phone, Diesel said.

Do you see any pay phones? Jearold asked.

Isaac looked around; the land had become a factory of black-
ness. They hadn't passed a light in many miles. Their struggling
motor was the only outside sound as they curved just like the
road. Pack another bowl, said Jearold, and Diesel did, and they
passed it back and forth. Isaac wondered if they would offer him
any. The smoke in the car warmed his lungs and body, and he
wished Jearold and Diesel would turn around to him so he could
stare back with a mean glare. Diesel shut up for a while. The
windows fogged. Verses of "Amazing Grace" wended their stems
through static, became the air, and Jearold almost drove the car
off the road reaching into his pocket. These is yellow roses, he
said to Diesel, holding two small custard-colored pills, and Jearold swallowed his.

Where'd you get those? said Diesel.

You ain't the only one in the goddamn county.

Isaac watched as Diesel let the pill slide down his esophagus.
His muscles weren't as stiff as dog bones anymore. Diesel looked
at himself in the rearview mirror and there he was, just like al-

ways, and he laughed. Rocks, he said to the dog, and turned
around but didn't look at Isaac once. Here boy. You can't see
me but I see you. The car's right headlight burned out. It made
Kentucky dark like all the static's croaks. The engine sounded
like an airplane up the grade as they sank together into mountains' grip. Diesel stayed calm until he dumped the bowl's ashes
out the window just as Jearold struck a furry fox. At the impact
Diesel lost his grip; the bowl's blue-green and swirly resinated
glass crashed behind them into the bowels of the night. The dead
fox beat against the bumper like a snare drum. It flew into the
woods and never landed, and Jearold started laughing. He pulled
them off the highway onto gravel. Isaac's lungs itched from the
pot smoke, and everywhere in the dark he saw glowing stones.

I'm taken a piss, said Jearold. Everybody out.

It wasn't much colder outside the car than in. The animal
had knocked the front bumper loose, and the night was too black
to see much else. Maybe what's-his-face is a mechanic, Diesel
said.

Who? said Jearold.

Old doo-lolly, said Diesel.

Why would he wanna fix my car? said Jearold.

I'll bet he's got a junkyard fifteen acres long, said Diesel.

They ain't nothen wrong with it, said Jearold.

I bet it's right upside a mountain like a strip mine, Diesel
said. He stared straight up at where the moon would have been
shining. I'll bet you can see it from space, he said. Maybe he's a
vet. We'll catch the fox and stick em in the cage.

It was too big for a fox, said Jearold. And it's dead.

Exactly, Diesel said. His shoulder twitched like jagged streaks
of lightning shocked his eyes. Isaac followed Diesel's line of sight
to the backseat of the car, whose light didn't come on when
Diesel opened the door and got the carrier out.

What are you doing? said Jearold.

I'm going to save our lives.

Put it back in the car.

Diesel shook his head and said, You can't deliver a dog you don't have.

All of them were shivering in the cold. Diesel disappeared into the woods with Rocks. It didn't make sense for Isaac to be scared for the dog, but Diesel wouldn't know where cliffs were in the darkness, or the openings of chasms, and Rocks would fall away, and now the radio was screaming. I got shot, raged an old man's voice. My eyeballs was black. Hallelujah.

Diesel reappeared. He froze as stiff as Rocks.

Black like you was dead, the man said, which was what Isaac's eyes were seeing too.

I've got a knife, Jearold yelled.

It's the radio, said Isaac.

The radio ain't on.

It was on scan, said Isaac.

It was on gospel, Jearold said, and then we turned it off.

No, said Diesel, it just went to static.

So where'd the static go? said Jearold. Did the hills move?

Hellfire ain't red, the radio man said, it's black. Cause you ain't got no eyeballs. The voice had holes in its throat and cancers in its mouth. Come down to the store, it said, and the gas man cried, The blood, the blood.

He's talken to us, said Diesel.

They's blood behind your eyeballs, said the radio, and Jearold felt his eyes for blood. This invasion will hit you anywhere you're at, said the radio. Steal away your shadow, hallelujah.

I can't see my shadow, said Diesel.

They's soon to be an invasion come inside your house like you've never had before, said the radio.

Isaac was sure it was the voice he'd talked to on the phone. It sounded kind and wise. He hoped the man was married, that he and his wife would see together Isaac's life and want to help him. Preachers helped other people; it was their job. They made money doing it, like deliverymen. The invasion was inside my house, the radio said, and Diesel cried out, He's talken to us. He's talken to the dog.

That was my eyeballs back in my head, said the radio. That was my eyeballs back in my head.

They ain't no dog to talk to, Jearold said.

His eyeballs are back in his head, said Diesel. Maybe it's okay.

Hallelujah, said the radio, we're gonna do some things to your eyeballs.

Your dog's dead, Diesel yelled at the radio.

Hallelujah out there on the roads. All of your eyeballs.

Diesel tore at the stereo. It was a Spark-o-matic from Walmart, and it came out easily. He threw it into the woods and held his breath and listened for its landing, which came much later, at the bottom of a rocky cliff. Isaac thought of the river, not so many yards away.

I paid thirty dollars for that tape deck, Jearold said.

I killed that tape deck, Diesel said. That tape deck is dead. He pointed toward the cliff that the sound had dug, and Isaac hated them both. He wanted to crawl down the chasm wall to find out where the eyeball preacher's eyes had gone, and now Diesel was petting Rocks, stroking a bone as if it were the nape of the dog's brown neck. Play dead, he whispered, and Isaac could see his breath again. Diesel's air hung right above the dog's head.

They should sell dead dogs, he said. They're fun to look at.

You could get one stuffed, said Jearold, climbing back into the car. One that's dead already.

That wouldn't be as interesting, Diesel said, laughing again. Isaac didn't understand him. He probably wasn't real, Isaac decided. He was like the people in the Bible who didn't have heads. Isaac shook to warm himself; the cold was tiring, and he needed to stay awake so Swortzel Swope would know he wanted to be saved. He followed Diesel back into the car, and the three of them drove down two hills and up three, past the Loyall turnoff and through Harlan, which was black and silent like a plague town. A floodwall hid the river from view, and lights blinked red, and banks' bricks glowed from a crumbly yellow light. It was two-thirty in the morning.

Let's just go to the wrong house on purpose, said Diesel.

What would the wrong house want with a dead dog? said Jearold.

Diesel shook his head. It stinks, he said.

Bones don't stink, said Jearold; it's your mind state.

So it stinks for you and not for me, said Diesel.

Isaac couldn't smell it, only burning trash somewhere uphill from Harlan. Ridges rose like ramparts all around the car, and Isaac was glad his father argued with everything Diesel said. He wanted to hurry and get to their destination. He hoped it would be a real house, not just a trailer, and he hoped it would have a staircase. Preachers probably had the money for an upstairs and a downstairs. Maybe this preacher would adopt him like a heathen child from the other continents. There was probably a spare room.

I'll bet there's a feud on, said Jearold.

What feud? said Diesel.

I don't know what feud, said Jearold, but he pointed to a sign they passed for Johnson's Engine and said, We'll tell him the Johnsons killed his dog. That'll be real funny.

Killed it how? said Diesel.

Shot him, Jearold said.

There's no bullet in the body, said Diesel.

We'll shoot one in, said Jearold.

With what gun? said Diesel.

Jearold shrugged. Poisoned, then, he said.

No wonder you get arrested so much, said Diesel, with stories like that.

People believe me, Jearold said, his voice raised. People like me.

What kind of people? said Diesel.

People are the same everywhere, Jearold said. It don't matter.

Maybe they ain't the same here.

Suddenly Jearold was bigger and more muscular than he'd ever seemed before to Isaac. You're gonna wait in the car when we get to Swortzel Swope's house, he said to Diesel. You'd best not say one word.

I'll save your life, said Diesel. Whatever you say.

You'll sit there and shut up.

You're scared, said Diesel. You're holden your ass funny.

I'm not holden it any way at all.

I'll bet the muscles is all tensed up, he said. A car on its way to Harlan passed them. It didn't have its headlights on, only the fog lights. There wasn't any fog; the night was clear and black. Jearold didn't answer. He took a sharp curve at sixty, and Diesel gripped the door and gasped. They shot beneath the tree cover, skidded on the chalk of faded lines, and a bird shat on the grainy glasspane of their windshield.

So you're quitting your job? said Diesel.

Jearold stared at him.

That's cool, Diesel said. Now we can hang out more. Play more pool down at the bar. You hardly ever even play no more.

He was right; Jearold hardly ever did.

We'll go cruising up in Gatlinburg and look for girls, said Diesel. It'll be pretty cool. He looked out the window for a while. Isaac's head was beginning to throb; he felt it with every beat of his pulse. Gnarled trees and dead mulched leaves were airbrushed onto the landscape like paint on glass. Jearold took the curves just slow enough so Rocks wouldn't bang against the door, just fast enough to feel like they were getting somewhere.

They got to Cumberland. They saw the five lights. Diesel read the directions aloud to Jearold, who squinted at the road like it was paved in a foreign language. They passed the curves, the corner, the church, the pink toilet. Isaac wondered if this was the last time he'd see Diesel and Jearold. He hoped so. The preacher would help him. He didn't know how courts and judges worked, but he figured they were good people, the kind who did what children hoped for. Jearold turned onto a gravel road and drove on it like it was a racetrack. Isaac couldn't see outside; he wondered if there were cattle, if the gravel hurt the cattle when it hit them. Jearold was grinning, snickering. He tugged at his crotch and turned into a driveway with a number on the mailbox that matched his sheet of paper, and Isaac's blood flowed fast; he wondered if his father would stab him, stab his son's heart once he defected.

Jearold darted up the driveway and held the horn down. It wasn't very loud. Goddamn sissy horn, he said. A porch light came on and illuminated an old log cabin on the hillside. Power lines ran to a shed outside it. A man staggered out.

Jearold turned off the car and opened the door. You Swope? he said.

The man grunted.

Which one are you? Jearold said. What number? Are you four?

This is box eight six one eight, the man said. As Isaac's eyes adjusted to the low light he got scared, because the man skulked like an ogre. He looked like the Boogerman. Isaac got out of the car; he couldn't see the man's nose yet.

I'll be goddamned if there's that many of you, said Jearold. You got a dog?

The man didn't answer. His head rose up to half the height of Jearold's neck, but he weighed two hundred pounds at least, and his greasy shoes were as wide as three of Isaac's. His green eyes shone like glowing ova. His beard was frostbound; it could crumble at the touch. Every breath was a ton of fog. He looked like the Canaanites in paintings printed inside Isaac's *Bible Stories* book. He chewed tobacco; he had stains on his face. Preachers weren't supposed to look like that. The Canaanites had knives and bludgeons when they fought, and Swortzel Swope's front pockets bulged, and he didn't have a shirt on; thick gray hair coated his chest and stomach, and Isaac gulped and clutched his father's Wranglers by the side; Jearold was strong, he hoped, and meaner than this demon who observed them all at once with eyes that narrowed like they channeled sunlight from the far side of the world.

We're the dog people, Jearold said. We've got Bones.

You the Delta man? said Swortzel Swope. His words were thick like swill. When he kicked gravel a piece of it hit Isaac in the chin.

You Gurney's cousin?

Huh? barked Swortzel Swope as if his mouth was full of meat.

You the fourth?

Huh?

Diesel, said Jearold, get them bones.

Diesel was standing with his hands inside the pockets of his jacket, hunched over with a frown and laughing nervously. He muttered to himself.

What bones? said Swortzel Swope.

Your dog, said Jearold.

My dog ain't Bones.

Jearold shrugged and said, They don't tell me the names.

I don't hear him, Swortzel Swope said.

That's cause he ain't talken, Jearold said.

I don't hear him breathe, said Swortzel Swope.

You don't hear anybody breathe, said Jearold. They just breathe.

I hear you doen it, the preacher said. I hear two others.

Isaac felt his father's shudders. He didn't understand why there was a Confederate flag hanging on the front porch of the cabin; they were in Kentucky now, which had never left the Union. Swortzel Swope refused to look at them but focused on the trees behind their backs, above them; his eyes stayed wide, and Isaac hoped his father would still be crazier than this man. He didn't like it when voices looked different than the things they said on radios. I hear a boy, said Swortzel Swope, his skin burnt dark in splotches like a fried potato, and Isaac shut his eyes, and across the hill invisibly two motorcycles screamed into the east and lacerated asphalt on Kingdom Come Parkway.

Don't you touch my boy, said Jearold.

Is there one? yelled Swortzel Swope. I hear the breaths.

You heard me, Jearold said.

I just said I heard one, Swortzel Swope said.

You touch my boy, said Jearold, you won't never get your dog back.

Swortzel Swope was grinning like an idiot in chains. Jearold clenched his fists, and Isaac felt ashamed; his father was protecting him, and he knew he wouldn't have done the same. He was small and scared. He held his breath. He hoped his father couldn't read his mind; it had harbored wickedness, and he looked at Swortzel Swope and understood why they were doing what they did.

I need my dog. I better get my dog.

Swortzel Swope looked like Isaac's nightmare mother. His eyes made Isaac want for things to burn. When Jearold tried to slaughter blackbirds with the car, Isaac secretly liked it, and his mother screamed at his every snore to tell him he was hellborn, that she didn't love him anymore, eight hours a night to keep him meek. He didn't need that. Jearold wouldn't make him do what God said, or what his mother said, or anyone else who didn't make sense.

You need your dog like holes in your goddamn head.

Jearold made sense. When Swortzel Swope leaned over to hack up sludge from his lungs, his left eye twitched. It popped out and it popped back in and Isaac's heart stopped for a moment. He squeezed his father's hand.

Are you the man on the radio? said Jearold.

I done some time on there, said Swortzel Swope. You play it for my dog?

What was all that shit you preached? said Jearold.

That was my sermon.

Invasions and all that eyeball shit, said Jearold. The preacher nodded. Isaac shivered, and Jearold as if he sensed it said, Were you tryen to scare me, you old fool?

It wasn't me, said Swortzel Swope.

Then who the hell was it? said Jearold.

I'm just a receiver, he said. Like a radio.

You're a radio? said Jearold.

Swortzel Swope didn't answer.

You don't look much like a fucken radio, said Jearold louder.

He's not a radio, said Diesel.

He just said he was a goddamn radio, said Jearold.

Well, Diesel said, he's not.

Like one of them worm things, said Swortzel Swope.

What worm things? said Jearold.

The ones that's in your body.

I ain't got a worm thing in my body, Jearold said.

Everybody's got one, Swortzel Swope said.

You don't know what I've got and don't got, Jearold said.

That was the invasion, said Swortzel Swope.

There ain't no invasion, said Jearold.

Will yuns shut up about the invasion? Diesel said.

It's what builds your shit up, Swortzel Swope said.

I'll build your damn shit up, Jearold said.

It's an intestine, Isaac said, and everyone turned to look at him, even Swortzel Swope whose eyes refused to look at anything at all.

Say what? said Jearold.

Isaac's cheeks turned red. Intestine, he said.

I knew there was a boy, said Swortzel Swope. I heard them breaths. That's how I know things. Jearold growled, and Isaac closed his eyes. He had known his speaking would make some-body mad, but he didn't know whom. That's it, said Swortzel Swope, but he didn't hear a dog, and he staggered down the driveway toward the car. Isaac stood between it and the preacher's body that groped toward him, taking baby steps on gravel, grunting, single hairs upright on his bald head; he picked at the insides of his ears and tilted them from side to side. Isaac stood transfixed, looking in terror up at Jearold, who looked back the same.

I know your kind, said Jearold to Swortzel Swope. I know how you try to make me afraid. I know you want me scared.

Isaac's blood felt warm when he saw his father raise his arm. Jearold wasn't crazy after all, only scared. He feared things. Isaac had never known his father had emotions. His eyes stung and teared, and he knew that such a feeling must be happiness. His father's fears were his own, and they could share them now. Don't lay your hand on the boy, said Swortzel Swope, whose

eyes lay numb like dead zeroes when he saw Jearold's arm. Isaac
stood on a pile of twigs that snapped and split. The preacher
stumbled when he heard it, so the bone of Jearold's elbow missed
him, struck the air, and when the old man leaned down to the
dirt to right himself, his eyeballs fell out and rolled and wobbled
to the feet of Isaac, who screamed inside himself. The spheres
were glass. Diesel charged into the black yard. In darkness and
confusion Jearold halted, spellbound like a shield against invasions, and Isaac hid behind his strength and wished that time
would stop so he could wrap himself forever in that safety.

I'll show you a damn invasion, Jearold said. You dickless old
fuck.

Diesel had walked back up to where they stood. He watched
Jearold open the car door and unleash the carrier from its seat
belt and take it out and drop it to the ground, and Swortzel
Swope, who hadn't found his eyeballs yet, jumped at the sound
it made.

That's to show how scared I am of you, said Jearold.

Help me, said Swortzel Swope. He sounded far away and
pitiful, and Isaac didn't feel sorry for him.

There's something you orta know about Bones, said Jearold.
What bones?

Invasion hit him, Jearold said. That damn invasion.

Swortzel Swope didn't move.

Go on, said Jearold. Look at your dog. Look what the invasion done to Bones.

Jearold, said Diesel. Look at his eyeballs.

Will you shut up? said Jearold. Look and see, he said to
Swortzel Swope. Get that stupid grin shet off your face.

Jearold, said Diesel louder. Eyeballs. Eyeballs.

If I hear one more godforsaken thing about an eyeball, Jearold said, I'll put em out myself. He drew back his arm as if to

prove his threat and punch the absent eyes, but the preacher staggered backwards, revealing gaping holes that twitched like phantoms.

Please don't hurt me, Swope pleaded, staring straight at Jearold helplessly, his front teeth twitching and the gap between them wider for a moment. Jearold dropped the dog carrier and opened his mouth wide and said nothing.

Don't do anything to my eyes, said Swortzel Swope.

Isaac wanted his father to crush them. He wondered would they squish or would they shatter into shards like marbles.

Your dog died on the way up here, Diesel said to Swortzel Swope. It was back around the state line. I don't know quite how it happened.

You don't have my dog, said Swortzel Swope. You're not the dog people.

There's its bones, said Diesel. See for yourself.

My dog's not bones. It's a dog.

Jearold staggered backwards to the car. Isaac bent to the carrier himself and opened its latch and tilted it, became the force that rained bones to the gravel earth.

It was the invasion, said Diesel, sounding like he believed it.

Get in the car, said Jearold.

Isaac obeyed.

Get in, his father said again to Diesel.

We have to find his eyeballs, Diesel said.

Find em, then, said Jearold.

Isaac followed his father into the car and watched him turn the ignition. Swortzel Swope didn't notice when Jearold turned on the headlights, but Diesel did; he ran toward the vehicle as it backed quickly down the driveway. Diesel looked like a gargoyle. Bugs were crawling like shadows in his beard. He probably had bugs inside him too, in his stomach, in his head to make him crazy. Go, said Isaac, and his father looked at him and seemed to smile, and they escaped, and Isaac smiled at Diesel as he made it to the front seat.

Isaac was glad Jearold could drive so drunk and tired; there were a lot of folks who couldn't. He settled back and put his seat belt on and took it off again. They were back on the main road. Isaac felt so tired that he wanted to cry, but not even dogs cried. Their eyes just got bigger and bigger until they held a body's weight of tears. Dogs knew crying was just how other people were.

But Jearold had eyes, and Isaac liked them; they looked like his own. They could do more things. He'd teach his eyes to do what Jearold's did. It was important to be tough. He wondered what a BB felt like. He'd ask his father to shoot him with the BB gun so he could know. He'd ask if he could call his father Dad instead of Jearold. It sounded strange to say Jearold if Dad was who he really was, and Isaac pinched himself as hard as he could pinch. BB's couldn't hurt worse than that. He knew some boys at school he'd like to shoot, and now he had a dog at home too. It was alive. It had eyes. It was a seeing-eye dog. He didn't hate dogs anymore, he decided. From now on, dogs would be his favorite thing. He would follow his new guardian through dark fields hunting groundhogs late at night, and they'd lie awake together and look at each other, and he wouldn't be scared to fall asleep, because he'd know who led him blindly through his nightmares.

ACKNOWLEDGMENTS

I am grateful to the Fellowship of Southern Writers, the Mrs. Giles Whiting Foundation, Hollins University, Madison Smartt Bell, the James A. Michener Center for Writers, and to Jane Gelfman, my agent. I consider myself uncommonly lucky to have Josh Kendall as an editor. In revising these stories I have also benefited from the wisdom of Pinckney Benedict, Kate Preusser, Jenny Noller, Cheri Johnson, Nathan Hilkert, and J. T. Hill. Thank you, all.